Thomas Moore, Richard Brinsley Sheridan

The Works of Richard Brinsley Sheridan

Vol. II

Thomas Moore, Richard Brinsley Sheridan

The Works of Richard Brinsley Sheridan
Vol. II

ISBN/EAN: 9783337058364

Printed in Europe, USA, Canada, Australia, Japan

Cover: Foto ©Andreas Hilbeck / pixelio.de

More available books at **www.hansebooks.com**

THE WORKS

OF

RICHARD BRINSLEY SHERIDAN,

With a Memoir

BY

JAMES P. BROWNE, M.D.

CONTAINING EXTRACTS FROM THE LIFE

BY

THOMAS MOORE.

IN TWO VOLUMES.

VOL. II.

LONDON:

BICKERS & SON, 1, LEICESTER SQUARE.

1884.

CONTENTS OF VOL. II.

THE

SCHOOL FOR SCANDAL:

A COMEDY.

VOL. II.

A PORTRAIT;

ADDRESSED TO MRS. CREWE, WITH THE COMEDY OF THE SCHOOL FOR SCANDAL.

BY R. B. SHERIDAN, ESQ.

TELL me, ye prim adepts in Scandal's school,
Who rail by precept, and detract by rule,
Lives there no character, so tried, so known,
So deck'd with grace, and so unlike your own,
That even you assist her fame to raise,
Approve by envy, and by silence praise?
Attend!—a model shall attract your view—
Daughters of calumny, I summon you!
You shall decide if this a portrait prove,
Or fond creation of the Muse and Love.
Attend, ye virgin critics, shrewd and sage,
Ye matron censors of this childish age,
Whose peering eye and wrinkled front declare
A fixed antipathy to young and fair;
By cunning, cautious; or by nature, cold,
In maiden madness, virulently bold!
Attend! ye skilled to coin the precious tale,
Creating proof, where innuendos fail!
Whose practised memories, cruelly exact,
Omit no circumstance, except the fact!
Attend all ye who boast—or old or young—
The living libel of a slanderous tongue!
So shall my theme as far contrasted be,
As saints by fiends, or hymns by calumny.
Come, gentle Amoret (for 'neath that name,
In worthier verse is sung thy beauty's fame);

Come—for but thee who seeks the Muse? and while
Celestial blushes check thy conscious smile,
With timid grace and hesitating eye,
The perfect model, which I boast, supply.
Vain Muse! couldst thou the humblest sketch create
Of her, or slightest charm couldst imitate—
Could thy blest strain in kindred colours trace
The faintest wonder of her form and face—
Poets would study the immortal line,
And *Reynolds* own *his* art subdued by thine;
That art, which well might added lustre give
To Nature's best, and Heaven's superlative:
On *Granby's* cheek might bid new glories rise,
Or point a purer beam from *Devon's* eyes!
Hard is the task to shape that beauty's praise,
Whose judgment scorns the homage flattery pays!
But praising Amoret we cannot err,
No tongue o'ervalues Heaven, or flatters her!
Yet she by Fate's perverseness—she alone
Would doubt our truth, nor deem such praise her own!
Adorning Fashion, unadorn'd by dress,
Simple from taste, and not from carelessness;
Discreet in gesture, in deportment mild,
Not stiff with prudence, nor uncouthly wild:
No state has *Amoret!* no studied mien;
She frowns no *goddess*, and she moves *no queen*.
The softer charm that in her manner lies
Is framed to captivate, yet not surprise;
It justly suits th' expression of her face—
'Tis less than dignity, and more than grace!
On her pure cheek the native hue is such,
That form'd by Heav'n to be admired so much,
The hand divine, with a less partial care,
Might well have fix'd a fainter crimson there,

And bade the gentle inmate of her breast—
Inshrined Modesty!—supply the rest.
But who the peril of her lips shall paint?
Strip them of smiles—still, still all words are faint!
But moving Love himself appears to teach
Their action, though denied to rule her speech;
And thou who seest her speak and dost not hear,
Mourn not her distant accents 'scape thine ear;
Viewing those lips, thou still may'st make pretence
To judge of what she says, and swear 'tis sense:
Cloth'd with such grace, with such expression fraught,
They move in meaning, and they pause in thought!
But dost thou farther watch, with charm'd surprise,
The mild irresolution of her eyes,
Curious to mark how frequent they repose,
In brief eclipse and momentary close—
Ah! seest thou not an ambush'd Cupid there,
Too tim'rous of his charge, with jealous care
Veils and unveils those beams of heav'nly light,
Too full, too fatal else, for mortal sight?
Nor yet, such pleasing vengeance fond to meet,
In pard'ning dimples hope a safe retreat.
What though her peaceful breast should ne'er allow
Subduing frowns to arm her alter'd brow,
By Love, I swear, and by his gentle wiles,
More fatal still the mercy of her smiles!
Thus lovely, thus adorn'd, possessing all
Of bright or fair that can to woman fall,
The height of vanity might well be thought
Prerogative in her, and Nature's fault.
Yet gentle *Amoret*, in mind supreme
As well as charms, rejects the vainer theme;
And half mistrustful of her beauty's store,
She barbs with wit those darts too keen before:—

Read in all knowledge that her sex should reach,
Though *Greville,* or the *Muse,* should deign to teach,
Fond to improve, nor tim'rous to discern
How far it is a woman's grace to learn;
In *Millar's* dialect she would not prove
Apollo's priestess, but Apollo's love,
Graced by those signs, which truth delights to own,
The timid blush, and mild submitted tone:
Whate'er she says, though sense appear throughout,
Displays the tender hüe of female doubt;
Deck'd with that charm, how lovely wit appears,
How graceful *science,* when that robe she wears!
Such too her talents, and her bent of mind,
As speak a sprightly heart by thought refined,
A taste for mirth, by contemplation school'd,
A turn for ridicule, by candour ruled,
A scorn of folly, which she tries to hide;
An awe of talent, which she owns with pride!
   Peace! idle Muse, no more thy strain prolong,
But yield a theme, thy warmest praises wrong;
Just to her merit, though thou canst not raise
Thy feeble verse, behold th' acknowledged praise
Has spread conviction through the envious train,
And cast a fatal gloom o'er Scandal's reign!
And lo! each pallid hag, with blister'd tongue,
Mutters assent to all thy zeal has sung—
Owns all the colours just—the outline true;
Thee my inspirer, and my *model*—CREWE!

PROLOGUE.

WRITTEN BY MR. GARRICK.

A SCHOOL for Scandal! tell me, I beseech you,
Needs there a school this modish art to teach you?
No need of lessons now, the knowing think;
We might as well be taught to eat and drink.
Caused by a dearth of scandal, should the vapours
Distress our fair ones—let them read the papers;
Their powerful mixtures such disorders hit;
Crave what you will—there's *quantum sufficit.*
'Lord!' cries my Lady *Wormwood* (who loves tattle,
And puts much salt and pepper in her prattle),
Just ris'n at noon, all night at cards when threshing
Strong tea and scandal—'Bless me, how refreshing!
'Give me the papers, *Lisp*—how bold and free! *(sips)*
'*Last night Lord L. (sips) was caught with Lady D.*
'For aching heads what charming *sal volatile! (sips.)*
'*If Mrs. B. will still continue flirting,*
'*We hope she'll* DRAW, *or we'll* UNDRAW *the curtain.*
'Fine satire, poz—in public all abuse it,
'But, by ourselves *(sips)*, our praise we can't refuse it.
'Now, *Lisp*, read you—there, at that dash and star.'
'Yes, ma'am—*A certain lord had best beware,*
'*Who lives not twenty miles from Grosvenor Square;*
'*For should he Lady W. find willing,*
'*Wormwood is bitter*'—'Oh! that's me, the villain!
'Throw it behind the fire, and never more
'Let that vile paper come within my door.'

Thus at our friends we laugh, who feel the dart;
To reach our feelings, we ourselves must smart.
Is our young bard so young, to think that he
Can stop the full spring-tide of calumny?
Knows he the world so little, and its trade?
Alas! the devil's sooner raised than laid.
So strong, so swift, the monster there's no gagging:
Cut Scandal's head off, still the tongue is wagging.
Proud of your smiles once lavishly bestow'd,
Again our young Don Quixote takes the road;
To show his gratitude he draws his pen,
And seeks this hydra, Scandal, in his den.
For your applause all perils he would through—
He'll fight—that's write—a cavalliero true,
Till every drop of blood—that's ink—is spilt for you.

DRAMATIS PERSONÆ,

AS ORIGINALLY ACTED AT DRURY LANE THEATRE, MAY 8, 1777.

Sir Peter Teazle	Mr. KING.
Sir Oliver Surface	Mr. YATES.
Joseph Surface	Mr. PALMER.
Charles	Mr. SMITH.
Crabtree	Mr. PARSONS.
Sir Benjamin Backbite . .	Mr. DODD.
Rowley	Mr. AICKIN.
Moses	Mr. BADDELEY.
Trip	Mr. LAMASH.
Snake	Mr. PACKER.
Careless	Mr. FARREN.
Sir Harry Bumper	Mr. GAWDRY.
Lady Teazle	Mrs. ABINGTON.
Maria	Miss P. HOPKINS.
Lady Sneerwell	Miss SHERRY.
Mrs. Candour	Miss POPE.

SCHOOL FOR SCANDAL.

ACT I.—SCENE I.

Lady SNEERWELL'S *House.*

Discovered Lady SNEERWELL *at the dressing-table;*
SNAKE *drinking chocolate.*

Lady Sneer. THE paragraphs, you say, Mr. Snake,
were all inserted?

Snake. They were, madam; and as I copied them
myself in a feigned hand, there can be no suspicion
whence they came.

Lady Sneer. Did you circulate the report of Lady
Brittle's intrigue with Captain Boastall?

Snake. That's in as fine a train as your ladyship
could wish. In the common course of things, I think
it must reach Mrs. Clackitt's ears within four-and-
twenty hours; and then, you know, the business is as
good as done.

Lady Sneer. Why, truly, Mrs. Clackitt has a very
pretty talent, and a great deal of industry.

Snake. True, madam, and has been tolerably successful in her day. To my knowledge she has been

the cause of six matches being broken off, and three sons disinherited; of four forced elopements, and as many close confinements; nine separate maintenances, and two divorces. Nay, I have more than once traced her causing a *tête-à-tête* in the *Town and Country Magazine*, when the parties, perhaps, had never seen each other's face before in the course of their lives.

Lady Sneer. She certainly has talents, but her manner is gross.

Snake. 'Tis very true. She generally designs well, has a free tongue, and a bold invention; but her colouring is too dark, and her outlines often extravagant. She wants that delicacy of tint, and mellowness of sneer, which distinguishes your ladyship's scandal.

Lady Sneer. You are partial, Snake.

Snake. Not in the least; everybody allows that Lady Sneerwell can do more with a word or a look than many can with the most laboured detail, even when they happen to have a little truth on their side to support it.

Lady Sneer. Yes, my dear Snake; and I am no hypocrite to deny the satisfaction I reap from the success of my efforts. Wounded myself in the early part of my life by the envenomed tongue of slander, I confess I have since known no pleasure equal to the reducing others to the level of my own injured reputation.

Snake. Nothing can be more natural. But, Lady Sneerwell, there is one affair in which you have lately employed me, wherein, I confess, I am at a loss to guess your motives.

Lady Sneer. I conceive you mean with respect to my neighbour, Sir Peter Teazle, and his family?

Snake. I do. Here are two young men, to whom Sir Peter has acted as a kind of guardian since their father's death ; the eldest possessing the most amiable character, and universally well spoken of; the youngest, the most dissipated and extravagant young fellow in the kingdom, without friends or character: the former an avowed admirer of your ladyship, and apparently your favourite; the latter attached to Maria, Sir Peter's ward, and confessedly beloved by her. Now, on the face of these circumstances, it is utterly unaccountable to me, why you, the widow of a city knight, with a good jointure, should not close with the passion of a man of such character and expectations as Mr. Surface; and more so why you should be so uncommonly earnest to destroy the mutual attachment subsisting between his brother Charles and Maria.

Lady Sneer. Then at once to unravel this mystery, I must inform you, that love has no share whatever in the intercourse between Mr. Surface and me.

Snake. No !

Lady Sneer. His real attachment is to Maria, or her fortune; but finding in his brother a favoured rival, he has been obliged to mask his pretensions, and profit by my assistance.

Snake. Yet still I am more puzzled why you should interest yourself in his success.

Lady Sneer. How dull you are ! Cannot you surmise the weakness which I hitherto, through shame, have concealed even from you? Must I confess that Charles, that libertine, that extravagant, that bankrupt in fortune and reputation, that he it is for whom I'm thus anxious and malicious, and to gain whom I would sacrifice everything ?

Snake. Now, indeed, your conduct appears consistent; but how came you and Mr. Surface so confidential ?

Lady Sneer. For our mutual interest. I have found

him out a long time since. I know him to be artful, selfish, and malicious; in short, a sentimental knave; while with Sir Peter, and indeed with all his acquaintance, he passes for a youthful miracle of prudence, good sense, and benevolence.

Snake. Yes; yet Sir Peter vows he has not his equal in England; and above all, he praises him as a man of sentiment.

Lady Sneer. True; and with the assistance of his sentiment and hypocrisy, he has brought Sir Peter entirely into his interest with regard to Maria; while poor Charles has no friend in the house, though, I fear, he has a powerful one in Maria's heart, against whom we must direct our schemes.

Enter SERVANT.

Serv. Mr. Surface.
Lady Sneer. Show him up. [*Exit* SERVANT.

Enter JOSEPH SURFACE.

Joseph S. My dear Lady Sneerwell, how do you do to-day? Mr. Snake, your most obedient.

Lady Sneer. Snake has just been rallying me on our mutual attachment; but I have informed him of our real views. You know how useful he has been to us, and, believe me, the confidence is not ill placed.

Joseph S. Madam, it is impossible for me to suspect a man of Mr. Snake's sensibility and discernment.

Lady Sneer. Well, well, no compliments now; but tell me when you saw your mistress, Maria; or, what is more material to me, your brother.

Joseph S. I have not seen either since I left you; but I can inform you that they never meet. Some of your stories have taken a good effect on Maria.

Lady Sneer. Ah! my dear Snake! the merit of this belongs to you; but do your brother's distresses increase?

Joseph S. Every hour. I am told he has had another execution in the house yesterday. In short, his dissipation and extravagance exceed anything I have ever heard of.

Lady Sneer. Poor Charles!

Joseph S. True, madam; notwithstanding his vices, one can't help feeling for him. Poor Charles! I'm sure I wish it were in my power to be of any essential service to him; for the man who does not share in the distresses of a brother, even though merited by his own misconduct, deserves——

Lady Sneer. O Lud! you are going to be moral, and forget that you are among friends.

Joseph S. Egad, that's true! I'll keep that sentiment till I see Sir Peter; however, it certainly is a charity to rescue Maria from such a libertine, who, if he is to be reclaimed, can be so only by a person of your ladyship's superior accomplishments and understanding.

Snake. I believe, Lady Sneerwell, here's company coming; I'll go and copy the letter I mentioned to you. Mr. Surface, your most obedient. [*Exit* SNAKE.

Joseph S. Sir, your very devoted. Lady Sneerwell, I am very sorry you have put any further confidence in that fellow.

Lady Sneer. Why so?

Joseph S. I have lately detected him in frequent conference with old Rowley, who was formerly my father's steward, and has never, you know, been a friend of mine.

Lady Sneer. And do you think he would betray us?

Joseph S. Nothing more likely; take my word for't,

Lady Sneerwell, that fellow hasn't virtue enough to be faithful even to his own villany. Ah! Maria!

Enter MARIA.

Lady Sneer. Maria, my dear, how do you do? What's the matter?

Maria. Oh! there is that disagreeable lover of mine, Sir Benjamin Backbite, has just called at my guardian's, with his odious uncle, Crabtree; so I slipped out, and ran hither to avoid them.

Lady Sneer. Is that all?

Joseph S. If my brother Charles had been of the party, madam, perhaps you would not have been so much alarmed.

Lady Sneer. Nay, now you are severe; for I dare swear the truth of the matter is, Maria heard *you* were here. But, my dear, what has Sir Benjamin done, that you would avoid him so?

Maria. Oh, he has done nothing; but 'tis for what he has said: his conversation is a perpetual libel on all his acquaintance.

Joseph S. Ay, and the worst of it is, there is no advantage in not knowing him; for he'll abuse a stranger just as soon as his best friend; and his uncle's as bad.

Lady Sneer. Nay, but we should make allowance; Sir Benjamin is a wit and a poet.

Maria. For my part, I confess, madam, wit loses its respect with me, when I see it in company with malice. What do you think, Mr. Surface?

Joseph S. Certainly, madam; to smile at the jest which plants a thorn in another's breast is to become a principal in the mischief.

Lady Sneer. Pshaw! there's no possibility of being

witty without a little ill nature: the malice of a good thing is the barb that makes it stick. What's your opinion, Mr. Surface?

Joseph S. To be sure, madam; that conversation, where the spirit of raillery is suppressed, will ever appear tedious and insipid.

Maria. Well, I'll not debate how far scandal may be allowable; but in a man, I am sure, it is always contemptible. We have pride, envy, rivalship, and a thousand motives to depreciate each other; but the male slanderer must have the cowardice of a woman before he can traduce one.

Enter SERVANT.

Serv. Madam, Mrs. Candour is below, and if your ladyship's at leisure, will leave her carriage.

Lady Sneer. Beg her to walk in. [*Exit* SERVANT.] Now, Maria, here is a character to your taste; for though Mrs. Candour is a little talkative, everybody allows her to be the best natured and best sort of woman.

Maria. Yes, with a very gross affectation of good nature and benevolence, she does more mischief than the direct malice of old Crabtree.

Joseph S. I'faith that's true, Lady Sneerwell: whenever I hear the current running against the characters of my friends, I never think them in such danger as when Candour undertakes their defence.

Lady Sneer. Hush! here she is!

Enter Mrs. CANDOUR.

Mrs. Can. My dear Lady Sneerwell, how have you been this century? Mr. Surface, what news do you hear? though indeed it is no matter, for I think one hears nothing else but scandal.

Joseph S. Just so, indeed, ma'am.

Mrs. Can. Oh, Maria! child, what is the whole affair off between you and Charles? His extravagance, I presume; the town talks of nothing else.

Maria. Indeed! I am very sorry, ma'am, the town is not better employed.

Mrs. Can. True, true, child; but there's no stopping people's tongues. I own I was hurt to hear it, as I indeed was to learn, from the same quarter, that your guardian, Sir Peter, and Lady Teazle have not agreed lately as well as could be wished.

Maria. 'Tis strangely impertinent for people to busy themselves so.

Mrs. Can. Very true, child; but what's to be done? People will talk; there's no preventing it. Why, it was but yesterday I was told Miss Gadabout had eloped with Sir Filigree Flirt. But, Lord! there's no minding what one hears; though, to be sure, I had this from very good authority.

Maria. Such reports are highly scandalous.

Mrs Can. So they are, child; shameful! shameful! But the world is so censorious, no character escapes. Lord, now who would have suspected your friend, Miss Prim, of an indiscretion? Yet such is the ill-nature of people, that they say her uncle stopped her last week, just as she was stepping into the York diligence with her dancing-master.

Maria. I'll answer for't there are no grounds for that report.

Mrs. Can. Ah, no foundation in the world, I dare swear: no more, probably, than for the story circulated last month, of Mrs. Festino's affair with Colonel Cassino; though, to be sure, that matter was never rightly cleared up.

Joseph S. The licence of invention some people take is monstrous indeed.

Maria. 'Tis so; but, in my opinion, those who report such things are equally culpable.

Mrs. Can. To be sure they are; tale-bearers are as bad as the tale-makers; 'tis an old observation, and a very true one. But what's to be done, as I said before? How will you prevent people from talking? To-day, Mrs. Clackitt assured me, Mr. and Mrs. Honeymoon were at last become mere man and wife, like the rest of their acquaintance. She likewise hinted that a certain widow, in the next street, had got rid of her dropsy and recovered her shape in a most surprising manner. And at the same time, Miss Tattle, who was by, affirmed that Lord Buffalo had discovered his lady at a house of no extraordinary fame; and that Sir H. Boquet and Tom Saunter were to measure swords on a similar provocation. But, Lord, do you think I would report these things? No, no! tale-bearers, as I said before, are just as bad as the tale-makers.

Joseph S. Ah! Mrs. Candour, if everybody had your forbearance and good-nature!

Mrs. Can. I confess, Mr. Surface, I cannot bear to hear people attacked behind their backs; and when ugly circumstances come out against our acquaintance, I own I always love to think the best. By-the-bye, I hope 'tis not true that your brother is absolutely ruined?

Joseph S. I am afraid his circumstances are very bad indeed, ma'am.

Mrs. Can. Ah! I heard so; but you must tell him to keep up his spirits; everybody almost is in the same way—Lord Spindle, Sir Thomas Splint, Captain Quinze, and Mr. Nickit—all up, I hear, within this week; so if Charles is undone, he'll find half his acquaintance ruined too, and that, you know, is a consolation.

Joseph S. Doubtless, ma'am; a very great one.

Enter SERVANT.

Serv. Mr. Crabtree and Sir Benjamin Backbite.

[*Exit* SERVANT.

Lady Sneer. So, Maria, you see your lover pursues you; positively you sha'n't escape.

Enter CRABTREE *and* Sir BENJAMIN BACKBITE.

Crabt. Lady Sneerwell, I kiss your hand. Mrs. Candour, I don't believe you are acquainted with my nephew, Sir Benjamin Backbite? Egad! ma'am, he has a pretty wit, and is a pretty poet too; isn't he, Lady Sneerwell?

Sir Benj. B. O fie, uncle!

Crabt. Nay, egad it's true; I back him at a rebus or a charade against the best rhymer in the kingdom. Has your ladyship heard the epigram he wrote last week on Lady Frizzle's feather catching fire? Do, Benjamin, repeat it, or the charade you made last night extempore at Mrs. Drowzie's conversazione. Come now; your first is the name of a fish, your second a great naval commander, and——

Sir Benj. B. Uncle, now—pr'ythee——

Crabt. I'faith, ma'am, 'twould surprise you to hear how ready he is at all these fine sort of things.

Lady Sneer. I wonder, Sir Benjamin, you never publish anything.

Sir Benj. B. To, say truth, ma'am, 'tis very vulgar to print; and as my little productions are mostly satires and lampoons on particular people, I find they circulate more by giving copies in confidence to the friends of the parties. However, I have some love elegies, which, when favoured with this lady's smiles, I mean to give the public.

Crabt. 'Fore heaven, ma'am, they'll immortalize you! You will be handed down to posterity, like Petrarch's Laura, or Waller's Sacharissa.

Sir Benj. B. Yes, madam, I think you will like them, when you shall see them on a beautiful quarto page, where a neat rivulet of text shall meander through a meadow of margin. 'Fore Gad, they will be the most elegant things of their kind!

Crabt. But, ladies, that's true. Have you heard the news?

Mrs. Can. What, sir, do you mean the report of——

Crabt. No, ma'am, that's not it. Miss Nicely is going to be married to her own footman.

Mrs. Can. Impossible!

Crabt. Ask Sir Benjamin.

Sir Benj. B. 'Tis very true, ma'am; everything is fixed, and the wedding liveries bespoke.

Crabt. Yes; and they do say there were pressing reasons for it.

Lady Sneer. Why I have heard something of this before.

Mrs. Can. It can't be, and I wonder any one should believe such a story, of so prudent a lady as Miss Nicely.

Sir Benj. B. O Lud! ma'am, that's the very reason 'twas believed at once. She has always been so cautious and so reserved, that everybody was sure there was some reason for it at bottom.

Mrs. Can. Why, to be sure, a tale of scandal is as fatal to the credit of a prudent lady of her stamp, as a fever is generally to those of the strongest constitutions. But there is a sort of puny, sickly reputation, that is always ailing, yet will outlive the robuster characters of a hundred prudes.

Sir Benj. B. True, madam, there are valetudinarians

in reputation as well as constitution; who, being conscious of their weak part, avoid the least breath of air, and supply their want of stamina by care and circumspection.

Mrs. Can. Well, but this may be all a mistake. You know, Sir Benjamin, very trifling circumstances often give rise to the most injurious tales.

Crabt. That they do, I'll be sworn, ma'am. Did you ever hear how Miss Piper came to lose her lover and her character last summer at Tunbridge? Sir Benjamin, you remember it?

Sir Benj. B. Oh, to be sure! The most whimsical circumstance.

Lady Sneer. How was it, pray?

Crabt. Why, one evening, at Mrs. Ponto's assembly, the conversation happened to turn on the breeding Nova Scotia sheep in this country. Says a young lady in company, I have known instances of it, for Miss Letitia Piper, a first cousin of mine, had a Nova Scotia sheep that produced her twins. What! cries the Lady Dowager Dundizzy (who you know is as deaf as a post), has Miss Piper had twins? This mistake, as you may imagine, threw the whole company into a fit of laughter. However, 'twas the next morning everywhere reported, and in a few days believed by the whole town, that Miss Letitia Piper had actually been brought to bed of a fine boy and a girl; and in less than a week there were some people who could name the father, and the farmhouse where the babies were put to nurse.

Lady Sneer. Strange, indeed!

Crabt. Matter of fact, I assure you. O Lud! Mr. Surface, pray is it true that your uncle, Sir Oliver, is coming home?

Joseph S. Not that I know of, indeed, sir.

Crabt. He has been in the East Indies a long time. You can scarcely remember him, I believe? Sad comfort whenever he returns, to hear how your brother has gone on!

Joseph S. Charles has been imprudent, sir, to be sure; but I hope no busy people have already prejudiced Sir Oliver against him. He may reform.

Sir Benj. B. To be sure he may; for my part, I never believed him to be so utterly void of principle as people say; and though he has lost all his friends, I am told nobody is better spoken of by the Jews.

Crabt. That's true, egad, nephew. If the Old Jewry was a ward, I believe Charles would be an alderman. No man more popular there, 'fore Gad! I hear he pays as many annuities as the Irish tontine; and that whenever he is sick, they have prayers for the recovery of his health in all the synagogues.

Sir Benj. B. Yet no man lives in greater splendour. They tell me, when he entertains his friends he will sit down to dinner with a dozen of his own securities; have a score of tradesmen waiting in the antechamber, and an officer behind every guest's chair.

Joseph S. This may be entertainment to you, gentlemen, but you pay very little regard to the feelings of a brother.

Maria. Their malice is intolerable. Lady Sneerwell, I must wish you a good morning: I'm not very well. [*Exit* Maria.

Mrs. Can. O dear! she changes colour very much.

Lady Sneer. Do, Mrs. Candour, follow her: she may want assistance.

Mrs. Can. That I will, with all my soul, ma'am. Poor dear girl, who knows what her situation may be! [*Exit* Mrs. Candour.

Lady Sneer. 'Twas nothing but that she could not

bear to hear Charles reflected on, notwithstanding their difference.

Sir Benj. B. The young lady's *penchant* is obvious.

Crabt. But, Benjamin, you must not give up the pursuit for that: follow her, and put her into good humour. Repeat her some of your own verses. Come, I'll assist you.

Sir Benj. B. Mr. Surface, I did not mean to hurt you; but depend on't your brother is utterly undone.

Crabt. O lud, lay! undone as ever man was. Can't raise a guinea!

Sir Benj. B. And everything sold, I'm told, that was movable.

Crabt. I have seen one that was at his house. Not a thing left but some empty bottles that were overlooked, and the family pictures, which I believe are framed in the wainscots.

Sir Benj. B. And I'm very sorry, also, to hear some bad stories against him.   [*Going.*

Crabt. Oh! he has done many mean things, that's certain.

Sir Benj. B. But, however, as he's your brother——
                    [*Going.*

Crabt. We'll tell you all another opportunity.

                    [*Exit* CRABTREE *and* Sir BENJAMIN.

Lady Sneer. Ha! ha! 'tis very hard for them to leave a subject they have not quite run down.

Joseph S. And I believe the abuse was no more acceptable to your ladyship than Maria.

Lady Sneer. I doubt her affections are farther engaged than we imagine. But the family are to be here this evening, so you may as well dine where you are, and we shall have an opportunity of observing farther; in the mean time, I'll go and plot mischief, and you shall study sentiment.   [*Exeunt.*

SCENE II.

Sir PETER's *House.*

Enter Sir PETER.

Sir Peter T. When an old bachelor marries a young wife, what is he to expect? 'Tis now six months since Lady Teazle made me the happiest of men; and I have been the most miserable dog ever since! We tifted a little going to church, and fairly quarrelled before the bells had done ringing. I was more than once nearly choked with gall during the honeymoon, and had lost all comfort in life before my friends had done wishing me joy. Yet I chose with caution—a girl bred wholly in the country, who never knew luxury beyond one silk gown, nor dissipation above the annual gala of a race ball. Yet now she plays her part in all the extravagant fopperies of the fashion and the town, with as ready a grace as if she had never seen a bush or a grass-plot out of Grosvenor Square! I am sneered at by all my acquaintance, and paragraphed in the newspapers. She dissipates my fortune, and contradicts all my humours; yet the worst of it is, I doubt I love her, or I should never bear all this. However, I'll never be weak enough to own it.

Enter ROWLEY.

Rowley. Oh! Sir Peter, your servant; how is it with you, sir?

Sir Peter T. Very bad, Master Rowley, very bad. I meet with nothing but crosses and vexations.

Rowley. What can have happened to trouble you since yesterday?

Sir Peter T. A good question to a married man!

Rowley. Nay, I'm sure your lady, Sir Peter, can't be the cause of your uneasiness.

Sir Peter T. Why, has anybody told you she was dead?

Rowley. Come, come, Sir Peter, you love her, notwithstanding your tempers don't exactly agree.

Sir Peter T. But the fault is entirely hers, Master Rowley. I am, myself, the sweetest tempered man alive, and hate a teasing temper; and so I tell her a hundred times a day.

Rowley. Indeed!

Sir Peter T. Ay; and what is very extraordinary, in all our disputes she is always in the wrong! But Lady Sneerwell, and the set she meets at her house, encourage the perverseness of her disposition. Then, to complete my vexation, Maria, my ward, whom I ought to have the power over, is determined to turn rebel too, and absolutely refuses the man whom I have long resolved on for her husband; meaning, I suppose, to bestow herself on his profligate brother.

Rowley. You know, Sir Peter, I have always taken the liberty to differ with you on the subject of these two young gentlemen. I only wish you may not be deceived in your opinion of the elder. For Charles, my life on't! he will retrieve his errors yet. Their worthy father, once my honoured master, was, at his years, nearly as wild a spark; yet, when he died, he did not leave a more benevolent heart to lament his loss.

Sir Peter T. You are wrong, Master Rowley. On their father's death, you know, I acted as a kind of guardian to them both, till their uncle Sir Oliver's liberality gave them an early independence: of course, no person could have more opportunities of judging of their hearts, and I was never mistaken in my life. Joseph is indeed a model for the young men of the age. He is a man of sentiment, and acts up to the *sentiments* he professes; but for the other, take my word for't, if he had any grain of virtue by descent, he has dissipated it with the rest of his inheritance. Ah! my old friend, Sir Oliver, will be deeply mortified when he finds how part of his bounty has been misapplied.

Rowley. I am sorry to find you so violent against the young man, because this may be the most critical period of his fortune. I came hither with news that will surprise you.

Sir Peter T. What! let me hear.

Rowley. Sir Oliver *is* arrived, and at this moment in town.

Sir Peter T. How! you astonish me! I thought you did not expect him this month.

Rowley. I did not; but his passage has been remarkably quick.

Sir Peter T. Egad, I shall rejoice to see my old friend. 'Tis fifteen years since we met. We have had many a day together; but does he still enjoin us not to inform his nephews of his arrival?

Rowley. Most strictly. He means, before it is known, to make some trial of their dispositions.

Sir Peter T. Ah! there needs no art to discover their merits; he shall have his way. But, pray, does he know I am married?

Rowley. Yes, and will soon wish you joy.

Sir Peter T. What, as we drink health to a friend in a consumption. Ah! Oliver will laugh at me. We used to rail at matrimony together, and he has been steady to his text. Well, he must be soon at my house, though! I'll instantly give orders for his reception. But, Master Rowley, don't drop a word that Lady Teazle and I ever disagree.

Rowley. By no means.

Sir Peter T. For I should never be able to stand Noll's jokes; so I'd have him think, Lord forgive me! that we are a very happy couple.

Rowley. I understand you; but then you must be very careful not to differ while he is in the house with you.

Sir Peter T. Egad, and so we must, and that's impossible. Ah! Master Rowley, when an old bachelor marries a young wife, he deserves—no—the crime carries its punishment along with it.   [*Exeunt.*

ACT II.—SCENE I.

Enter Sir PETER *and* Lady TEAZLE.

Sir Peter T. Lady Teazle, Lady Teazle, I'll not bear it!

Lady T. Sir Peter, Sir Peter, you may bear it or not, as you please; but I ought to have my own way in everything, and what's more, I will, too. What! though I was educated in the country, I know very well that women of fashion in London are accountable to nobody after they are married.

Sir Peter T. Very well, ma'am, very well; so a husband is to have no influence, no authority?

Lady T. Authority! No, to be sure; if you wanted

authority over me, you should have adopted me, and not married me : I am sure you were old enough.

Sir Peter T. Old enough! ay, there it is. Well, well, Lady Teazle, though my life may be made unhappy by your temper, I'll not be ruined by your extravagance.

Lady T. My extravagance! I'm sure I'm not more extravagant than a woman of fashion ought to be.

Sir Peter T. No, no, madam, you shall throw away no more sums on such unmeaning luxury. 'Slife! to spend as much to furnish your dressing-room with flowers in winter as would suffice to turn the Pantheon into a green-house, and give a *fête champétre* at Christmas.

Lady T. And I am to blame, Sir Peter, because flowers are dear in cold weather? You should find fault with the climate, and not with me. For my part, I'm sure, I wish it was spring all the year round, and that roses grew under our feet.

Sir Peter T. Oons! madam; if you had been born to this, I shouldn't wonder at your talking thus; but you forget what your situation was when I married you.

Lady T. No, no, I don't; 'twas a very disagreeable one, or I should never have married you.

Sir Peter T. Yes, yes, madam; you were then in somewhat a humbler style: the daughter of a plain country squire. Recollect, Lady Teazle, when I saw you first sitting at your tambour, in a pretty figured linen gown, with a bunch of keys at your side; your hair combed smooth over a roll, and your apartment hung round with fruits in worsted, of your own working.

Lady T. O, yes! I remember it very well, and a curious life I led. My daily occupation to inspect the dairy, superintend the poultry, make extracts from the family receipt book; and comb my aunt Deborah's lap-dog.

Sir Peter T. Yes, yes, ma'am, 'twas so indeed.

Lady T. And then, you know, my evening amusements! To draw patterns for ruffles, which I had not materials to make up; to play Pope Joan with the curate; to read a sermon to my aunt; or to be stuck down to an old spinet to strum my father to sleep after a fox-chase.

Sir Peter T. I am glad you have so good a memory. Yes, madam, these were the recreations I took you from; but now you must have your coach—*vis-à-vis*—and three powdered footmen before your chair; and, in the summer, a pair of white cats to draw you to Kensington Gardens. No recollection, I suppose, when you were content to ride double, behind the butler, on a docked coach-horse?

Lady T. No; I swear I never did that. I deny the butler and the coach-horse.

Sir Peter T. This, madam, was your situation; and what have I done for you? I have made you a woman of fashion, of fortune, of rank; in short, I have made you my wife.

Lady T. Well, then, and there is but one thing more you can make me to add to the obligation, and that is——

Sir Peter T. My widow, I suppose?

Lady T. Hem! hem!

Sir Peter T. I thank you, madam; but don't flatter yourself; for though your ill conduct may disturb my peace, it shall never break my heart, I promise you; however, I am equally obliged to you for the hint.

Lady T. Then why will you endeavour to make yourself so disagreeable to me, and thwart me in every little elegant expense?

Sir Peter T. 'Slife, madam, I say, had you any of these little elegant expenses when you married me ?

Lady T. Lud, Sir Peter! would you have me be out of the fashion ?

Sir Peter T. The fashion, indeed! what had you to do with the fashion before you married me ?

Lady T. For my part, I should think you would like to have your wife thought a woman of taste.

Sir Peter T. Ay, there again; taste! Z—ds! madam, you had no taste when you married me !

Lady T. That's very true indeed, Sir Peter; and after having married you, I should never pretend to taste again, I allow. But now, Sir Peter, if we have finished our daily jangle, I presume I may go to my engagement at Lady Sneerwell's.

Sir Peter T. Ay, there's another precious circumstance; a charming set of acquaintance you have made there.

Lady T. Nay, Sir Peter, they are all people of rank and fortune, and remarkably tenacious of reputation.

Sir Peter T. Yes, egad, they are tenacious of reputation with a vengeance; for they don't choose anybody should have a character but themselves! Such a crew! Ah! many a wretch has rid on a hurdle who has done less mischief than these utterers of forged tales, coiners of scandal, and clippers of reputation.

Lady T. What! would you restrain the freedom of speech?

Sir Peter T. Ah! they have made you just as bad as any one of the society.

Lady T. Why, I believe I do bear a part with a tolerable grace. But I vow I bear no malice against the people I abuse. When I say an ill-natured thing, 'tis out of pure good humour; and I take it for granted, they deal exactly in the same manner with me. But, Sir Peter, you know you promised to come to Lady Sneerwell's too.

Sir Peter T. Well, well, I'll call in just to look after my own character.

Lady T. Then indeed you must make haste after me, or you'll be too late. So, good-bye to ye.

[*Exit* Lady TEAZLE.

Sir Peter T. So, I have gained much by my intended expostulation; yet, with what a charming air she contradicts everything I say, and how pleasingly she shows her contempt for my authority! Well, though I can't make her love me, there is great satisfaction in quarrelling with her; and I think she never appears to such advantage as when she is doing everything in her power to plague me. [*Exit.*

SCENE II.

At Lady SNEERWELL'S.

Enter Lady SNEERWELL, Mrs. CANDOUR, CRABTREE, Sir BENJAMIN BACKBITE, *and* JOSEPH SURFACE.

Lady Sneer. Nay, positively, we will hear it.

Joseph S. Yes, yes, the epigram, by all means.

Sir Benj. B. O plague on't, uncle! 'tis mere nonsense.

Crabt. No, no; 'fore Gad, very clever for an extempore!

Sir Benj. B. But, ladies, you should be acquainted with the circumstances. You must know, that one day last week, as Lady Betty Curricle was taking the dust in Hyde Park, in a sort of duodecimo phaeton, she desired me to write some verses on her ponies, upon which I took out my pocket-book, and in one moment produced the following :—

Sure never were seen two such beautiful ponies;
Other horses are clowns, but these macaronies:
To give them this title I'm sure can't be wrong,
Their legs are so slim, and their tails are so long.

Crabt. There, ladies, done in the smack of a whip, and on horseback too.

Joseph S. A very Phœbus mounted, indeed, Sir Benjamin.

Sir Benj. B. O dear sir! trifles, trifles.

Enter Lady TEAZLE *and* MARIA.

Mrs. Can. I must have a copy.

Lady Sneer. Lady Teazle, I hope we shall see Sir Peter?

Lady T. I believe he'll wait on your ladyship presently.

Lady Sneer. Maria, my love, you look grave. Come, you shall set down to piquet with Mr. Surface.

Maria. I take very little pleasure in cards; however, I'll do as you please.

Lady T. I am surprised Mr. Surface should sit down with her; I thought he would have embraced this opportunity of speaking to me, before Sir Peter came.

[*Aside.*

Mrs. Can. Now, I'll die, but you are so scandalous, I'll forswear your society.

Lady T. What's the matter, Mrs. Candour?

Mrs. Can. They'll not allow our friend, Miss Vermilion, to be handsome.

Lady Sneer. O surely she is a pretty woman.

Crabt. I'm very glad you think so, ma'am.

Mrs. Can. She has a charming fresh colour.

Lady T. Yes, when it is fresh put on.

Mrs. Can. O fie! I'll swear her colour is natural; I have seen it come and go.

Lady T. I dare swear you have, ma'am; it goes off at night, and comes again in the morning.

Sir Benj. B. True, ma'am, it not only comes and goes, but what's more, egad! her maid can fetch and carry it.

Mrs. Can. Ha! ha! ha! how I hate to hear you talk so! But surely, now, her sister *is*, or *was*, very handsome.

Crabt. Who? Mrs. Evergreen? O Lord! she's six and fifty if she's an hour.

Mrs. Can. Now positively you wrong her; fifty-two or fifty-three is the utmost; and I don't think she looks more.

Sir Benj. B. Ah! there's no judging by her looks, unless one could see her face.

Lady Sneer. Well, well, if Mrs. Evergreen *does* take some pains to repair the ravages of time, you must allow she effects it with great ingenuity, and surely that's better than the careless manner in which the widow Ochre chalks her wrinkles.

Sir Benj. B. Nay, now, Lady Sneerwell, you are severe upon the widow. Come, come, 'tis not that she paints so ill, but when she has finished her face, she joins it so badly to her neck, that she looks like a mended statue, in which the connoisseur sees at once that the head's modern though the trunk's antique.

Crabt. Ha! ha! ha! well said, nephew.

Mrs. Can. Ha! ha! ha! well, you make me laugh, but I vow I hate you for it. What do you think of Miss Simper?

Sir Benj. B. Why, she has very pretty teeth.

Lady T. Yes, and on that account, when she is neither speaking nor laughing (which very seldom happens), she never absolutely shuts her mouth, but leaves it always on a jar, as it were—thus

[*Shows her teeth.*

Mrs. Can. How can you be so ill-natured?

Lady T. Nay, I allow even that's better than the pains Mrs. Prim takes to conceal her losses in front. She draws her mouth till it positively resembles the aperture of a poor's box, and all her words appear to slide out edgewise, as it were thus, *How do you do, madam? Yes, madam.*

Lady Sneer. Very well, Lady Teazle; I see you can be a little severe.

Lady T. In defence of a friend it is but justice. But here comes Sir Peter to spoil our pleasantry.

Enter Sir PETER TEAZLE.

Sir Peter T. Ladies, your most obedient. Mercy on me! here is the whole set! a character dead at every word, I suppose.   [*Aside.*

Mrs. Can. I am rejoiced you are come, Sir Peter. They have been so censorious; and Lady Teazle as bad as any one.

Sir Peter T. It must be very distressing to *you*, Mrs. Candour, I dare swear.

Mrs. Can. O, they will allow good qualities to nobody; not even good nature to our friend Mrs. Pursy.

Lady T. What, the fat dowager who was at Mrs. Quadrille's last night?

Mrs. Can. Nay, her bulk is her misfortune; and when she takes such pains to get rid of it, you ought not to reflect on her.

Lady Sneer. That's very true, indeed.

Lady T. Yes, I know she almost lives on acids and small whey; laces herself by pullies; and often in the hottest noon in summer, you may see her on a little squat pony, with her hair plaited up behind like a drummer's, and puffing round the Ring on a full trot.

Mrs. Can. I thank you, Lady Teazle, for defending her.

Sir Peter T. Yes, a good defence, truly!

Mrs. Can. Truly, Lady Teazle is as censorious as Miss Sallow.

Crabt. Yes, and she is a curious being to pretend to be censorious—an awkward gawky, without any one good point under heaven.

Mrs. Can. Positively you shall not be so very severe. Miss Sallow is a near relation of mine by marriage, and as for her person, great allowance is to be made; for, let me tell you, a woman labours under many disadvantages who tries to pass for a girl at six-and-thirty.

Lady Sneer. Though, surely, she is handsome still; and for the weakness in her eyes, considering how much she reads by candlelight, it is not to be wondered at.

Mrs. Can. True, and then as to her manner; upon my word I think it is particularly graceful, considering she had never had the least education; for you know her mother was a Welsh milliner, and her father a sugar-baker at Bristol.

Sir Benj. B. Ah! you are both of you too good natured!

Sir Peter T. Yes, d—d good natured! This their own relation! mercy on me!   [*Aside.*

Mrs. Can. For my part; I own I cannot bear to hear a friend ill spoken of.

Sir Peter T. No, to be sure!

Sir Benj. B. Oh! you are of a moral turn. Mrs. Candour and I can sit for an hour and hear Lady Stucco talk sentiment.

Lady T. Nay, I vow Lady Stucco is very well with the dessert after dinner; for she's just like the French fruits one cracks for mottoes—made up of paint and proverb.

Mrs. Can. Well, I never will join in ridiculing a friend; and so I constantly tell my cousin Ogle, and you all know what pretensions she has to be critical on beauty.

Crabt. O to be sure! she has herself the oddest countenance that ever was seen; 'tis a collection of features from all the different countries of the globe.

Sir Benj. B. So she has, indeed—an Irish front—

Crabt. Caledonian locks—

Sir Benj. B. Dutch nose—

Crabt. Austrian lips—

Sir Benj. B. Complexion of a Spaniard—

Crabt. And teeth *à la Chinois.*

Sir Benj. B. In short, her face resembles a *table d'hôte* at Spa, where no two guests are of a nation—

Crabt. Or a congress at the close of a general war—wherein all the members, even to her eyes, appear to have a different interest, and her nose and chin are the only parties likely to join issue.

Mrs. Can. Ha! ha! ha!

Sir Peter T. Mercy on my life!—a person they dine with twice a week. [*Aside.*

Lady Sneer. Go, go; you are a couple of provoking toads.

Mrs. Can. Nay, but I vow you shall not carry the laugh off so; for give me leave to say that Mrs. Ogle——

Sir Peter T. Madam, madam, I beg your pardon;

there's no stopping these good gentlemen's tongues. But when I tell you, Mrs. Candour, that the lady they are abusing is a particular friend of mine, I hope you'll not take her part.

Lady Sneer. Ha! ha! ha! Well said, Sir Peter! But you are a cruel creature—too phlegmatic yourself for a jest, and too peevish to allow wit in others.

Sir Peter T. Ah! madam, true wit is more nearly allied to good-nature than your ladyship is aware of.

Lady T. True, Sir Peter. I believe they are so near akin that they can never be united.

Sir Benj. B. Or rather, madam, suppose them to be man and wife, because one seldom sees them together.

Lady T. But Sir Peter is such an enemy to scandal, I believe he would have it put down by Parliament.

Sir Peter T. 'Fore heaven, madam, if they were to consider the sporting with reputation of as much importance as poaching on manors, and pass an Act for the preservation of fame, I believe there are many would thank them for the bill.

Lady Sneer. O Lud! Sir Peter; would you deprive us of our privileges?

Sir Peter T. Ay, madam; and then no person should be permitted to kill characters and run down reputations, but qualified old maids and disappointed widows.

Lady Sneer. Go, you monster!

Mrs. Can. But, surely, you would not be quite so severe on those who only report what they hear?

Sir Peter T. Yes, madam, I would have law merchant for them too; and in all cases of slander currency, whenever the drawer of the lie was not to be found, the injured parties should have a right to come on any of the indorsers.

Crabt. Well, for my part, I believe there never was a scandalous tale without some foundation.

Sir Peter T. O, nine out of ten of the malicious inventions are founded on some ridiculous misrepresentation.

Lady Sneer. Come, ladies, shall we sit down to cards in the next room?

Enter a SERVANT, *who whispers* Sir PETER.

Sir Peter T. I'll be with them directly. I'll get away unperceived. [*Apart.*

Lady Sneer. Sir Peter, you are not going to leave us?

Sir Peter T. Your ladyship must excuse me; I'm called away by particular business. But I leave my character behind me. [*Exit* Sir PETER.

Sir Benj. B. Well; certainly, Lady Teazle, that lord of yours is a strange being; I could tell you some stories of him would make you laugh heartily if he were not your husband.

Lady T. O, pray don't mind that; come, do let's hear them.

[*Joins the rest of the company going into the next room.*

Joseph S. Maria, I see you have no satisfaction in this society.

Maria. How is it possible I should? If to raise malicious smiles at the infirmities or misfortunes of those who have never injured us be the province of wit or humour, Heaven grant me a double portion of dulness!

Joseph S. Yet they appear more ill-natured than they are; they have no malice at heart.

Maria. Then is their conduct still more contemptible; for, in my opinion, nothing could excuse the interference of their tongues, but a natural and uncontrollable bitterness of mind.

Joseph S. Undoubtedly, madam; and it has always been a sentiment of mine, that to propagate a malicious truth wantonly is more despicable than to falsify from revenge. But can you, Maria, feel thus for others, and be unkind to me alone? Is hope to be denied the tenderest passion?

Maria. Why will you distress me by renewing the subject?

Joseph S. Ah, Maria! you would not treat me thus, and oppose your guardian, Sir Peter's will, but that I see that profligate Charles is still a favoured rival.

Maria. Ungenerously urged! But whatever my sentiments are for that unfortunate young man, be assured I shall not feel more bound to give him up, because his distresses have lost him the regard even of a brother.

Joseph S. Nay, but Maria, do not leave me with a frown; by all that's honest, I swear——Gad's life, here's Lady Teazle! [*Aside.*] You must not; no, you shall not; for, though I have the greatest regard for Lady Teazle——

Maria. Lady Teazle!

Joseph S. Yet were Sir Peter to suspect——

Enter Lady TEAZLE, *and comes forward.*

Lady T. What is this, pray? Do you take her for me? Child, you are wanted in the next room. [*Exit* MARIA.] What is all this, pray?

Joseph S. O, the most unlucky circumstance in nature! Maria has somehow suspected the tender concern I have for your happiness, and threatened to acquaint Sir Peter with her suspicions, and I was just endeavouring to reason with her when you came in.

Lady T. Indeed! but you seemed to adopt a very

tender mode of reasoning; do you usually argue on your knees?

Joseph S. O, she's a child, and I thought a little bombast——But, Lady Teazle, when are you to give me your judgment on my library, as you promised?

Lady T. No, no; I begin to think it would be imprudent, and you know I admit you as a lover no farther than fashion sanctions.

Joseph S. True, a mere platonic cicisbeo—what every wife is entitled to.

Lady T. Certainly, one must not be out of the fashion. However, I have so much of my country prejudices left, that, though Sir Peter's ill-humour may vex me ever so, it never shall provoke me to——

Joseph S. The only revenge in your power. Well; I applaud your moderation.

Lady T. Go; you are an insinuating wretch. But we shall be missed; let us join the company.

Joseph S. But we had best not return together.

Lady T. Well, don't stay; for Maria sha'n't come to hear any more of your reasoning, I promise you.

[*Exit* Lady TEAZLE.

Joseph S. A curious dilemma my politics have run me into! I wanted, at first, only to ingratiate myself with Lady Teazle, that she might not be my enemy with Maria; and I have, I don't know how, become her serious lover. Sincerely I begin to wish I had never made such a point of gaining so very good a character, for it has led me into so many cursed rogueries that I doubt I shall be exposed at last.

[*Exit.*

SCENE III.

Sir Peter Teazle's.

Enter Rowley *and* Sir Oliver Surface.

Sir Oliver S. Ha! ha! ha! So my old friend is married, hey? a young wife out of the country. Ha! ha! ha! that he should have stood bluff to old bachelor so long, and sink into a husband at last.

Rowley. But you must not rally him on the subject, Sir Oliver; 'tis a tender point, I assure you, though he has been married only seven months.

Sir Oliver S. Then he has been just half a year on the stool of repentance! Poor Peter! But you say he has entirely given up Charles; never sees him, hey?

Rowley. His prejudice against him is astonishing, and I am sure greatly increased by a jealousy of him with Lady Teazle, which he has industriously been led into by a scandalous society in the neighbourhood, who have contributed not a little to Charles's ill name. Whereas the truth is, I believe, if the lady is partial to either of them, his brother is the favourite.

Sir Oliver S. Ay, I know there is a set of malicious, prating, prudent gossips, both male and female, who murder characters to kill time; and will rob a young fellow of his good name, before he has years to know the value of it. But I am not to be prejudiced against my nephew by such, I promise you. No, no; if Charles has done nothing false or mean, I shall compound for his extravagance.

Rowley. Then, my life on't, you will reclaim him. Ah, sir! it gives me new life to find that *your* heart is not turned against him; and that the son of my good old master has one friend, however, left.

Sir Oliver S. What, shall I forget, Master Rowley, when I was at his years myself? Egad, my brother and I were neither of us very prudent youths; and yet, I believe, you have not seen many better men than your old master was.

Rowley. Sir, 'tis this reflection gives me assurance that Charles may yet be a credit to his family. But here comes Sir Peter.

Sir Oliver S. Egad, so he does. Mercy on me! he's greatly altered, and seems to have a settled married look! One may read *husband* in his face at this distance!

Enter Sir PETER TEAZLE.

Sir Peter T. Ha! Sir Oliver, my old friend! Welcome to England a thousand times!

Sir Oliver S. Thank you—thank you, Sir Peter! and i'faith I am glad to find you well, believe me.

Sir Peter T. Oh! 'tis a long time since we met— fifteen years, I doubt, Sir Oliver, and many a cross accident in the time.

Sir Oliver S. Ay, I have had my share. But what! I find you are married, hey? Well, well, it can't be helped; and so—I wish you joy with all my heart.

Sir Peter T. Thank you, thank you, Sir Oliver. Yes, I have entered into—the happy state; but we'll not talk of that now.

Sir Oliver S. True, true, Sir Peter; old friends should not begin on grievances at first meeting; no, no, no.

Rowley. Take care, pray, sir.

Sir Oliver S. Well; so one of my nephews is a wild fellow, hey?

Sir Peter T. Wild! Ah! my old friend, I grieve for your disappointment there; he's a lost young man, indeed. However, his brother will make you amends. Joseph is, indeed, what a youth should be. Everybody in the world speaks well of him.

Sir Oliver S. I am sorry to hear it; he has too good a character to be an honest fellow. Everybody speaks well of him! Pshaw! then he has bowed as low to knaves and fools as to the honest dignity of genius and virtue.

Sir Peter T. What, Sir Oliver! do you blame him for not making enemies?

Sir Oliver S. Yes, if he has merit enough to deserve them.

Sir Peter T. Well, well; you'll be convinced when you know him. 'Tis edification to hear him converse; he professes the noblest sentiments.

Sir Oliver S. Oh! plague of his sentiments! If he salutes me with a scrap of morality in his mouth, I shall be sick directly. But, however, don't mistake me, Sir Peter; I don't mean to defend Charles's errors; but before I form my judgment of either of them, I intend to make a trial of their hearts; and my friend Rowley and I have planned something for the purpose.

Rowley. And Sir Peter shall own for once he has been mistaken.

Sir Peter T. Oh! my life on Joseph's honour.

Sir Oliver S. Well—come, give us a bottle of good wine, and we'll drink the lads' health, and tell you our scheme.

Sir Peter T. Allons, then!

Sir Oliver S. And don't, Sir Peter, be so severe against your old friend's son. Odds my life! I am not sorry that he has run out of the course a little; for my part I hate to see prudence clinging to the green suckers of youth; 'tis like ivy round a sapling, and spoils the growth of the tree. [*Exeunt.*

ACT III.—SCENE I.

Sir PETER TEAZLE'S.

Enter Sir PETER TEAZLE, Sir OLIVER SURFACE, *and* ROWLEY.

Sir Peter T. Well, then, we will see this fellow first, and have our wine afterwards; but how is this, Master Rowley? I don't see the jet of your scheme.

Rowley. Why, sir, this Mr. Stanley, who I was speaking of, is nearly related to them by their mother. He was a merchant in Dublin, but has been ruined by a series of undeserved misfortunes. He has applied, by letter, to Mr. Surface and Charles; from the former he has received nothing but evasive promises of future service, while Charles has done all that his extravagance has left him power to do, and he is, at this time, endeavouring to raise a sum of money, part of which, in the midst of his own distresses, I know he intends for the service of poor Stanley.

Sir Oliver S. Ah! he is my brother's son.

Sir Peter T. Well, but how is Sir Oliver personally to——

Rowley. Why, sir, I will inform Charles and his brother that Stanley has obtained permission to apply personally to his friends, and as they have neither of them ever seen him, let Sir Oliver assume his character, and he will have a fair opportunity of judging, at least, of the benevolence of their dispositions; and believe me, sir, you will find in the youngest brother one who, in the midst of folly and dissipation, has still, as our immortal bard expresses it, "a heart to pity, and a hand, open as day, for melting charity."

Sir Peter T. Pshaw! What signifies his having an open hand or purse either, when he has nothing left to give? Well, well, make the trial, if you please. But where is the fellow whom you brought for Sir Oliver to examine, relative to Charles's affairs?

Rowley. Below, waiting his commands, and no one can give him better intelligence. This, Sir Oliver, is a friendly Jew, who, to do him justice, has done everything in his power to bring your nephew to a proper sense of his extravagance.

Sir Peter T. Pray let us have him in.

Rowley. Desire Mr. Moses to walk upstairs.

[*Apart to* SERVANT.

Sir Peter T. But, pray, why should you suppose he will speak the truth?

Rowley. Oh! I have convinced him that he has no chance of recovering certain sums advanced to Charles, but through the bounty of Sir Oliver, who he knows is arrived, so that you may depend on his fidelity to his own interests. I have also another evidence in my power—one Snake, whom I have detected in a matter little short of forgery, and shall speedily produce him to remove some of your prejudices.

Sir Peter T. I have heard too much on that subject.

Rowley. Here comes the honest Israelite.

Enter MOSES.

This is Sir Oliver.

Sir Oliver S. Sir, I understand you have lately had great dealings with my nephew, Charles.

Moses. Yes, Sir Oliver, I have done all I could for him; but he was ruined before he came to me for assistance.

Sir Oliver S. That was unlucky, truly; for you have had no opportunity of showing your talents.

Moses. None at all; I hadn't the pleasure of knowing his distresses till he was some thousands worse than nothing.

Sir Oliver S. Unfortunate, indeed! But I suppose you have done all in your power for him, honest Moses?

Moses. Yes, he knows that. This very evening I was to have brought him a gentleman from the city, who does not know him, and will, I believe, advance him some money.

Sir Peter T. What! one Charles has never had money from before?

Moses. Yes; Mr. Premium, of Crutched Friars, formerly a broker.

Sir Peter T. Egad, Sir Oliver, a thought strikes me! Charles, you say, does not know Mr. Premium?

Moses. Not at all.

Sir Peter T. Now then, Sir Oliver, you may have a better opportunity of satisfying yourself than by an old romancing tale of a poor relation. Go with my friend Moses, and represent Premium, and then, I'll answer for it, you'll see your nephew in all his glory.

Sir Oliver S. Eg d, I like this idea better than the other, and I may visit Joseph afterwards as Old Stanley.

Sir Peter T. True, so you may.

Rowley. Well, this is taking Charles rather at a disadvantage, to be sure. However, Moses, you understand Sir Peter, and will be faithful?

Moses. You may depend upon me. This is near the time I was to have gone.

Sir Oliver S. I'll accompany you as soon as you please, Moses. But hold! I have forgot one thing—how the plague shall I be able to pass for a Jew?

Moses. There's no need—the principal is Christian.

Sir Oliver S. Is he? I'm very sorry to hear it. But then, again, a'n't I rather too smartly dressed to look like a money lender?

Sir Peter T. Not at all; 'twould not be out of character if you went in your own carriage—would it, Moses?

Moses. Not in the least.

Sir Oliver S. Well, but how must I talk? There's certainly some cant of usury and mode of treating that I ought to know.

Sir Peter T. O! there's not much to learn. The great point, as I take it, is to be exorbitant enough in your demands—hey, Moses?

Moses. Yes, that's a very great point.

Sir Oliver S. I'll answer for't I'll not be wanting in that. I'll ask him eight or ten per cent. on the loan, at least.

Moses. If you ask him no more than that, you'll be discovered immediately.

Sir Oliver S. Hey! what the plague! How much, then?

Moses. That depends upon the circumstances. If he

appears not very anxious for the supply, you should require only forty or fifty per cent.; but if you find him in great distress, and want the moneys very bad, you may ask double.

Sir Peter T. A good honest trade you're learning, Sir Oliver!

Sir Oliver S. Truly, I think so; and not un-profitable.

Moses. Then, you know, you hav'n't the moneys yourself, but are forced to borrow them for him of an old friend.

Sir Oliver S. Oh! I borrow it of a friend, do I?

Moses. And your friend is an unconscionable dog; but you can't help that.

Sir Oliver S. My friend an unconscionable dog?

Moses. Yes, and he himself has not the moneys by him, but is forced to sell stock at a great loss.

Sir Oliver S. He is forced to sell stock at a great loss, is he? Well, that's very kind of him.

Sir Peter T. I'faith, Sir Oliver—Mr. Premium, I mean—you'll soon be master of the trade. But, Moses! would not you have him run out a little against the Annuity Bill? That would be in character, I should think.

Moses. Very much.

Rowley. And lament that a young man now must be at years of discretion before he is suffered to ruin himself?

Moses. Ay, great pity!

Sir Peter T. And abuse the public for allowing merit to an Act, whose only object is to snatch misfortune and imprudence from the rapacious gripe of usury, and give the minor a chance of inheriting his estate without being undone by coming into possession.

Sir Oliver S. So, so; Moses shall give me further instructions as we go together.

Sir Peter T. You will not have much time, for your nephew lives hard by.

Sir Oliver S. O! never fear; my tutor appears so able, that though Charles lived in the next street, it must be my own fault if I am not a complete rogue before I turn the corner.

              [*Exeunt* Sir OLIVER SURFACE *and* MOSES.

Sir Peter T. So, now, I think Sir Oliver will be convinced. You are partial, Rowley, and would have prepared Charles for the other plot.

Rowley. No, upon my word, Sir Peter.

Sir Peter T. Well, go bring me this Snake, and I'll hear what he has to say presently. I see Maria, and want to speak with her. [*Exit* ROWLEY.] I should be glad to be convinced my suspicions of Lady Teazle and Charles were unjust. I have never yet opened my mind on this subject to my friend Joseph. I am determined I will do it; he will give me his opinion sincerely.

Enter MARIA.

So, child, has Mr. Surface returned with you?

Maria. No, sir; he was engaged.

Sir Peter T. Well, Maria, do you not reflect, the more you converse with that amiable young man, what return his partiality for you deserves?

Maria. Indeed, Sir Peter, your frequent importunity on this subject distresses me extremely; you compel me to declare, that I know no man who has ever paid me a particular attention, whom I would not prefer to Mr. Surface.

Sir Peter T. So, here's perverseness! No, no,

Maria, 'tis Charles only whom you would prefer. 'Tis evident his vices and follies have won your heart.

Maria. This is unkind, sir. You know I have obeyed you in neither seeing nor corresponding with him. I have heard enough to convince me that he is unworthy my regard. Yet I cannot think it culpable, if, while my understanding severely condemns his vices, my heart suggests some pity for his distresses.

Sir Peter T. Well, well, pity him as much as you please; but give your heart and hand to a worthier object.

Maria. Never to his brother!

Sir Peter T. Go, perverse and obstinate! But take care, madam; you have never yet known what the authority of a guardian is. Don't compel me to inform you of it.

Maria. I can only say, you shall not have just reason. 'Tis true, by my father's will, I am for a short period bound to regard you as his substitute; but must cease to think you so, when you would compel me to be miserable. [*Exit* MARIA.

Sir Peter T. Was ever man so crossed as I am? everything conspiring to fret me! I had not been involved in matrimony a fortnight, before her father, a hale and hearty man, died, on purpose, I believe, for the pleasure of plaguing me with the care of his daughter. But here comes my helpmate! She appears in great good humour. How happy I should be if I could tease her into loving me, though but a little!

Enter Lady TEAZLE.

Lady T. Lud! Sir Peter, I hope you hav'n't been

quarrelling with Maria? It is not using me well to be ill humoured when I am not by.

Sir Peter T. Ah! Lady Teazle, you might have the power to make me good humoured at all times.

Lady T. I am sure I wish I had; for I want you to be in a charming sweet *temper* at this moment. Do be good humoured now, and let me have two hundred pounds, will you?

Sir Peter T. Two hundred pounds! What, a'n't I to be in a good humour without paying for it? But speak to me thus, and i'faith there's nothing I could refuse you. You shall have it; but seal me a bond for the repayment.

Lady T. O no—there. My note of hand will do as well. [*Offering her hand.*

Sir Peter T. And you shall no longer reproach me with not giving you an independent settlement. I mean shortly to surprise you. But shall we always live thus, hey?

Lady T. If you please. I'm sure I don't care how soon we leave off quarrelling, provided you'll own you were tired first.

Sir Peter T. Well, then let our future contest be, who shall be most obliging.

Lady T. I assure you, Sir Peter, good nature becomes you. You look now as you did before we were married, when you used to walk with me under the elms, and tell me stories of what a gallant you were in your youth, and chuck me under the chin, you would; and ask me if I thought I could love an old fellow, who would deny me nothing—didn't you?

Sir Peter T. Yes, yes; and you were as kind and attentive——

Lady T. Ay, so I was, and would always take your

part, when my acquaintance used to abuse you, and turn you into ridicule.

Sir Peter T. Indeed!

Lady T. Ay, and when my cousin Sophy has called you a stiff, peevish old bachelor, and laughed at me for thinking of marrying one who might be my father, I have always defended you, and said, I didn't think you so ugly by any means, and I dared say you'd make a very good sort of a husband.

Sir Peter T. And you prophesied right; and we shall now be the happiest couple——

Lady T. And never differ again?

Sir Peter T. No, never! Though at the same time, indeed, my dear Lady Teazle, you must watch your temper very seriously; for in all our little quarrels, my dear, if you recollect, my love, you always began first.

Lady T. I beg your pardon, my dear Sir Peter: indeed, you always gave the provocation.

Sir Peter T. Now see, my angel! take care; contradicting isn't the way to keep friends.

Lady T. Then don't you begin it, my love!

Sir Peter T. There, now! you—you are going on. You don't perceive, my life, that you are just doing the very thing which you know always makes me angry.

Lady T. Nay, you know if you will be angry without any reason, my dear——

Sir Peter T. There! now you want to quarrel again.

Lady T. No, I am sure I don't; but if you will be so peevish——

Sir Peter T. There now! who begins first?

Lady T. Why you, to be sure. I said nothing; but there's no bearing your temper.

Sir Peter T. No, no, madam; the fault's in your own temper.

Lady T. Ay, you are just what my cousin Sophy said you would be.

Sir Peter T. Your cousin Sophy is a forward, impertinent gipsy.

Lady T. You are a great bear, I'm sure, to abuse my relations.

Sir Peter T. Now may all the plagues of marriage be doubled on me, if ever I try to be friends with you any more!

Lady T. So much the better.

Sir Peter T. No, no, madam; 'tis evident you never cared a pin for me, and I was a madman to marry you —a pert, rural coquette, that had refused half the honest squires in the neighbourhood.

Lady T. And I am sure I was a fool to marry you; an old dangling bachelor, who was single at fifty, only because he never could meet with any one who would have him.

Sir Peter T. Ay, ay, madam; but you were pleased enough to listen to me; you never had such an offer before.

Lady T. No! didn't I refuse Sir Tivy Terrier, who everybody said would have been a better match? for his estate is just as good as yours, and he has broke his neck since we have been married.

Sir Peter T. I have done with you, madam! You are an unfeeling, ungrateful—but there's an end of everything. I believe you capable of everything that is bad. Yes, madam, I now believe the reports relative to you and Charles, madam. Yes, madam, *you* and Charles are—not without grounds——

Lady T. Take care, Sir Peter! you had better not insinuate any such thing! I'll not be suspected without cause, I promise you.

Sir Peter T. Very well, madam! very well! A

separate maintenance as soon as you please. Yes, madam, or a divorce! I'll make an example of myself for the benefit of all old bachelors. Let us separate, madam.

Lady T. Agreed! agreed! And now, my dear Sir Peter, we are of a mind once more, we may be the happiest couple, and never differ again, you know—ha! ha! ha! Well, you are going to be in a passion, I see, and I shall only interrupt you; so, bye—bye. [*Exit.*

Sir Peter T. Plagues and tortures! Can't I make her angry either! Oh, I am the most miserable fellow! but I'll not bear her presuming to keep her temper; no! she may break my heart, but she sha'n't keep her temper. [*Exit.*

SCENE II.

CHARLES SURFACE'S *House.*

Enter TRIP, MOSES, *and* Sir OLIVER SURFACE.

Trip. Here, Master Moses! if you'll stay a moment, I'll try whether—what's the gentleman's name?

Sir Oliver S. Mr. Moses, what is my name?

Moses. Mr. Premium.

Trip. Premium—very well.

[*Exit* TRIP, *taking snuff.*

Sir Oliver S. To judge by the servants, one wouldn't believe the master was ruined. But what!—sure, this was my brother's house?

Moses. Yes, sir; Mr. Charles bought it of Mr. Joseph, with the furniture, pictures, &c., just as the old gentleman left it. Sir Peter thought it a piece of extravagance in him.

Sir Oliver S. In my mind, the other's economy in selling it to him was more reprehensible by half.

Enter TRIP.

Trip. My master says you must wait, gentlemen; he has company, and can't speak with you yet.

Sir Oliver S. If he knew who it was wanted to see him, perhaps he would not send such a message?

Trip. Yes, yes, sir; he knows you are here. I did not forget little Premium; no, no, no.

Sir Oliver S. Very well; and I pray, sir, what may be your name?

Trip. Trip, sir; my name is Trip, at your service.

Sir Oliver S. Well then, Mr. Trip, you have a pleasant sort of place here, I guess?

Trip. Why, yes; here are three or four of us pass our time agreeably enough; but then our wages are sometimes a little in arrear—and not very great either —but fifty pounds a year, and find our own bags and bouquets.

Sir Oliver S. Bags and bouquets! halters and bastinadoes! 　　　　　　　　　　　　　　　　[*Aside.*

Trip. And, *à propos*, Moses; have you been able to get me that little bill discounted?

Sir Oliver S. Wants to raise money too! mercy on me! Has his distresses too, I warrant, like a lord, and affects creditors and duns. 　　　　　　　　　[*Aside.*

Moses. 'Twas not to be done, indeed, Mr. Trip.

Trip. Good lack, you surprise me! My friend Brush has indorsed it, and I thought when he put his name at the back of a bill 'twas the same as cash.

Moses. No! 'twouldn't do.

Trip. A small sum; but twenty pounds. Hark'ee, Moses, do you think you couldn't get it me by way of annuity?

Sir Oliver S. An annuity! ha! ha! a footman raise money by way of annuity! Well done, luxury, egad! [*Aside.*

Moses. Well, but you must insure your place.

Trip. O with all my heart! I'll insure my place, and my life too, if you please.

Sir Oliver S. It's more than I would your neck. [*Aside.*

Moses. But is there nothing you could deposit?

Trip. Why, nothing capital of my master's wardrobe has dropped lately; but I could give you a mortgage on some of his winter clothes, with equity of redemption before November; or you shall have the reversion of the French velvet, or a post-obit on the blue and silver: these, I should think, Moses, with a few pair of point ruffles, as a collateral security; hey, my little fellow?

Moses. Well, well. [*Bell rings.*

Trip. Egad, I heard the bell! I believe, gentlemen, I can now introduce you. Don't forget the annuity, little Moses! This way, gentlemen. I'll insure my place, you know.

Sir Oliver S. If the man be a shadow of the master, this is the temple of dissipation indeed. [*Exeunt.*

SCENE III.

CHARLES SURFACE, CARELESS, &c. &c. *at a table with wine, &c.*

Charles S. 'Fore heaven, 'tis true! there's the great degeneracy of the age. Many of our acquaintance have taste, spirit, and politeness; but, plague on't, they won't drink.

Careless. It is so indeed, Charles! they give into all

the substantial luxuries of the table, and abstain from nothing but wine and wit. O certainly society suffers by it intolerably; for now, instead of the social spirit of raillery that used to mantle over a glass of bright Burgundy, their conversation is become just like the Spa water they drink, which has all the pertness and flatulence of Champagne, without the spirit or flavour.

1st Gent. But what are they to do who love play better than wine?

Careless. True; there's Sir Harry diets himself for gaming, and is now under a hazard regimen.

Charles S. Then he'll have the worst of it. What! you wouldn't train a horse for the course by keeping him from corn? For my part, egad, I am never so successful as when I am a little merry; let me throw on a bottle of Champagne, and I never lose; at least, I never feel my losses, which is exactly the same thing.

2nd Gent. Ay, that I believe.

Charles S. And then, what man can pretend to be a believer in love, who is an abjurer of wine? 'Tis the test by which the lover knows his own heart. Fill a dozen bumpers to a dozen beauties, and she that floats atop is the maid that has bewitched you.

Careless. Now then, Charles, be honest, and give us your real favourite.

Charles S. Why, I have withheld her only in compassion to you. If I toast her, you must give a round of her peers, which is impossible—on earth.

Careless. Oh! then we'll find some canonized vestals or heathen goddesses that will do, I warrant!

Charles S. Here then, bumpers, you rogues! bumpers! Maria! Maria!

Sir Harry B. Maria who?

Charles S. O d—n the surname; 'tis too formal to

be registered in Love's calendar; but now, Sir Harry, beware, we must have beauty superlative.

Careless. Nay, never study, Sir Harry; we'll stand to the toast, though your mistress should want an eye, and you know you have a song will excuse you.

Sir Harry B. Egad, so I have! and I'll give him the song instead of the lady.

SONG.

Here's to the maiden of bashful fifteen;
 Here's to the widow of fifty;
Here's to the flaunting extravagant quean,
 And here's to the housewife that's thrifty.
Chorus. Let the toast pass,
   Drink to the lass,
I'll warrant she'll prove an excuse for the glass.

Here's to the charmer whose dimples we prize;
 Now to the maid who has none, sir;
Here's to the girl with a pair of blue eyes,
 And here's to the nymph with but *one*, sir.
Chorus. Let the toast pass, &c.

Here's to the maid with a bosom of snow;
 Now to her that's as brown as a berry;
Here's to the wife with a face full of woe,
 And now to the girl that is merry.
Chorus. Let the toast pass, &c.

For let 'em be clumsy, or let 'em be slim,
 Young or ancient, I care not a feather;
So fill a pint bumper quite up to the brim,
 And let us e'en toast them together.
Chorus. Let the toast pass, &c.

All. Bravo! bravo!

Enter TRIP, *and whispers* CHARLES SURFACE.

Charles S. Gentlemen, you must excuse me a little. Careless, take the chair, will you?

Careless. Nay, pr'ythee, Charles, what now? This is one of your peerless beauties, I suppose, has dropt in by chance?

Charles S. No, faith! To tell you the truth, 'tis a Jew and a broker, who are come by appointment.

Careless. O d—n it! let's have the Jew in.

1st Gent. Ay, and the broker too, by all means.

2nd Gent. Yes, yes, the Jew and the broker.

Charles S. Egad, with all my heart! Trip, bid the gentlemen walk in; though there's one of them a stranger, I can tell you.

Careless. Charles, let us give them some generous Burgundy, and perhaps they'll grow conscientious.

Charles S. O hang 'em, no! wine does but draw forth a man's natural qualities, and to make them drink would only be to whet their knavery.

Enter TRIP, Sir OLIVER SURFACE, *and* MOSES.

Charles S. So, honest Moses, walk in; walk in, pray, Mr. Premium—that's the gentleman's name, isn't it, Moses?

Moses. Yes, sir.

Charles S. Set chairs, Trip—sit down, Mr. Premium —glasses, Trip—sit down, Moses. Come, Mr. Premium, I'll give you a sentiment; here's *Success to usury!* Moses, fill the gentleman a bumper.

Moses. Success to usury!

Careless. Right, Moses; usury is prudence and industry, and deserves to succeed.

Sir Oliver S. Then, *here's all the success it deserves!*

Careless. No, no, that won't do! Mr. Premium,

you have demurred at the toast, and must drink it in a pint bumper.

1st Gent. A pint bumper, at least.

Moses. O pray, sir, consider; Mr. Premium's a gentleman.

Careless. And therefore loves good wine.

2nd Gent. Give Moses a quart glass; this is mutiny, and a high contempt for the chair.

Careless. Here, now for't! I'll see justice done, to the last drop of my bottle.

Sir Oliver S. Nay, pray, gentlemen; I did not expect this usage.

Charles S. No, hang it, you sha'n't! Mr. Premium's a stranger.

Sir Oliver S. Odd! I wish I was well out of their company. [*Aside.*

Careless. Plague on 'em, then! if they don't drink, we'll not sit down with them. Come, Harry, the dice are in the next room. Charles, you'll join us when you have finished your business with the gentlemen!

Charles S. I will! I will! [*Exeunt.*] Careless!

Careless. [*Returning.*] Well!

Charles S. Perhaps I may want you.

Careless. O, you know I am always ready: word, note, or bond, 'tis all the same to me. [*Exit.*

Moses. Sir, this is Mr. Premium, a gentleman of the strictest honour and secresy; and always performs what he undertakes. Mr. Premium, this is——

Charles S. Pshaw! have done. Sir, my friend Moses is a very honest fellow, but a little slow at expression: he'll be an hour giving us our titles. Mr. Premium, the plain state of the matter is this: I am an extravagant young fellow who wants to borrow money; you I take to be a prudent old fellow, who have got money to lend. I am blockhead enough to give fifty per cent. sooner than not have it; and you, I presume, are rogue enough to take a hundred if you can get it. Now, sir, you see we are acquainted at once, and may proceed to business without further ceremony.

Sir Oliver S. Exceeding frank, upon my word. I see, sir, you are not a man of many compliments.

Charles S. Oh no, sir! plain dealing in business I always think best.

Sir Oliver S. Sir, I like you the better for it; however, you are mistaken in one thing; I have no money to lend, but I believe I could procure some of a friend; but then he's an unconscionable dog, isn't he, Moses?

Moses. But you can't help that.

Sir Oliver S. And must sell stock to accommodate you—mustn't he, Moses?

Moses. Yes, indeed! You know I always speak the truth, and scorn to tell a lie!

Charles S. Right. People that speak truth generally do: but these are trifles, Mr. Premium. What! I know money isn't to be bought without paying for't!

Sir Oliver S. Well; but what security could you give? You have no land, I suppose?

Charles S. Not a molehill, nor a twig, but what's in the bough-pots out of the window!

Sir Oliver S. Nor any stock, I presume?

Charles S. Nothing but live stock, and that's only a few pointers and ponies. But pray, Mr. Premium, are you acquainted at all with any of my connections?

Sir Oliver S. Why, to say truth, I am.

Charles S. Then you must know that I have a dev'lish rich uncle in the East Indies, Sir Oliver Surface, from whom I have the greatest expectations?

Sir Oliver S. That you have a wealthy uncle I

have heard; but how your expectations will turn out is more, I believe, than you can tell.

Charles S. O no! there can be no doubt. They tell me I'm a prodigious favourite, and that he talks of leaving me everything.

Sir Oliver S. Indeed! this is the first I've heard of it.

Charles S. Yes, yes, 'tis just so. Moses knows 'tis true; don't you, Moses?

Moses. O yes! I'll swear to't.

Sir Oliver S. Egad, they'll persuade me presently I'm at Bengal. [*Aside.*

Charles S. Now I propose, Mr. Premium, if it's agreeable to you, a post-obit on Sir Oliver's life; though at the same time the old fellow has been so liberal to me, that I give you my word, I should be very sorry to hear that anything had happened to him.

Sir Oliver S. Not more than I should, I assure you. But the bond you mention happens to be just the worst security you could offer me, for I might live to a hundred, and never see the principal.

Charles S. O yes, you would; the moment Sir Oliver dies, you know, you would come on me for the money.

Sir Oliver S. Then I believe I should be the most unwelcome dun you ever had in your life?

Charles S. What! I suppose you're afraid that Sir Oliver is too good a life?

Sir Oliver S. No, indeed, I am not; though I have heard he is as hale and healthy as any man of his years in Christendom.

Charles S. There again now you are misinformed. No, no, the climate has hurt him considerably, poor uncle Oliver! Yes, yes, he breaks apace, I'm told,

and is so much altered lately, that his nearest relations
don't know him.

Sir Oliver S. No! ha! ha! ha! so much altered
lately, that his nearest relations don't know him!
ha! ha! ha! egad—ha! ha! ha!

Charles S. Ha! ha! you're glad to hear that, little
Premium?

Sir Oliver S. No, no, I'm not.

Charles S. Yes, yes, you are—ha! ha! ha! You
know that mends your chance.

Sir Oliver S. But I'm told Sir Oliver is coming
over? Nay, some say he is actually arrived?

Charles S. Pshaw! Sure I must know better than
you whether he's come or not. No, no; rely on't,
he's at this moment at Calcutta. Isn't he, Moses?

Moses. O yes, certainly.

Sir Oliver S. Very true, as you say, you must know
better than I, though I have it from pretty good
authority. Haven't I, Moses?

Moses. Yes, most undoubted!

Sir Oliver S. But, sir, as I understand you want
a few hundreds immediately, is there nothing you
could dispose of?

Charles S. How do you mean?

Sir Oliver S. For instance, now, I have heard that
your father left behind him a great quantity of massive
old plate?

Charles S. O Lud! that's gone long ago. Moses
can tell you how better than I can.

Sir Oliver S. Good lack! all the family race cups
and corporation bowls! [*Aside.*] Then it was also
supposed that his library was one of the most valuable
and compact——

Charles S. Yes, yes, so it was—vastly too much
so for a private gentleman. For my part, I was

always of a communicative disposition, so I thought it a shame to keep so much knowledge to myself.

Sir Oliver S. Mercy upon me! Learning that had run in the family like an heirloom! [*Aside.*] Pray, what are become of the books?

Charles S. You must inquire of the auctioneer, Master Premium, for I don't believe even Moses can direct you.

Moses. I know nothing of books.

Sir Oliver S. So, so, nothing of the family property left, I suppose?

Charles S. Not much, indeed; unless you have a mind to the family pictures. I have got a room full of ancestors above, and if you have a taste for paintings, egad, you shall have 'em a bargain.

Sir Oliver S. Hey! what the devil! sure, you wouldn't sell your forefathers, would you?

Charles S. Every man of them to the best bidder.

Sir Oliver S. What! your great uncles and aunts?

Charles S. Ay, and my great grandfathers and grandmothers too.

Sir Oliver S. Now I give him up. [*Aside.*] What, the plague, have you no bowels for your own kindred? Odd's life, do you take me for Shylock in the play, that you would raise money of me on your own flesh and blood?

Charles S. Nay, my little broker, don't be angry: what need you care if you have your money's worth?

Sir Oliver S. Well, I'll be the purchaser: I think I can dispose of the family canvas. Oh, I'll never forgive him this! never! [*Aside.*]

Enter CARELESS.

Careless. Come, Charles, what keeps you?

Charles S. I can't come yet : i'faith we are going to have a sale above stairs ; here's little Premium will buy all my ancestors.

Careless. O, burn your ancestors !

Charles S. No, he may do that afterwards, if he pleases. Stay, Careless, we want you ; egad, you shall be auctioneer ; so come along with us.

Careless. Oh, have with you, if that's the case. Handle a hammer as well as a dice-box !

Sir Oliver S. Oh, the profligates ! [*Aside.*]

Charles S. Come, Moses, you shall be appraiser, if we want one. Gad's life, little Premium, you don't seem to like the business ?

Sir Oliver S. O yes, I do, vastly. Ha ! ha ! ha ! yes, yes, I think it a rare joke to sell one's family by auction—ha ! ha !—O the prodigal ! [*Aside.*

Charles S. To be sure ! when a man wants money, where the plague should he get assistance if he can't make free with his own relations ? [*Exeunt.*

ACT IV.—SCENE I.

Picture Room at CHARLES'S.

Enter CHARLES SURFACE, SIR OLIVER SURFACE, MOSES, *and* CARELESS.

Charles S. Walk in, gentlemen ; pray walk in. Here they are, the family of the Surfaces, up to the Conquest.

Sir Oliver S. And, in my opinion, a goodly collection.

Charles S. Ay, ay ; these are done in the true spirit of portrait painting ; no *volontier grace* and expression.

Not like the works of your modern Raphaels, who give you the strongest resemblance, yet contrive to make your portrait independent of you ; so that you may sink the original and not hurt the picture. No, no ; the merit of these is the inveterate likeness—all stiff and awkward as the originals, and like nothing in human nature besides.

Sir Oliver S. Ah ! we shall never see such figures of men again.

Charles S. I hope not. Well, you see, Master Premium, what a domestic character I am. Here I sit of an evening surrounded by my family. But come, get to your pulpit, Mr. Auctioneer ; here's an old gouty chair of my father's will answer the purpose.

Careless. Ay, ay, this will do. But, Charles, I hav'n't a hammer ; and what's an auctioneer without his hammer ?

Charles S. Egad, that's true. What parchment have we here ? O, our genealogy in full. Here, Careless, you shall have no common bit of mahogany ; here's the family tree, for you, you rogue ; this shall be your hammer, and now you may knock down my ancestors with their own pedigree.

Sir Oliver S. What an unnatural rogue ! an *ex post facto* parricide ! [*Aside.*

Careless. Yes, yes, here's a bit of your generation indeed ; faith, Charles, this is the most convenient thing you could have found for the business, for 'twill serve not only as a hammer, but a catalogue into the bargain. Come, begin,—A-going, a-going, a-going !

Charles S. Bravo, Careless ! Well, here's my great uncle, Sir Richard Raveline, a marvellous good general in his day, I assure you. He served in all the Duke of Marlborough's wars, and got that cut over his eye at the battle of Malplaquet. What say you, Mr. Premium ?

look at him; there's a hero, not cut out of his feathers, as your modern clipp'd captains are, but enveloped in wig and regimentals, as a general should be. What do you bid?

Moses. Mr. Premium would have *you* speak.

Charles S. Why, then, he shall have him for ten pounds, and I'm sure that's not dear for a staff-officer.

Sir Oliver S. Heaven deliver me! his famous uncle Richard for ten pounds! [*Aside.*] Well, sir, I take him at that.

Charles S. Careless, knock down my uncle Richard. Here, now, is a maiden sister of his, my great aunt Deborah, done by Kneller, thought to be in his best manner, and a very formidable likeness. There she is, you see, a shepherdess feeding her flock. You shall have her for five pounds ten; the sheep are worth the money.

Sir Oliver S. Ah! poor Deborah; a woman who set such a value on herself! [*Aside.*] Five pounds ten; she's mine.

Charles S. Knock down my aunt Deborah! Here, now, are two that were a sort of cousins of theirs. You see, Moses, these pictures were done some time ago, when beaux wore wigs, and the ladies their own hair.

Sir Oliver S. Yes, truly, headdresses appear to have been a little lower in those days.

Charles S. Well, take that couple for the same.

Moses. 'Tis good bargain.

Charles S. Careless! This, now, is a grandfather of my mother, a learned judge, well known on the Western Circuit. What do you rate him at, Moses?

Moses. Four guineas.

Charles S. Four guineas! Gad's life, you don't bid

me the price of his wig. Mr. Premium, you have more respect for the woolsack; do let us knock his lordship down at fifteen.

Sir Oliver S. By all means.

Careless. Gone!

Charles S. And there are two brothers of his, William and Walter Blunt, Esquires, both members of parliament, and noted speakers, and what's very extraordinary, I believe, this is the first time they were ever bought or sold.

Sir Oliver S. That is very extraordinary, indeed! I'll take them at your own price, for the honour of Parliament.

Careless. Well said, little Premium! I'll knock them down at forty.

Charles S. Here's a jolly fellow; I don't know what relation, but he was mayor of Manchester. Take him at eight pounds.

Sir Oliver S. No, no; six will do for the mayor.

Charles S. Come, make it guineas, and I'll throw you the two aldermen there into the bargain.

Sir Oliver S. They're mine.

Charles S. Careless, knock down the mayor and aldermen. But, plague on't, we shall be all day retailing in this manner. Do let us deal wholesale; what say you, little Premium? Give us three hundred pounds for the rest of the family in the lump.

Careless. Ay, ay, that will be the best way.

Sir Oliver S. Well, well, anything to accommodate you—they are mine. But there is one portrait which you have always passed over.

Careless. What, that ill-looking little fellow over the settee?

Sir Oliver S. Yes, sir, I mean that; though I don't think him so ill-looking a little fellow, by any means.

Charles S. What, that? Oh! that's my uncle Oliver; 'twas done before he went to India.

Careless. Your uncle Oliver! Gad, then, you'll never be friends, Charles. That, now, to me, is as stern a looking rogue as ever I saw—an unforgiving eye, and a d—d disinheriting countenance! an inveterate knave, depend on't. Don't you think so, little Premium?

Sir Oliver S. Upon my soul, sir, I do not. I think it is as honest a looking face as any in the room, dead or alive. But I suppose uncle Oliver goes with the rest of the lumber?

Charles S. No, hang it! I'll not part with poor Noll. The old fellow has been very good to me, and, egad, I'll keep his picture while I've a room to put it in.

Sir Oliver S. The rogue's my nephew after all! [*Aside.*] But, sir, I have somehow taken a fancy to that picture.

Charles S. I'm sorry for't, for you certainly will not have it. Oons, haven't you got enough of them?

Sir Oliver S. I forgive him everything! [*Aside.*] But, sir, when I take a whim in my head I don't value money. I'll give you as much for that as for all the rest.

Charles S. Don't tease me, master broker. I tell you I'll not part with it, and there's an end of it.

Sir Oliver S. How like his father the dog is! [*Aside.*] Well, well, I have done.—I did not perceive it before, but I think I never saw such a striking resemblance. [*Aside.*]—Here is a draft for your sum.

Charles S. Why, 'tis for eight hundred pounds.

Sir Oliver S. You will not let Sir Oliver go?

Charles S. Z—ds! no! I tell you once more.

Sir Oliver S. Then never mind the difference, we'll

balance that another time. But give me your hand on
the bargain; you are an honest fellow, Charles. I beg
pardon, sir, for being so free. Come, Moses.

Charles S. Egad, this is a whimsical old fellow!
But hark'ee, Premium, you'll prepare lodgings for these
gentlemen?

Sir Oliver S. Yes, yes, I'll send for them in a day
or two.

Charles S. But, hold; do now send a genteel con-
veyance for them, for, I assure you, they were most of
them used to ride in their own carriages.

Sir Oliver S. I will, I will; for all but Oliver.

Charles S. Ay, all but the little nabob.

Sir Oliver S. You're fixed on that?

Charles S. Peremptorily.

Sir Oliver S. A dear extravagant rogue! [*Aside.*]
Good day! Come, Moses. Let me hear now who
calls him profligate!

[*Exeunt* Sir OLIVER SURFACE *and* MOSES.

Careless. Why, this is the oddest genius of the sort
I ever saw!

Charles S. Egad, he's the prince of brokers, I
think. I wonder how Moses got acquainted with so
honest a fellow. Hah! here's Rowley; do, Careless,
say I'll join the company in a few moments.

Careless. I will; but don't let that old blockhead
persuade you to squander any of that money on old
musty debts, or any such nonsense; for tradesmen,
Charles, are the most exorbitant fellows.

Charles S. Very true, and paying them is only
encouraging them.

Careless. Nothing else.

Charles S. Ay, ay, never fear. [*Exit* CARELESS.
Soh! this was an odd old fellow, indeed. Let me
see; two-thirds of this is mine by right, five hundred

and thirty odd pounds. 'Fore heaven! I find one's ancestors are more valuable relations than I took them for! Ladies and gentlemen, your most obedient and very grateful servant.

Enter ROWLEY.

Hah! old Rowley; egad, you are just come in time to take leave of your old acquaintance.

Rowley. Yes, I heard they were a going. But I wonder you can have such spirits under so many distresses.

Charles S. Why, there's the point! my distresses are so many, that I can't afford to part with my spirits ; but I shall be rich and splenetic, all in good time. However, I suppose you are surprised that I am not more sorrowful at parting with so many near relations; to be sure 'tis very affecting; but you see they never move a muscle, so why should I?

Rowley. There's no making you serious a moment.

Charles S. Yes, faith, I am so now. Here, my honest Rowley, here, get me this changed directly, and take a hundred pounds of it immediately to old Stanley.

Rowley. A hundred pounds! Consider only——

Charles S. Gad's life, don't talk about it; poor Stanley's wants are pressing, and if you don't make haste, we shall have some one call that has a better right to the money.

Rowley. Ah! there's the point! I never will cease dunning you with the old proverb——

Charles S. ' Be just before you're generous.' Why, so I would if I could ; but Justice is an old, lame, hobbling beldame, and I can't get her to keep pace with Generosity for the soul of me.

Rowley. Yet, Charles, believe me, one hour's reflection——

Charles S. Ay, ay, it's all very true; but, hark'ee, Rowley, while I have, by heaven, I'll give; so d—n your economy, and now for hazard. [*Exeunt.*

SCENE II.

The Parlour.

Enter Sir OLIVER SURFACE *and* MOSES.

Moses. Well, sir, I think, as Sir Peter said, you have seen Mr. Charles in high glory; 'tis great pity he's so extravagant. ·

Sir Oliver S. True, but he would not sell my picture.

Moses. And loves wine and women so much.

Sir Oliver S. But he would not sell my picture.

Moses. And games so deep.

Sir Oliver S. But he would not sell my picture. O, here's Rowley.

Enter ROWLEY.

Rowley. So, Sir Oliver, I find you have made a purchase——

Sir Oliver S. Yes, yes; our young rake has parted with his ancestors like old tapestry.

Rowley. And here has he commissioned me to redeliver you part of the purchase money. I mean, though, in your necessitous character of old Stanley.

Moses. Ah! there is the pity of all; he is so d—d charitable.

Rowley. And I left a hosier and two tailors in the hall, who, I'm sure, won't be paid, and this hundred would satisfy them.

Sir Oliver S. Well, well, I'll pay his debts, and his benevolence too. But now I am no more a broker, and you shall introduce me to the elder brother as old Stanley.

Rowley. Not yet a while; Sir Peter, I know, means to call there about this time.

Enter TRIP.

Trip. O, gentlemen, I beg pardon for not showing you out; this way. Moses, a word.

[Exeunt TRIP *and* MOSES.

Sir Oliver S. There's a fellow for you; would you believe it, that puppy intercepted the Jew on our coming, and wanted to raise money before he got to his master.

Rowley. Indeed!

Sir Oliver S. Yes, they are now planning an annuity business. Ah! Master Rowley, in my days servants were content with the follies of their masters, when they were worn a little threadbare; but now, they have their vices, like their birth-day clothes, with the gloss on. *[Exeunt.*

SCENE III.

A Library.

JOSEPH SURFACE *and a* SERVANT.

Joseph S. No letter from Lady Teazle?

Serv. No, sir.

Joseph S. I am surprised she has not sent, if she is prevented from coming. Sir Peter certainly does not suspect me. Yet, I wish I may not lose the heiress, through the scrape I have drawn myself into with the wife ; however, Charles's imprudence and bad character are great points in my favour. [*Knocking heard without.*

Serv. Sir, I believe that must be Lady Teazle.

Joseph S. Hold! See whether it is or not before you go to the door: I have a particular message for you, if it should be my brother.

Serv. 'Tis her ladyship, sir; she always leaves her chair at the milliner's in the next street.

Joseph S. Stay, stay; draw that screen before the window—that will do; my opposite neighbour is a maiden lady of so anxious a temper. [SERVANT *draws the screen, and exit.*] I have a difficult hand to play in this affair. Lady Teazle has lately suspected my views on Maria; but she must by no means be let into that secret—at least, till I have her more in my power.

Enter Lady TEAZLE.

Lady T. What, sentiment in soliloquy now? Have you been very impatient? O Lud! don't pretend to look grave. I vow I couldn't come before.

Joseph S. O, madam, punctuality is a species of constancy, a very unfashionable quality in a lady.

Lady T. Upon my word you ought to pity me. Do you know, Sir Peter is grown so ill-natured to me of late, and so jealous of Charles too; that's the best of the story, isn't it?

Joseph S. I am glad my scandalous friends keep that up. [*Aside.*

Lady T. I am sure I wish he would let Maria marry

him, and then perhaps he would be convinced. Don't you, Mr. Surface?

Joseph S. Indeed I do not. [*Aside.*] Oh, certainly I do! for then my dear Lady Teazle would also be convinced how wrong her suspicions were of my having any design on the silly girl.

Lady T. Well, well, I'm inclined to believe you. But isn't it provoking, to have the most ill-natured things said of one. And there's my friend, Lady Sneerwell, has circulated I don't know how many scandalous tales of me, and all without any foundation too; that's what vexes me.

Joseph S. Ay, madam, to be sure, that is the provoking circumstance—without foundation. Yes, yes, there's the mortification, indeed; for when a scandalous story is believed against one, there certainly is no comfort like the consciousness of having deserved it.

Lady T. No, to be sure, then I'd forgive their malice; but to attack me, who am really so innocent, and who never say an ill-natured thing of anybody—that is, of any friend; and then Sir Peter too, to have him so peevish, and so suspicious, when I know the integrity of my own heart! indeed 'tis monstrous!

Joseph S. But, my dear Lady Teazle, 'tis your own fault if you suffer it. When a husband entertains a groundless suspicion of his wife, and withdraws his confidence from her, the original compact is broken, and she owes it to the honour of her sex to outwit him.

Lady T. Indeed! so that if he suspects me without cause, it follows, that the best way of curing his jealousy is to give him reason for't.

Joseph S. Undoubtedly; for your husband should never be deceived in you; and in that case it becomes you to be frail in compliment to his discernment.

Lady T. To be sure, what you say is very reasonable, and when the consciousness of my innocence——

Joseph S. Ah! my dear madam, there is the great mistake: 'tis this very conscious innocence that is of the greatest prejudice to you. What is it makes you negligent of forms, and careless of the world's opinion? Why, the consciousness of your own innocence. What makes you thoughtless in your own conduct, and apt to run into a thousand little imprudences? Why, the consciousness of your own innocence. What makes you impatient of Sir Peter's temper, and outrageous at his suspicions? Why, the consciousness of your innocence.

Lady T. 'Tis very true!

Joseph S. Now, my dear Lady Teazle, if you would but once make a trifling *faux pas*, you can't conceive how cautious you would grow, and how ready to humour and agree with your husband.

Lady T. Do you think so?

Joseph S. Oh! I am sure on't; and then you would find all scandal would cease at once; for, in short, your character at present is like a person in a plethora, absolutely dying from too much health.

Lady T. So, so; then I perceive your prescription is, that I must sin in my own defence, and part with my virtue to secure my reputation?

Joseph S. Exactly so, upon my credit, ma'am.

Lady T. Well, certainly this is the oddest doctrine and the newest receipt for avoiding calumny!

Joseph S. An infallible one, believe me. Prudence, like experience, must be paid for.

Lady T. Why, if my understanding were once convinced——

Joseph S. O, certainly, madam, your understanding should be convinced. Yes, yes; heaven forbid I should persuade you to do anything you thought wrong. No, no, I have too much honour to desire it.

Lady T. Don't you think we may as well leave *honour* out of the question?

Joseph S. Ah! the ill effects of your country education, I see, still remain with you.

Lady T. I doubt they do indeed; and I will fairly own to you, that if I could be persuaded to do wrong, it would be by Sir Peter's ill usage sooner than your *honourable logic*, after all.

Joseph S. Then, by this hand, which he is unworthy of——   [*Taking her hand.*

Enter SERVANT.

'Sdeath, you blockhead! What do you want?

Serv. I beg your pardon, sir, but I thought you would not choose Sir Peter to come up without announcing him.

Joseph S. Sir Peter! Oons, the devil!

Lady T. Sir Peter! O Lud, I'm ruined! I'm ruined!

Serv. Sir, 'twasn't I let him in.

Lady T. Oh! I'm quite undone! What will become of me? Now, Mr. Logic. Oh! he's on the stairs. I'll get behind here; and if ever I'm so imprudent again——   [*Goes behind the screen.*

Joseph S. Give me that book. [*Sits down. Servant pretends to adjust his hair.*

Enter Sir PETER.

Sir Peter T. Ay, ever improving himself. Mr. Surface! Mr. Surface!

Joseph S. Oh! my dear Sir Peter, I beg your pardon. [*Gaping, throws away the book.*] I have been dozing over a stupid book. Well, I am much obliged to you for this call. You haven't been here,

I believe, since I fitted up this room. Books, you know, are the only things in which I am a coxcomb.

Sir Peter T. 'Tis very neat indeed. Well, well, that's proper; and you can make even your screen a source of knowledge; hung, I perceive, with maps?

Joseph S. O, yes, I find great use in that screen.

Sir Peter T. I dare say you must, certainly, when you want to find anything in a hurry.

Joseph S. Ay, or to hide anything in a hurry, either. [*Aside.*

Sir Peter T. Well, I have a little private business——

Joseph S. You need not stay (*to the* SERVANT).

Serv. No, sir. [*Exit.*

Joseph S. Here's a chair, Sir Peter. I beg——

Sir Peter T. Well, now we are alone, there is a subject, my dear friend, on which I wish to unburden my mind to you—a point of the greatest moment to my peace; in short, my dear friend, Lady Teazle's conduct of late has made me extremely unhappy.

Joseph S. Indeed! I am very sorry to hear it.

Sir Peter T. Ay, 'tis too plain she has not the least regard for me; but, what's worse, I have pretty good authority to suppose she has formed an attachment to another.

Joseph S. Indeed! you astonish me!

Sir Peter T. Yes; and, between ourselves, I think I've discovered the person.

Joseph S. How! you alarm me exceedingly.

Sir Peter T. Ay, my dear friend, I knew you would sympathize with me!

Joseph S. Yes, believe me, Sir Peter, such a discovery would hurt me just as much as it would you.

Sir Peter T. I am convinced of it. Ah! it is a happiness to have a friend whom we can trust even

with one's family secrets. But have you no guess who
I mean ?

Joseph S. I haven't the most distant idea. It can't
be Sir Benjamin Backbite !

Sir Peter T. Oh, no ! What say you to Charles ?

Joseph S. My brother ! impossible !

Sir Peter T. Oh ! my dear friend, the goodness of
your own heart misleads you. You judge of others
by yourself.

Joseph S. Certainly, Sir Peter, the heart that is conscious of its own integrity is ever slow to credit another's treachery.

Sir Peter T. True ; but your brother has no sentiment ; you never hear him talk so.

Joseph S. Yet I can't but think Lady Teazle herself
has too much principle.

Sir Peter T. Ay ; but what is principle against the
flattery of a handsome, lively young fellow ?

Joseph S. That's very true.

Sir Peter T. And there's, you know, the difference
of our ages makes it very improbable that she should
have any very great affection for me ; and if she were
to be frail, and I were to make it public, why the town
would only laugh at me, the foolish old bachelor, who
had married a girl.

Joseph S. That's true, to be sure ; they would laugh.

Sir Peter T. Laugh—ay, and make ballads, and
paragraphs, and the devil knows what of me.

Joseph S. No ; you must never make it public.

Sir Peter T. But then again—that the nephew of
my old friend, Sir Oliver, should be the person to
attempt such a wrong, hurts me more nearly.

Joseph S. Ay, there's the point. When ingratitude barbs the dart of injury, the wound has double
danger in it.

Sir Peter T. Ay, I, that was, in a manner, left his guardian; in whose house he had been so often entertained; who never in my life denied him—my advice.

Joseph S. O, 'tis not to be credited. There may be a man capable of such baseness, to be sure; but, for my part, till you can give me positive proofs, I cannot but doubt it. However, if it should be proved on him, he is no longer a brother of mine. I disclaim kindred with him; for the man who can break the laws of hospitality, and tempt the wife of his friend, deserves to be branded as the pest of society.

Sir Peter T. What a difference there is between you! What noble sentiments!

Joseph S. Yet, I cannot suspect Lady Teazle's honour.

Sir Peter T. I am sure I wish to think well of her, and to remove all ground of quarrel between us. She has lately reproached me more than once with having made no settlement on her; and, in our last quarrel, she almost hinted that she should not break her heart if I was dead. Now, as we seem to differ in our ideas of expense, I have resolved she shall have her own way, and be her own mistress in that respect for the future; and if I were to die, she will find I have not been inattentive to her interest while living. Here, my friend, are the drafts of two deeds, which I wish to have your opinion on. By one, she will enjoy eight hundred a year independent while I live; and, by the other, the bulk of my fortune at my death.

Joseph S. This conduct, Sir Peter, is indeed truly generous. I wish it may not corrupt my pupil.

[*Aside.*

Sir Peter T. Yes, I am determined she shall have no cause to complain, though I would not have her acquainted with the latter instance of my affection yet awhile.

Joseph S. Nor I, if I could help it.   [*Aside.*

Sir Peter T. And now, my dear friend, if you please, we will talk over the situation of your affairs with Maria.

Joseph S. [*Softly.*]   O, no, Sir Peter; another time, if you please.

Sir Peter T. I am sensibly chagrined at the little progress you seem to make in her affections.

Joseph S. I beg you will not mention it.   What are my disappointments when your happiness is in debate! [*Softly.*]   'Sdeath, I shall be ruined every way.   [*Aside.*

Sir Peter T. And though you are so averse to my acquainting Lady Teazle with your passion for Maria, I'm sure she's not your enemy in the affair.

Joseph S. Pray, Sir Peter, now, oblige me.   I am really too much affected by the subject we have been speaking of, to bestow a thought on my own concerns.   The man who is intrusted with his friend's distresses can never——

Enter SERVANT.

Well, sir?

Serv. Your brother, sir, is speaking to a gentleman in the street, and says he knows you are within.

Joseph S. 'Sdeath, blockhead, I'm not within; I'm out for the day.

Sir Peter T. Stay—hold—a thought has struck me: you shall be at home.

Joseph S. Well, well, let him up. [*Exit* SERVANT.] He'll interrupt Sir Peter, however.   [*Aside.*

Sir Peter T. Now, my good friend, oblige me, I entreat you. Before Charles comes, let me conceal myself somewhere; then do you tax him on the point we have been talking, and his answer may satisfy me at once.

Joseph S. O fie, Sir Peter! would you have me join in so mean a trick?—to trepan my brother, too?

Sir Peter T. Nay, you tell me you are sure he is innocent; if so, you do him the greatest service by giving him an opportunity to clear himself, and you will set my heart at rest. Come, you shall not refuse me; here, behind this screen will be—Hey! what the devil! there seems to be one listener there already. I'll swear I saw a petticoat!

Joseph S. Ha! ha! ha! Well, this is ridiculous enough. I'll tell you, Sir Peter, though I hold a man of intrigue to be a most despicable character, yet, you know, it does not follow that one is to be an absolute Joseph either! Hark'ee, tis a little French milliner—a silly rogue that plagues me—and having some character to lose, on your coming, sir, she ran behind the screen.

Sir Peter T. Ah! you rogue! But egad, she has overheard all I have been saying of my wife.

Joseph S. O, 'twill never go any farther, you may depend upon it.

Sir Peter T. No, then, faith, let her hear it out Here's a closet will do as well.

Joseph S. Well, go in there.

Sir Peter T. Sly rogue! sly rogue!

          [Going into the closet.

Joseph S. A narrow escape, indeed! and a curious situation I'm in, to part man and wife in this manner.

Lady T. (*Peeping.*) Couldn't I steal off?

Joseph S. Keep close, my angel!

Sir Peter T. (*Peeping.*) Joseph, tax him home.

Joseph S. Back, my dear friend!

Lady T. Couldn't you lock Sir Peter in?

Joseph S. Be still, my life !

Sir Peter T. (*Peeping.*) You're sure the little milliner won't blab ?

Joseph S. In, in, my good Sir Peter.   'Fore Gad, I wish I had a key to the door.

Enter CHARLES SURFACE.

Charles S. Holloa! brother, what has been the matter? Your fellow would not let me up at first. What! have you had a Jew or a wench with you ?

Joseph S. Neither, brother, I assure you.

Charles S. But what has made Sir Peter steal off? I thought he had been with you.

Joseph S. He *was*, brother; but hearing you were coming, he did not choose to stay.

Charles S. What! was the old gentleman afraid I wanted to borrow money of him ?

Joseph S. No, sir; but I am sorry to find, Charles, you have lately given that worthy man grounds for great uneasiness.

Charles S. Yes, they tell me I do that to a great many worthy men.   But how so, pray ?

Joseph S. To be plain with you, brother, he thinks you are endeavouring to gain Lady Teazle's affections from him.

Charles S. Who, I ? O Lud! not I, upon my word. Ha! ha! ha! ha! so the old fellow has found out that he has got a young wife, has he? Or, what is worse, Lady Teazle has found out she has an old husband?

Joseph S. This is no subject to jest on, brother.   He who can laugh——

Charles S. True, true, as you were going to say— then, seriously, I never had the least idea of what you charge me with, upon my honour.

Joseph S. Well, it will give Sir Peter great satisfaction to hear this. [*Aloud.*

Charles S. To be sure, I once thought the lady seemed to have taken a fancy to me; but, upon my soul, I never gave her the least encouragement; besides, you know my attachment to Maria.

Joseph S. But sure, brother, even if Lady Teazle had betrayed the fondest partiality for you——

Charles S. Why, look'ee, Joseph, I hope I shall never deliberately do a dishonourable action; but if a pretty woman was purposely to throw herself in my way; and that pretty woman married to a man old enough to be her father——

Joseph S. Well——

Charles S. Why, I believe I should be obliged to borrow a little of your morality, that's all. But, brother, do you know now that you surprise me exceedingly, by naming *me* with Lady Teazle? for, 'faith, I always understood you were her favourite.

Joseph S. O, for shame, Charles! This retort is foolish.

Charles S. Nay, I swear I have seen you exchange such significant glances——

Joseph S. Nay, nay, sir, this is no jest.

Charles S. Egad, I'm serious. Don't you remember one day when I called here——

Joseph S. Nay, prithee, Charles——

Charles S. And found you together——

Joseph S. Z—ds, sir! I insist——

Charles S. And another time when your servant——

Joseph S. Brother, brother, a word with you! Gad, I must stop him. [*Aside.*

Charles S. Informed, I say, that——

Joseph S. Hush! I beg your pardon, but Sir Peter has overheard all we have been saying. I knew you

would clear yourself, or I should not have con-
sented.

Charles S. How, Sir Peter! Where is he?

Joseph S. Softly; there!   [*Points to the closet.*

Charles S. O, 'fore heaven, I'll have him out. Sir
Peter, come forth!

Joseph S. No, no——

Charles S. I say, Sir Peter, come into court (*pulls
in* Sir PETER). What! my old guardian! What! turn
inquisitor, and take evidence incog.?

Sir Peter T. Give me your hand, Charles. I believe
I have suspected you wrongfully; but you mustn't be
angry with Joseph; 'twas my plan!

Charles S. Indeed!

Sir Peter T. But I acquit you. I promise you I
don't think near so ill of you as I did. What I have
heard has given me great satisfaction.

Charles S. Egad, then, 'twas lucky you didn't hear
any more; wasn't it, Joseph?   [*Apart to* JOSEPH.

Sir Peter T. Ah! you would have retorted on him.

Charles S. Ay, ay, that was a joke.

Sir Peter T. Yes, yes, I know his honour too well.

Charles S. But you might as well have suspected
him as *me* in this matter, for all that; mightn't he,
Joseph?   [*Apart to* JOSEPH.

Sir Peter T. Well, well, I believe you.

Joseph S. Would they were both well out of the
room!   [*Aside.*

Enter SERVANT, *and whispers* JOSEPH SURFACE.

Sir Peter T. And in future perhaps we may not be
such strangers.

Joseph S. Gentlemen, I beg pardon, I must wait on
you downstairs; here is a person come on particular
business.

Charles S. Well, you can see him in another room. Sir Peter and I have not met a long time, and I have something to say to him.

Joseph S. They must not be left together. [*Aside.*] I'll send this man away, and return directly. Sir Peter, not a word of the French milliner.

[*Apart to* Sir PETER, *and goes out.*

Sir Peter T. I! not for the world! [*Apart to* JOSEPH.] Ah! Charles, if you associated more with your brother, one might indeed hope for your reformation. He is a man of sentiment. Well, there is nothing in the world so noble as a man of sentiment.

Charles S. Pshaw! he is too moral by half, and so apprehensive of his good name, as he calls it, that I suppose he would as soon let a priest into his house as a girl.

Sir Peter T. No, no; come, come; you wrong him. No, no! Joseph is no rake, but he is no such saint either in that respect.—I have a great mind to tell him; we should have a laugh at Joseph. [*Aside.*

Charles S. Oh, hang him! He's a very anchorite, a young hermit.

Sir Peter T. Hark'ee; you must not abuse him; he may chance to hear of it again, I promise you.

Charles S. Why, you won't tell him?

Sir Peter T. No—but—this way. Egad, I'll tell him. [*Aside.*] Hark'ee; have you a mind to have a good laugh at Joseph?

Charles S. I should like it of all things.

Sir Peter T. Then, i'faith, we will; I'll be quit with him for discovering me. He had a girl with him when I called.

Charles S. What! Joseph? you jest.

Sir Peter T. Hush! a little French milliner, and the best of the jest is, she's in the room now.

Charles S. The devil she is!

Sir Peter T. Hush! I tell you!   [*Points.*

Charles S. Behind the screen! 'Slife, let's unveil her!

Sir Peter T. No, no—he's coming—you sha'n't, indeed!

Charles S. O, egad, we'll have a peep at the little milliner!

Sir Peter T. Not for the world; Joseph will never forgive me——

Charles S. I'll stand by you——

Sir Peter T. Odds, here he is (JOSEPH SURFACE *enters just as* CHARLES SURFACE *throws down the screen*).

Charles S. Lady Teazle, by all that's wonderful!

Sir Peter T. Lady Teazle, by all that's damnable!

Charles S. Sir Peter, this is one of the smartest French milliners I ever saw. Egad, you seem all to have been diverting yourselves here at hide and seek, and I don't see who is out of the secret. Shall I beg your ladyship to inform me? Not a word! Brother, will you be pleased to explain this matter? What! is Morality dumb too? Sir Peter, though I found you in the dark, perhaps you are not so now! All mute! Well, though I can make nothing of the affair, I suppose you perfectly understand one another, so I'll leave you to yourselves [*Going*]. Brother, I'm sorry to find you have given that worthy man cause for so much uneasiness. Sir Peter! there's nothing in the world so noble as a man of sentiment!

                                        [*Exit* CHARLES.

(*They stand for some time looking at each other.*)

Joseph S. Sir Peter—notwithstanding—I confess—that appearances are against me—if you will afford me your patience—I make no doubt—but I shall explain everything to your satisfaction.

Sir Peter T. If you please, sir.

Joseph S. The fact is, sir, that Lady Teazle, knowing my pretensions to your ward Maria—I say, sir, Lady Teazle, being apprehensive of the jealousy of your temper — and knowing my friendship to the family—She, sir, I say—called here—in order that—I might explain these pretensions—but on your coming—being apprehensive—as I said—of your jealousy—she withdrew—and this, you may depend on it, is the whole truth of the matter.

Sir Peter T. A very clear account, upon my word; and I dare swear the lady will vouch for every article of it.

Lady T. For not one word of it, Sir Peter!

Sir Peter T. How! don't you think it worth while to agree in the lie?

Lady T. There is not one syllable of truth in what that gentleman has told you.

Sir Peter T. I believe you, upon my soul, ma'am!

Joseph S. [*Aside.*] 'Sdeath, madam, will you betray me?

Lady T. Good Mr. Hypocrite, by your leave, I'll speak for myself.

Sir Peter T. Ay, let her alone, sir; you'll find she'll make out a better story than you, without prompting.

Lady T. Hear me, Sir Peter! I came hither on no matter relating to your ward, and even ignorant of this gentleman's pretensions to her. But I came seduced by his insidious arguments, at least to listen to his pretended passion, if not to sacrifice your honour to his baseness.

Sir Peter T. Now, I believe, the truth is coming indeed!

Joseph S. The woman's mad!

Lady T. No, sir, she has recovered her senses, and

your own arts have furnished her with the means. Sir Peter, I do not expect you to credit me, but the tenderness you expressed for me, when I am sure you could not think I was a witness to it, has penetrated so to my heart, that had I left the place without the shame of this discovery, my future life should have spoken the sincerity of my gratitude. As for that smooth-tongued hypocrite, who would have seduced the wife of his too credulous friend, while he affected honourable addresses to his ward, I behold him now in a light so truly despicable, that I shall never again respect myself for having listened to him.   [*Exit* Lady TEAZLE.

Joseph S. Notwithstanding all this, Sir Peter, Heaven knows——

Sir Peter T. That you are a villain! and so I leave you to your conscience.

Joseph S. You are too rash, Sir Peter; you shall hear me. The man who shuts out conviction by refusing to——

[*Exeunt* Sir PETER *and* SURFACE *talking.*

ACT V.—SCENE I.

The Library.

Enter JOSEPH SURFACE *and* SERVANT.

Joseph S. Mr. Stanley? and why should you think I would see him? you must know he comes to ask something.

Serv. Sir, I should not have let him in, but that Mr. Rowley came to the door with him.

Joseph S. Pshaw! blockhead! to suppose that I should now be in a temper to receive visits from poor relations! Well, why don't you show the fellow up?

Serv. I will, sir. Why, sir, it was not my fault that Sir Peter discovered my lady——

Joseph S. Go, fool! [*Exit* SERVANT.] Sure Fortune never played a man of my policy such a trick before. My character with Sir Peter, my hopes with Maria, destroyed in a moment! I'm in a rare humour to listen to other people's distresses! I sha'n't be able to bestow even a benevolent sentiment on Stanley. So! here he comes, and Rowley with him. I must try to recover myself, and put a little charity into my face, however. [*Exit.*

Enter Sir OLIVER SURFACE *and* ROWLEY.

Sir Oliver S. What! does he avoid us? That was he, was it not?

Rowley. It was, sir. But I doubt you are come a little too abruptly. His nerves are so weak, that the sight of a poor relation may be too much for him. I should have gone first to break it to him.

Sir Oliver S. O, plague of his nerves! Yet this is he whom Sir Peter extols as a man of the most benevolent way of thinking!

Rowley. As to his way of thinking, I cannot pretend to decide; for, to do him justice, he appears to have as much speculative benevolence as any private gentleman in the kingdom, though he is seldom so sensual as to indulge himself in the exercise of it.

Sir Oliver S. Yet has a string of charitable sentiments at his fingers' ends.

Rowley. Or rather at his tongue's end, Sir Oliver; for I believe there is no sentiment he has such faith in, as that ' Charity begins at home.'

Sir Oliver S. And his, I presume, is of that domestic sort which never stirs abroad at all?

Rowley. I doubt you'll find it so; but he's coming. I mustn't seem to interrupt you; and, you know, immediately as you leave him, I come in to announce your arrival in your real character.

Sir Oliver S. True; and afterwards you'll meet me at Sir Peter's.

Rowley. Without losing a moment.   [*Exit.*

Sir Oliver S. I don't like the complaisance of his features.

Enter JOSEPH SURFACE.

Joseph S. Sir, I beg you ten thousand pardons for keeping you a moment waiting. Mr. Stanley, I presume.

Sir Oliver S. At your service.

Joseph S. Sir, I beg you will do me the honour to sit down. I entreat you, sir!

Sir Oliver S. Dear sir, there's no occasion.—Too civil by half!   [*Aside.*

Joseph S. I have not the pleasure of knowing you, Mr. Stanley, but I am extremely happy to see you look so well. You were nearly related to my mother, I think, Mr. Stanley?

Sir Oliver S. I was, sir; so nearly, that my present poverty, I fear, may do discredit to her wealthy children, else I should not have presumed to trouble you.

Joseph S. Dear sir, there needs no apology; he that is in distress, though a stranger, has a right to claim kindred with the wealthy. I am sure I wish I was of that class, and had it in my power to offer you even a small relief.

Sir Oliver S. If your uncle, Sir Oliver, were here, I should have a friend.

Joseph S. I wish he was, sir, with all my heart: you should not want an advocate with him, believe me, sir.

Sir Oliver S. I should not need one—my distresses would recommend me. But I imagined his bounty would enable you to become the agent of his charity.

Joseph S. My dear sir, you were strangely misinformed. Sir Oliver is a worthy man, a very worthy man; but avarice, Mr. Stanley, is the vice of age. I will tell you, my good sir, in confidence, what he has done for me has been a mere nothing; though people, I know, have thought otherwise, and, for my part, I never chose to contradict the report.

Sir Oliver S. What! has he never transmitted you bullion—rupees—pagodas?

Joseph S. O, dear sir, nothing of the kind. No, no; a few presents now and then—china, shawls, congou tea, avadavats, and Indian crackers; little more, believe me.

Sir Oliver S. Here's gratitude for twelve thousand pounds! Avadavats and Indian crackers! [*Aside.*

Joseph S. Then, my dear sir, you have heard, I doubt not, of the extravagance of my brother; there are very few would credit what I have done for that unfortunate young man.

Sir Oliver S. Not I, for one! [*Aside.*

Joseph S. The sums I have lent him! Indeed I have been exceedingly to blame; it was an amiable weakness; however, I don't pretend to defend it; and now I feel it doubly culpable, since it has deprived me of the pleasure of serving you, Mr. Stanley, as my heart dictates.

Sir Oliver S. Dissembler! [*Aside.*] Then, sir, you can't assist me !

Joseph S. At present, it grieves me to say, I cannot; but, whenever I have the ability, you may depend upon hearing from me.

Sir Oliver S. I am extremely sorry——

Joseph S. Not more than I, believe me; to pity without the power to relieve, is still more painful than to ask and be denied.

Sir Oliver S. Kind sir, your most obedient humble servant.

Joseph S. You leave me deeply affected, Mr. Stanley. William, be ready to open the door.

Sir Oliver S. O, dear sir, no ceremony.

Joseph S. Your very obedient.

Sir Oliver S. Sir, your most obsequious.

Joseph S. You may depend upon hearing from me, whenever I can be of service.

Sir Oliver S. Sweet sir, you are too good !

Joseph S. In the mean time I wish you health and spirits.

Sir Oliver S. Your ever grateful and perpetual humble servant.

Joseph S. Sir, yours as sincerely.

Sir Oliver S. Charles, you are my heir !

[*Aside. Exit.*

Joseph S. This is one bad effect of a good character; it invites application from the unfortunate, and there needs no small degree of address to gain the reputation of benevolence without incurring the expense. The silver ore of pure charity is an expensive article in the catalogue of a man's good qualities; whereas the sentimental French plate I use instead of it makes just as good a show, and pays no tax.

Enter Rowley.

Rowley. Mr. Surface, your servant. I was apprehensive of interrupting you, though my business demands immediate attention, as this note will inform you.

Joseph S. Always happy to see Mr. Rowley. [*Reads the letter.*] Sir Oliver Surface! My uncle arrived!

Rowley. He is, indeed ; we have just parted—quite well, after a speedy voyage, and impatient to embrace his worthy nephew.

Joseph S. I am astonished! William! stop Mr. Stanley, if he's not gone.

Rowley. Oh! he's out of reach, I believe.

Joseph S. Why did you not let me know this when you came in together?

Rowley. I thought you had particular business; but I must be gone to inform your brother, and appoint him here to meet your uncle. He will be with you in a quarter of an hour.

Joseph S. So he says. Well, I am strangely overjoyed at his coming.—Never, to be sure, was anything so d—d unlucky. [*Aside.*

Rowley. You will be delighted to see how well he looks.

Joseph S. Ah! I'm rejoiced to hear it——Just at this time! [*Aside.*

Rowley. I'll tell him how impatiently you expect him.

Joseph S. Do, do; pray give my best duty and affection. Indeed, I cannot express the sensations I feel at the thought of seeing him. [*Exit* Rowley.] Certainly his coming just at this time is the cruellest piece of ill fortune! [*Exit.*

SCENE II.

Sir Peter Teazle's.

Enter Mrs. Candour *and* Maid.

Maid. Indeed, ma'am, my lady will see nobody at present.

Mrs. Can. Did you tell her it was her friend Mrs. Candour?

Maid. Yes, ma'am; but she begs you will excuse her.

Mrs. Can. Do go again; I shall be glad to see her, if it be only for a moment, for I am sure she must be in great distress. [*Exit* Maid.] Dear heart, how provoking! I'm not mistress of half the circumstances! We shall have the whole affair in the newspapers, with the names of the parties at length, before I have dropped the story at a dozen houses.

Enter Sir Benjamin Backbite.

Oh, Sir Benjamin! you have heard, I suppose——

Sir Benj. B. Of Lady Teazle and Mr. Surface——

Mrs. Can. And Sir Peter's discovery——

Sir Benj. B. O! the strangest piece of business, to be sure!

Mrs. Can: Well, I never was so surprised in my life. I am so sorry for all parties, indeed.

Sir Benj. B. Now, I don't pity Sir Peter at all; he was so extravagantly partial to Mr. Surface.

Mrs. Can. Mr. Surface! Why, 'twas with Charles Lady Teazle was detected.

Sir Benj. B. No, no, I tell you; Mr. Surface is the gallant.

Mrs. Can. No such thing! Charles is the man. 'Twas Mr. Surface brought Sir Peter on purpose to discover them.

Sir Benj. B. I tell you I had it from one——

Mrs. Can. And I have it from one——

Sir Benj. B. Who had it from one, who had it——

Mrs. Can. From one immediately—but here comes Lady Sneerwell; perhaps she knows the whole affair.

Enter Lady SNEERWELL.

Lady Sneer. So, my dear Mrs. Candour, here's a sad affair of our friend, Lady Teazle.

Mrs. Can. Ay, my dear friend, who would have thought——

Lady Sneer. Well, there is no trusting appearances; though, indeed, she was always too lively for me.

Mrs. Can. To be sure, her manners were a little too free; but then she was young!

Lady Sneer. And had, indeed, some good qualities.

Mrs. Can. So she had, indeed. But have you heard the particulars?

Lady Sneer. No; but everybody says that Mr. Surface——

Sir Benj. B. Ay, there; I told you Mr. Surface was the man.

Mrs. C. No, no; indeed the assignation was with Charles.

Lady Sneer. With Charles! You alarm me, Mrs. Candour!

Mrs. Can. Yes, yes, he was the lover. Mr. Surface, to do him justice, was only the informer.

Sir Benj. B. Well, I'll not dispute with you,

Mrs. Candour; but, be it which it may, I hope that Sir Peter's wound will not——

Mrs. Can. Sir Peter's wound! O, mercy! I didn't hear a word of their fighting.

Lady Sneer. Nor I, a syllable.

Sir Benj. B. No! what, no mention of the duel?

Mrs. Can. Not a word.

Sir Benj. B. O, yes; they fought before they left the room.

Lady Sneer. Pray, let us hear.

Mrs. Can. Ay, do oblige us with the duel.

Sir Benj. B. 'Sir,' says Sir Peter, immediately after the discovery, 'you are a most ungrateful fellow.'

Mrs. Can. Ay, to Charles.

Sir Benj. B. No, no, to Mr. Surface—'a most ungrateful fellow; and, old as I am, sir,' says he, 'I insist on an immediate satisfaction.'

Mrs. Can. Ay, that must have been to Charles; for 'tis very unlikely Mr. Surface should fight in his own house.

Sir Benj. B. Gad's life, ma'am, not at all. 'Giving me satisfaction.' On this, ma'am, Lady Teazle, seeing Sir Peter in such danger, ran out of the room in strong hysterics, and Charles after her, calling out for hartshorn and water; then, madam, they began to fight with swords.

Enter CRABTREE.

Crabt. With pistols, nephew—pistols. I have it from undoubted authority.

Mrs. Can. O, Mr. Crabtree, then it is all true!

Crabt. Too true, indeed, madam, and Sir Peter is dangerously wounded—

Sir Benj. B. By a thrust in second quite through his left side—

Crabt. By a bullet lodged in the thorax.

Mrs. Can. Mercy on me! Poor Sir Peter!

Crabt. Yes, madam; though Charles would have avoided the matter, if he could.

Mrs. Can. I knew Charles was the person.

Sir Benj. B. My uncle, I see, knows nothing of the matter.

Crabt. But Sir Peter taxed him with the basest ingratitude.

Sir Benj. B. That I told you, you know—

Crabt. Do, nephew, let me speak! and insisted on immediate—

Sir Benj. B. Just as I said—

Crabt. Odds life, nephew, allow others to know something too. A pair of pistols lay on the bureau (for Mr. Surface, it seems, had come home the night before late from Salthill, where he had been to see the Montem with a friend, who has a son at Eton), so, unluckily, the pistols were left charged.

Sir Benj. B. I heard nothing of this.

Crabt. Sir Peter forced Charles to take one, and they fired, it seems, pretty nearly together. Charles's shot took effect as I tell you, and Sir Peter's missed; but what is very extraordinary, the ball struck against a little bronze Shakspeare that stood over the fireplace, grazed out of the window at a right angle, and wounded the postman, who was just coming to the door with a double letter from Northampton-shire.

Sir Benj. B. My uncle's account is more cir-cumstantial, I confess; but I believe mine is the true one, for all that.

Lady Sneer. I am more interested in this affair than they imagine, and must have better information. (*Aside*).   [*Exit* Lady SNEERWELL.

Sir Benj. B. Ah! Lady Sneerwell's alarm is very easily accounted for.

Crabt. Yes, yes, they certainly do say; but that's neither here nor there.

Mrs. Can. But, pray, where is Sir Peter at present?

Crabt. Oh! they brought him home, and he is now in the house, though the servants are ordered to deny him.

Mrs. Can. I believe so, and Lady Teazle, I suppose, attending him.

Crabt. Yes, yes; and I saw one of the faculty enter just before me.

Sir Benj. B. Hey! who comes here?

Crabt. O, this is he: the physician, depend on't.

Mrs. Can. O, certainly: it must be the physician; and now we shall know.

Enter Sir OLIVER SURFACE.

Crabt. Well, doctor, what hopes?

Mrs. Can. Ay, doctor, how's your patient?

Sir Benj. B. Now, doctor, isn't it a wound with a small sword?

Crabt. A bullet lodged in the thorax, for a hundred.

Sir Oliver S. Doctor! a wound with a small sword! and a bullet in the thorax! Oons! are you mad, good people?

Sir Benj. B. Perhaps, sir, you are not a doctor?

Sir Oliver S. Truly, I am to thank you for my degree if I am.

Crabt. Only a friend of Sir Peter's, then, I presume. But, sir, you must have heard of his accident?

Sir Oliver S. Not a word!

Crabt. Not of his being dangerously wounded?

Sir Oliver S. The d—l he is!

Sir Benj. B. Run through the body——

Crabt. Shot in the breast——

Sir Benj. B. By one Mr. Surface——

Crabt. Ay, the younger.

Sir Oliver S. Hey! what the plague! you seem to differ strangely in your accounts: however, you agree that Sir Peter is dangerously wounded.

Sir Benj. B. O, yes, we agree there.

Crabt. Yes, yes, I believe there can be no doubt of that.

Sir Oliver S. Then, upon my word, for a person in that situation, he is the most imprudent man alive; for here he comes, walking as if nothing at all was the matter.

Enter Sir PETER TEAZLE.

Odds heart, Sir Peter, you are come in good time, I promise you; for we had just given you over.

Sir Benj. B. Egad, uncle, this is the most sudden recovery!

Sir Oliver S. Why, man, what do you out of bed with a small sword through your body, and a bullet lodged in your thorax?

Sir Peter T. A small sword, and a bullet!

Sir Oliver S. Ay, these gentlemen would have killed you without law, or physic, and wanted to dub me a doctor, to make me an accomplice.

Sir Peter T. Why, what is all this?

Sir Benj. B. We rejoice, Sir Peter, that the story of the duel is not true, and are sincerely sorry for your other misfortune.

Sir Peter T. So, so; all over the town already.

[*Aside.*

Crabt. Though, Sir Peter, you were certainly vastly to blame to marry at your years.

Sir Peter T. Sir, what business is that of yours?

Mrs. Can. Though, indeed, as Sir Peter made so good a husband, he's very much to be pitied.

Sir Peter T. Plague on your pity, ma'am! I desire none of it.

Sir Benj. B. However, Sir Peter, you must not mind the laughing and jests you will meet with on the occasion.

Sir Peter T. Sir, sir, I desire to be master in my own house.

Crabt. 'Tis no uncommon case, that's one comfort.

Sir Peter T. I insist on being left to myself; without ceremony. I insist on your leaving my house directly.

Mrs. Can. Well, well, we are going, and depend on't we'll make the best report of it we can.   [*Exit.*

Sir Peter T. Leave my house!

Crabt. And tell how hardly you've been treated.

[*Exit.*

Sir Peter T. Leave my house!

Sir Benj. B. And how patiently you bear it. [*Exit.*

Sir Peter T. Fiends! vipers! furies! Oh! that their own venom would choke them!

Sir Oliver S. They are very provoking, indeed, Sir Peter.

Enter ROWLEY.

Rowley. I heard high words; what has ruffled you, sir?

Sir Peter T. Pshaw! what signifies asking? Do I ever pass a day without my vexations?

Rowley. Well, I'm not inquisitive.

Sir Oliver S. Well, Sir Peter, I have seen both my nephews in the manner we proposed.

Sir Peter T. A precious couple they are!

Rowley. Yes, and Sir Oliver is convinced that your judgment was right, Sir Peter.

Sir Oliver S. Yes, I find Joseph is indeed the man, after all.

Rowley. Ay, as Sir Peter says, he is a man of sentiment.

Sir Oliver S. And acts up to the sentiments he professes.

Rowley. It certainly is edification to hear him talk.

Sir Oliver S. Oh, he's a model for the young men of the age! But how's this, Sir Peter? you don't join us in your friend Joseph's praise, as I expected.

Sir Peter T. Sir Oliver, we live in a d—d wicked world, and the fewer we praise the better.

Rowley. What! do you say so, Sir Peter, who were never mistaken in your life?

Sir Peter T. Pshaw! Plague on you both! I see by your sneering you have heard the whole affair. I shall go mad among you!

Rowley. Then, to fret you no longer, Sir Peter, we are indeed acquainted with it all. I met Lady Teazle coming from Mr. Surface's so humbled, that she deigned to request me to be her advocate with you.

Sir Peter T. And does Sir Oliver know all this?

Sir Oliver S. Every circumstance.

Sir Peter T. What, of the closet and the screen, hey?

Sir Oliver S. Yes, yes, and the little French milliner. O, I have been vastly diverted with the story! Ha! ha! ha!

Sir Peter T. 'Twas very pleasant.

Sir Oliver S. I never laughed more in my life, I assure you. Ha! ha! ha!

Sir Peter T. O, vastly diverting!   Ha! ha! ha!

Rowley. To be sure, Joseph with his sentiments; ha! ha! ha!

Sir Peter T. Yes, yes, his sentiments!   Ha! ha! ha!   Hypocritical villain!

Sir Oliver S. Ay, and that rogue Charles to pull Sir Peter out of the closet: ha! ha! ha!

Sir Peter T. Ha! ha! 'twas devilish entertaining, to be sure!

Sir Oliver S. Ha! ha! ha!   Egad, Sir Peter, I should like to have seen your face when the screen was thrown down: ha! ha!

Sir Peter T. Yes, yes, my face when the screen was thrown down: ha! ha! ha!   Oh, I must never show my head again!

Sir Oliver S. But come, come, it isn't fair to laugh at you neither, my old friend; though, upon my soul, I can't help it.

Sir Peter T. O pray don't restrain your mirth on my account; it does not hurt me at all!   I laugh at the whole affair myself.   Yes, yes, I think being a standing jest for all one's acquaintance a very happy situation.   O yes, and then of a morning to read the paragraphs about Mr. S—, Lady T—, and Sir P—, will be so entertaining!

Rowley. Without affectation, Sir Peter, you may despise the ridicule of fools; but I see Lady Teazle going towards the next room.   I am sure you must desire a reconciliation as earnestly as she does.

Sir Oliver S. Perhaps my being here prevents her coming to you.   Well, I'll leave honest Rowley to mediate between you; but he must bring you all presently to Mr. Surface's, where I am now returning, if not to reclaim a libertine, at least to expose hypocrisy.

Sir Peter T. Ah, I'll be present at your discovering yourself there with all my heart; though 'tis a vile unlucky place for discoveries.

Rowley. We'll follow. [*Exit* Sir OLIVER.

Sir Peter T. She is not coming here, you see, Rowley.

Rowley. No, but she has left the door of that room open, you perceive. See, she is in tears.

Sir Peter T. Certainly a little mortification appears very becoming in a wife. Don't you think it will do her good to let her pine a little?

Rowley. Oh, this is ungenerous in you!

Sir Peter T. Well, I know not what to think. You remember the letter I found of her's, evidently intended for Charles?

Rowley. A mere forgery, Sir Peter, laid in your way on purpose: This is one of the points which I intend Snake shall give you conviction of.

Sir Peter T. I wish I were once satisfied of that. She looks this way: What a remarkably elegant turn of the head she has! Rowley, I'll go to her.

Rowley. Certainly.

Sir Peter T. Though when it is known that we are reconciled, people will laugh at me ten times more.

Rowley. Let them laugh, and retort their malice only by showing them you are happy in spite of it.

Sir Peter T. I'faith, so I will! And if I'm not mistaken, we may yet be the happiest couple in the country.

Rowley. Nay, Sir Peter, he who once lays aside suspicion——

Sir Peter T. Hold, Master Rowley! if you have any regard for me, let me never hear you utter anything like a sentiment. I have had enough of them to serve me the rest of my life. [*Exeunt.*

SCENE III.

The Library.

Enter JOSEPH SURFACE *and* Lady SNEERWELL.

Lady Sneer. Impossible! Will not Sir Peter immediately be reconciled to Charles, and, of course, no longer oppose his union with Maria? The thought is distraction to me.

Joseph S. Can passion furnish a remedy?

Lady Sneer. No, nor cunning neither. O! I was a fool, an idiot, to league with such a blunderer!

Joseph S. Lady Sneerwell, I am the greatest sufferer; yet you see I bear the accident with calmness.

Lady Sneer. Because the disappointment doesn't reach your heart; your interest only attached you to Maria. Had you felt for her what I have for that ungrateful libertine, neither your temper nor hypocrisy could prevent your showing the sharpness of your vexation.

Joseph S. But why should your reproaches fall on me for this disappointment?

Lady Sneer. Are you not the cause of it? Had you not a sufficient field for your roguery in imposing upon Sir Peter, and supplanting your brother, but you must endeavour to seduce his wife? I hate such an avarice of crimes; 'tis an unfair monopoly, and never prospers.

Joseph S. Well, I admit I have been to blame. I confess I deviated from the direct road of wrong, but I don't think we're so totally defeated neither.

Lady Sneer. No!

Joseph S. You tell me you have made a trial of Snake since we met, and that you still believe him faithful to us.

Lady Sneer. I do believe so.

Joseph S. And that he has undertaken, should it be necessary, to swear and prove, that Charles is at this time contracted by vows and honour to your ladyship, which some of his former letters to you will serve to support.

Lady Sneer. This, indeed, might have assisted.

Joseph S. Come, come; it is not too late yet. [*Knocking at the door.*] But hark! this is probably my uncle, Sir Oliver; retire to that room, we'll consult farther when he is gone.

Lady Sneer. Well, but if *he* should find you out too?

Joseph S. Oh, I have no fear of that. Sir Peter will hold his tongue for his own credit's sake; and you may depend on it I shall soon discover Sir Oliver's weak side!

Lady Sneer. I have no diffidence of your abilities! only be constant to one roguery at a time:

[*Exit* Lady SNEERWELL.

Joseph S. I will, I will. So! 'tis confounded hard, after such bad fortune, to be baited by one's confederate in evil. Well, at all events my character is so much better than Charles's, that I certainly—hey!—what!— this is not Sir Oliver, but old Stanley again. Plague on't that he should return to tease me just now. I shall have Sir Oliver come and find him here—and——

Enter Sir OLIVER SURFACE.

Gad's life, Mr. Stanley, why have you come back to plague me at this time? You must not stay now, upon my word.

Sir Oliver S. Sir, I hear your uncle Oliver is expected here, and though he has been so penurious to you, I'll try what he'll do for me.

Joseph S. Sir, 'tis impossible for you to stay now, so I must beg—come any other time, and I promise you, you shall be assisted.

Sir Oliver S. No; Sir Oliver and I must be acquainted.

Joseph S. Z—ds, sir! then I insist on your quitting the room directly.

Sir Oliver S. Nay, sir——

Joseph S. Sir, I insist on't: here, William! show this gentleman out. Since you compel me, sir, not one moment; this is such insolence!

[Going to push him out.

Enter Charles Surface.

Charles S. Hey day! what's the matter now! What the d—l, have you got hold of my little broker here? Z—ds, brother! don't hurt little Premium. What's the matter, my little fellow?

Joseph S. So! he has been with you too, has he?

Charles S. To be sure he has. Why he's as honest a little—— But sure, Joseph, you have not been borrowing money too, have you?

Joseph S. Borrowing! no! But, brother, you know we expect Sir Oliver here every——

Charles S. O Gad, that's true! Noll mustn't find the little broker here, to be sure.

Joseph S. Yet Mr. Stanley insists——

Charles S. Stanley! why his name's Premium.

Joseph S. No, sir, Stanley.

Charles S. No, no, Premium.

Joseph S. Well, no matter which—but——

Charles S. Ay, ay, Stanley or Premium, 'tis the same thing, as you say; for I suppose he goes by half a hundred names, besides A. B. at the coffee-house.

[Knocking.

Joseph S. 'Sdeath, here's Sir Oliver at the door. Now I beg, Mr. Stanley——

Charles S. Ay, ay, and I beg, Mr. Premium——

Sir Oliver S. Gentlemen——

Joseph S. Sir, by heaven you shall go!

Charles S. Ay, out with him, certainly!

Sir Oliver S. This violence——

Joseph S. Sir, 'tis your own fault.

Charles S. Out with him, to be sure.

[*Both forcing* Sir OLIVER *out.*

Enter Sir PETER *and* Lady TEAZLE, MARIA, *and* ROWLEY.

Sir Peter T. My old friend, Sir Oliver; hey! What in the name of wonder; here are dutiful nephews; assault their uncle at a first visit!

Lady T. Indeed, Sir Oliver, 'twas well we came in to rescue you.

Rowley. Truly, it was; for I perceive, Sir Oliver, the character of old Stanley was no protection to you.

Sir Oliver S. Nor of Premium either: the necessities of the former could not extort a shilling from that benevolent gentleman; and now, egad, I stood a chance of faring worse than my ancestors, and being knocked down without being bid for.

Joseph S. Charles!

Charles S. Joseph!

Joseph S. 'Tis now complete!

Charles S. Very!

Sir Oliver S. Sir Peter, my friend, and Rowley too— look on that elder nephew of mine. You know what he has already received from my bounty; and you also know how gladly I would have regarded half my fortune as held in trust for him; judge then my disappointment in discovering him to be destitute of faith, charity, and gratitude.

Sir Peter T. Sir Oliver, I should be more surprised at this declaration, if I had not myself found him to be mean, treacherous, and hypocritical.

Lady T. And if the gentleman pleads not guilty to these, pray let him call *me* to his character.

Sir Peter T. Then, I believe, we need add no more: if he knows himself, he will consider it as the most perfect punishment, that he is known to the world.

Charles S. If they talk this way to honesty, what will they say to me, by and by?   [*Aside.*

Sir Oliver S. As for that prodigal, his brother, there——

Charles S. Ay, now comes my turn; the d—d family pictures will ruin me.   [*Aside.*

Joseph S. Sir Oliver; uncle, will you honour me with a hearing?

Charles S. Now if Joseph would make one of his long speeches, I might recollect myself a little. [*Aside.*

Sir Peter T. I suppose you would undertake to justify yourself entirely.   [*To* JOSEPH.

Joseph S. I trust I could.

Sir Oliver S. Well, sir! and you could justify yourself too, I suppose?

Charles S. Not that I know of, Sir Oliver.

Sir Oliver S. What! Little Premium has been let too much into the secret, I suppose?

Charles S. True, sir; but they were *family* secrets, and should not be mentioned again, you know.

Rowley. Come, Sir Oliver, I know you cannot speak of Charles's follies with anger.

Sir Oliver S. Odd's heart, no more I can; nor with gravity either. Sir Peter, do you know the rogue bargained with me for all his ancestors; sold me judges and generals by the foot, and maiden aunts as cheap as broken china.

Charles S. To be sure, Sir Oliver, I did make a little free with the family canvas, that's the truth on't. My ancestors may rise in judgment against me, there's no denying it; but believe me sincere when I tell you —and upon my soul I would not say so if I was not— that if I do not appear mortified at the exposure of my follies, it is because I feel at this moment the warmest satisfaction in seeing you, my liberal benefactor.

Sir Oliver S. Charles, I believe you; give me your hand again; the ill-looking little fellow over the settee has made your peace.

Charles S. Then, sir, my gratitude to the original is still increased.

Lady T. Yet, I believe, Sir Oliver, here is one whom Charles is still more anxious to be reconciled to.

Sir Oliver S. Oh, I have heard of his attachment there; and, with the young lady's pardon, if I construe right—that blush——

Sir Peter T. Well, child, speak your sentiments!

Maria. Sir, I have little to say, but that I shall rejoice to hear that he is happy; for me—whatever claim I had to his affection, I willingly resign to one who has a better title.

Charles S. How, Maria!

Sir Peter T. Hey day! what's the mystery now? While he appeared an incorrigible rake, you would give your hand to no one else; and now that he is likely to reform, I'll warrant you won't have him.

Maria. His own heart and Lady Sneerwell know the cause.

Charles. Lady Sneerwell!

Joseph S. Brother, it is with great concern I am obliged to speak on this point, but my regard to justice compels me, and Lady Sneerwell's injuries can no longer be concealed.   [*Opens the door.*

Enter Lady SNEERWELL.

Sir Peter T. So! another French milliner! Egad, he has one in every room in the house, I suppose.

Lady Sneer. Ungrateful Charles! Well may you be surprised, and feel for the indelicate situation your perfidy has forced me into.

Charles S. Pray, uncle, is this another plot of yours? For, as I have life, I don't understand it.

Joseph S. I believe, sir, there is but the evidence of one person more necessary to make it extremely clear.

Sir Peter T. And that person, I imagine, is Mr. Snake. Rowley, you were perfectly right to bring him with us, and pray let him appear

Rowley. Walk in, Mr. Snake.

Enter SNAKE.

I thought his testimony might be wanted; however, it happens unluckily that he comes to confront Lady Sneerwell, not to support her.

Lady Sneer. A villain! Treacherous to me at last! Speak, fellow; have you too conspired against me?

Snake. I beg your ladyship ten thousand pardons; you paid me extremely liberally for the lie in question; but I unfortunately have been offered double to speak the truth.

Sir Peter T. Plot and counter-plot, egad!

Lady Sneer. The torments of shame and disappointment on you all.

Lady T. Hold, Lady Sneerwell; before you go, let

me thank you for the trouble you and that gentleman have taken, in writing letters from me to Charles, and answering them yourself; and let me also request you to make my respects to the scandalous college, of which you are president, and inform them that Lady Teazle, licentiate, begs leave to return the diploma they gave her, as she leaves off practice, and kills characters no longer.

Lady Sneer. You too, madam—provoking—insolent. May your husband live these fifty years.   [*Exit.*

Sir Peter T. Oons! what a fury!

Lady T. A malicious creature, indeed!

Sir Peter T. Hey! Not for her last wish?

Lady T. O no!

Sir Oliver S. Well, sir, and what have you to say now?

Joseph S. Sir, I am so confounded, to find that Lady Sneerwell could be guilty of suborning Mr. Snake in this manner, to impose on us all, that I know not what to say; however, lest her revengeful spirit should prompt her to injure my brother, I had certainly better follow her directly.   [*Exit.*

Sir Peter T. Moral to the last drop!

Sir Oliver S. Ay, and marry her, Joseph, if you can. Oil and vinegar, egad! you'll do very well together.

Rowley. I believe we have no more occasion for Mr. Snake at present?

Snake. Before I go, I beg pardon once for all, for whatever uneasiness I have been the humble instrument of causing to the parties present.

Sir Peter T. Well, well, you have made atonement by a good deed at last.

Snake. But I must request of the company that it shall never be known.

Sir Peter T. Hey! What the plague! Are you ashamed of having done a right thing once in your life?

Snake. Ah, sir! consider; I live by the badness of my character. I have nothing but my infamy to depend on! and if it were once known that I had been betrayed into an honest action, I should lose every friend I have in the world.

Sir Oliver S. Well, well; we'll not traduce you by saying anything in your praise, never fear.

[*Exit* SNAKE.

Sir Peter T. There's a precious rogue!

Lady T. See, Sir Oliver, there needs no persuasion now to reconcile your nephew and Maria.

Sir Oliver S. Ay, ay, that's as it should be, and egad we'll have the wedding to-morrow morning.

Charles S. Thank you, dear uncle!

Sir Peter T. What, you rogue! don't you ask the girl's consent first?

Charles S. Oh, I have done that a long time—a minute ago—and she has looked yes.

Maria. For shame, Charles! I protest, Sir Peter, there has not been a word.

Sir Oliver S. Well, then, the fewer the better. May your love for each other never know abatement!

Sir Peter T. And may you live as happily together as Lady Teazle and I intend to do!

Charles S. Rowley, my old friend, I am sure you congratulate me; and I suspect that I owe you much.

Sir Oliver S. You do indeed, Charles.

Rowley. If my efforts to serve you had not succeeded, you would have been in my debt for the attempt; but deserve to be happy, and you overpay me.

Sir Peter T. Ay, honest Rowley always said you would reform.

Charles S. Why, as to reforming, Sir Peter, I'll make no promises, and that I take to be a proof that I intend to set about it; but here shall be my monitor —my gentle guide. Ah! can I leave the virtuous path those eyes illumine?

> Though thou, dear maid, shouldst wave thy beauty's
>   sway,
> Thou still must rule, because I will obey:
> An humble fugitive from Folly view,
> No sanctuary near but Love and you.
>   [*To the audience.*
> You can, indeed, each anxious fear remove,
> For even Scandal dies if you approve.

EPILOGUE,

BY MR. COLMAN.

SPOKEN BY LADY TEAZLE.

I, who was late so volatile and gay,
Like a trade wind must now blow all one way,
Bend all my cares, my studies, and my vows,
To one dull rusty weathercock—my spouse!
So wills our virtuous bard—the motley Bayes
Of crying epilogues and laughing plays!
Old bachelors, who marry smart young wives,
Learn from our play to regulate your lives:
Each bring his dear to town, all faults upon her,
London will prove the very source of honour.
Plunged fairly in, like a cold bath it serves,
When principles relax, to brace the nerves.
Such is my case; and yet I must deplore
That the gay dream of dissipation's o'er.
And say, ye fair, was ever lively wife,
Born with a genius for the highest life,
Like me untimely blasted in her bloom,
Like me condemn'd to such a dismal doom?
Save money—when I just knew how to waste it!
Leave London—just as I began to taste it!
   Must I then watch the early crowing cock,
The melancholy ticking of a clock;
In a lone rustic hall for ever pounded,
With dogs, cats, rats, and squalling brats surrounded?

With humble curate can I now retire
(While good Sir Peter boozes with the squire),
And at backgammon mortify my soul,
That pants for loo, or flutters at a vole?
Seven's the main!   Dear sound that must expire,
Lost at hot cockles round a Christmas fire!
The transient hour of fashion too soon spent,
Farewell the tranquil mind, farewell content!
Farewell the plumed head, the cushioned tête,
That takes the cushion from its proper seat!
The spirit-stirring drum! card drums I mean,
Spadille—odd trick—pam—basto—king and queen!
And you, ye knockers, that, with brazen throat,
The welcome visitors' approach denote;
Farewell all quality of high renown,
Pride, pomp, and circumstance of glorious town!
Farewell! your revels I partake no more,
And Lady Teazle's occupation's o'er!
All this I told our bard; he smiled, and said 'twas
            clear,
I ought to play deep tragedy next year;
Meanwhile he drew wise morals from his play,
And in these solemn periods stalk'd away:
Blest were the fair like you! her faults who stopp'd,
And closed her follies when the curtain dropp'd!
No more in vice or error to engage,
Or play the fool at large on life's great stage.

THE

CRITIC;

OR,

A TRAGEDY REHEARSED.

TO MRS. GREVILLE.

MADAM,

IN requesting your permission to address the following pages to you, which, as they aim themselves to be critical, require every protection and allowance that approving taste or friendly prejudice can give them, I yet ventured to mention no other motive than the gratification of private friendship and esteem. Had I suggested a hope that your implied approbation would give a sanction to their defects, your particular reserve, and dislike to the reputation of critical taste, as well as of poetical talent, would have made you refuse the protection of your name to such a purpose. However, I am not so ungrateful as now to attempt to combat this disposition in you. I shall not here presume to argue that the present state of poetry claims and expects every assistance that taste and example can afford it; nor endeavour to prove that a fastidious concealment of the most elegant productions of judgment and fancy is an ill return for the possession of those endowments. Continue to deceive yourself in the idea that you are known only to be eminently admired and regarded for the valuable qualities that attach private friendships, and the graceful talents that adorn conversation. Enough of what you have written has stolen into full public notice to answer my purpose; and you will, perhaps, be the only person, conversant in elegant

literature, who shall read this address and not perceive
that by publishing your particular approbation of the
following drama, I have a more interested object than
to boast the true respect and regard with which

I have the honour to be,
Madam,
Your very sincere,
And obedient humble servant,
R. B. SHERIDAN.

PROLOGUE.

BY THE HONOURABLE RICHARD FITZPATRICK.

THE sister muses, whom these realms obey,
Who o'er the drama hold divided sway,
Sometimes, by evil counsellors, 'tis said,
Like earth-born potentates have been misled.
In those gay days of wickedness and wit,
When Villiers criticised what Dryden writ,
The tragic queen, to please a tasteless crowd,
Had learn'd to bellow, rant, and roar so loud,
That frighten'd nature, her best friend before,
The blust'ring beldam's company forswore.
Her comic sister, who had wit, 'tis true,
With all her merits, had her failings too;
And would sometimes in mirthful moments use
A style too flippant for a well-bred muse;
Then female modesty abash'd began
To seek the friendly refuge of the fan,
Awhile behind that slight entrenchment stood,
Till driv'n from thence, she left the stage for good.
In our more pious and far chaster times,
These sure no longer are the muse's crimes!
But some complain that, former faults to shun,
The reformation to extremes has run.
The frantic hero's wild delirium past,
Now insipidity succeeds bombast;
So slow Melpomene's cold numbers creep,
Here dulness seems her drowsy court to keep,
And we are scarce awake, whilst you are fast asleep.

Thalia, once so ill behaved and rude,
Reform'd, is now become an arrant prude;
Retailing nightly to the yawning pit
The purest morals, undefiled by wit!
Our author offers, in these motley scenes,
A slight remonstrance to the drama's queens:
Nor let the goddesses be over nice;
Free-spoken subjects give the best advice.
Although not quite a novice in his trade,
His cause to-night requires no common aid.
To this, a friendly, just, and pow'rful court,
I come ambassador to beg support.
Can he undaunted brave the critic's rage?
In civil broils with brother bards engage?
Hold forth their errors to the public eye,
Nay more, e'en newspapers themselves defy?
Say, must his single arm encounter all?
By numbers vanquish'd, e'en the brave may fall;
And though no leader should success distrust,
Whose troops are willing, and whose cause is just;
To bid such hosts of angry foes defiance,
His chief dependence must be, your alliance.

DRAMATIS PERSONÆ.

AS ORIGINALLY ACTED AT DRURY LANE THEATRE, OCTOBER 30, 1779.

Dangle . . . . Mr. DODD.
Sneer . . . . Mr. PALMER.
Sir Fretful Plagiary . . . Mr. PARSONS.
Signor Pasticcio Ritornello . Mr. DELPINI.
Interpreter . . . . . . Mr. BADDELEY.
Under Prompter . . . . Mr. PHILLIMORE.
Puff . . . . Mr. KING.

Mrs. Dangle . . . . . Mrs. HOPKINS.
Italian Girls . . . . . { Miss FIELD *and the* Miss ABRAMS.

CHARACTERS OF THE TRAGEDY.

Lord Burleigh . . . . . Mr. MOODY.
Governor of Tilbury Fort . Mr. WRIGHTEN.
Earl of Leicester . . . . Mr. FARREN.
Sir Walter Raleigh . . . Mr. BURTON.
Sir Christopher Hatton . . Mr. WALDRON.
Master of the Horse . . . Mr. KENNY.
Beef-eater . . . . . . Mr. WRIGHT.
Justice . . . . Mr. PACKER.
Son . . . . Mr. LAMASH.
Constable . . . . . . Mr. FAWCETT.
Thames . . . . Mr. GAWDRY.
Don Ferolo Whiskerandos . Mr. BANNISTER, jun.

1st Niece . . . . . . Miss COLLET.
2nd Niece . . . . . . Miss KIRBY.
Justice's Lady . . . . . Mrs. JOHNSTON.
Confidante . . . . . . Mrs. BRADSHAW.
Tilburina . . . . . . Miss POPE.

Guards, Constables, Servants, Chorus, Rivers, Attendants, &c.

THE CRITIC.

ACT I.—SCENE I.

Mr. *and* Mrs. DANGLE *at breakfast, and reading news-papers.*

Dangle. [*Reading.*] ' *Brutus to Lord North.*' ' *Letter the second on the State of the Army.*' Pshaw ! ' *To the first L— dash D. of the A— dash Y.*' ' *Genuine Extract of a Letter from St. Kitt's.*' ' *Coxheath Intelligence.*' ' *It is now confidently asserted that Sir Charles Hardy.*' Pshaw! Nothing but about the fleet and the nation! and I hate all politics but theatrical politics. Where's the Morning Chronicle ?

Mrs. Dangle. Yes, that's your gazette.

Dangle. So, here we have it. ' *Theatrical intelligence extraordinary. We hear there is a new tragedy in rehearsal at Drury Lane Theatre, called the Spanish Armada, said to be written by Mr. Puff, a gentleman well known in the theatrical world; if we may allow ourselves to give credit to the report of the performers, who, truth to say, are in general but indifferent judges, this piece abounds with the most striking and received beauties of modern composition.*' So! I am very glad my friend Puff's tragedy is in such forwardness. Mrs.

Dangle, my dear, you will be very glad to hear that
Puff's tragedy——

Mrs. Dangle. Lord, Mr. Dangle, why will you
plague me about such nonsense? Now the plays are
begun I shall have no peace. Isn't it sufficient to
make yourself ridiculous by your passion for the
theatre, without continually teasing me to join you?
Why can't you ride your hobby-horse without desiring to place me on a pillion behind you, Mr.
Dangle?

Dangle. Nay, my dear, I was only going to
read——

Mrs. Dangle. No, no; you will never read anything that's worth listening to: you hate to hear about
your country; there are letters every day with Roman
signatures, demonstrating the certainty of an invasion,
and proving that the nation is utterly undone. But
you never will read anything to entertain one.

Dangle. What has a woman to do with politics, Mrs.
Dangle?

Mrs. Dangle. And what have you to do with the
theatre, Mr. Dangle? Why should you affect the
character of a critic? I have no patience with you!
Haven't you made yourself the jest of all your acquaintance by your interference in matters where
you have no business? Are not you called a theatrical quidnunc, and a mock Mecænas to second-hand
authors?

Dangle. True; my power with the managers is
pretty notorious; but is it no credit to have applica-
tions from all quarters for my interest: from lords to
recommend fiddlers, from ladies to get boxes, from
authors to get answers, and from actors to get engage-
ments?

Mrs. Dangle. Yes, truly; you have contrived to

get a share in all the plague and trouble of theatrical property, without the profit, or even the credit of the abuse that attends it.

Dangle. I am sure, Mrs. Dangle, you are no loser by it, however; *you* have all the advantages of it. Mightn't you, last winter, have had the reading of the new pantomime a fortnight previous to its performance? And doesn't Mr. Fosbrook let you take places for a play before it is advertised, and set you down for a box for every new piece through the season? And didn't my friend, Mr. Smatter, dedicate his last farce to you at my particular request, Mrs. Dangle?

Mrs. Dangle. Yes; but wasn't the farce damned, Mr. Dangle? And to be sure it is extremely pleasant to have one's house made the motley rendezvous of all the lackeys of literature; the very high 'change of trading authors and jobbing critics! Yes, my drawing-room is an absolute register-office for candidate actors, and poets without character; then to be continually alarmed with misses and ma'ams piping hysteric changes on Juliets and Dorindas, Pollys and Ophelias; and the very furniture trembling at the probationary starts and unprovoked rants of would-be Richards and Hamlets! And what is worse than all, now that the manager has monopolized the Opera House, haven't we the signors and signoras calling here, sliding their smooth semibreves, and gargling glib divisions in their outlandish throats; with foreign emissaries and French spies, for aught I know, disguised like fiddlers and figure dancers?

Dangle. Mercy! Mrs. Dangle!

Mrs. Dangle. And to employ yourself so idly at such an alarming crisis as this too; when, if you had the least spirit, you would have been at the head of one of the Westminster associations, or trailing a vo-

lunteer pike in the Artillery Ground? But you—
o' my conscience, I believe if the French were landed
to-morrow, your first inquiry would be, whether they
had brought a theatrical troop with them.

Dangle. Mrs. Dangle, it does not signify; I say the
stage is '*the Mirror of Nature*,' and the actors are
'*the Abstract and brief Chronicles of the Time :*' and
pray what can a man of sense study better? Besides,
you will not easily persuade me that there is no credit
or importance in being at the head of a band of critics,
who take upon them to decide for the whole town,
whose opinion and patronage all writers solicit, and
whose recommendation no manager dares refuse.

Mrs. Dangle. Ridiculous! Both managers and
authors of the least merit laugh at your pretensions.
The *public* is their *critic;* without whose fair approbation they know no play can rest on the stage, and with
whose applause they welcome such attacks as yours,
and laugh at the malice of them, where they can't
at the wit.

Dangle. Very well, madam; very well.

Enter Servant.

Serv. Mr. Sneer, sir, to wait on you.

Dangle. O, show Mr. Sneer up. [*Exit* Servant.]
Plague on't, now we must appear loving and affectionate, or Sneer will hitch us into a story.

Mrs. Dangle. With all my heart; you can't be more
ridiculous than you are.

Dangle. You are enough to provoke——

Enter Mr. Sneer.

Ha! my dear Sneer, I am vastly glad to see you. My
dear, here's Mr. Sneer.

Mrs. Dangle. Good morning to you, sir.

Dangle. Mrs. Dangle and I have been diverting ourselves with the papers. Pray, Sneer, won't you go to Drury Lane Theatre the first night of Puff's tragedy?

Sneer. Yes; but I suppose one sha'n't be able to get in, for on the first night of a new piece they always fill the house with orders to support it. But here, Dangle, I have brought you two pieces, one of which you must exert yourself to make the managers accept, I can tell you that; for 'tis written by a person of consequence.

Dangle. So! now my plagues are beginning.

Sneer. Ay, I am glad of it, for now you'll be happy. Why, my dear Dangle, it is a pleasure to see how you enjoy your volunteer fatigue, and your solicited solicitations.

Dangle. It's a great trouble; yet, egad, it's pleasant too. Why, sometimes of a morning I have a dozen people call on me at breakfast-time, whose faces I never saw before, nor ever desire to see again.

Sneer. That must be very pleasant indeed!

Dangle. And not a week but I receive fifty letters, and not a line in them about any business of my own.

Sneer. An amusing correspondence!

Dangle. [*Reading.*] ' *Bursts into tears and exit.*' What, is this a tragedy?

Sneer. No, that's a genteel comedy, not a translation; only *taken from the French:* it is written in a style which they have lately tried to run down; the true sentimental, and nothing ridiculous in it from the beginning to the end.

Mrs. Dangle. Well, if they had kept to that, I should not have been such an enemy to the stage; there was some edification to be got from those pieces, Mr. Sneer!

Sneer. I am quite of your opinion, Mrs. Dangle: the

theatre, in proper hands, might certainly be made the school of morality ; but now, I am sorry to say it, people seem to go there principally for their entertainment !

Mrs. Dangle. It would have been more to the credit of the managers to have kept it in the other line.

Sneer. Undoubtedly, madam ; and hereafter perhaps to have had it recorded, that in the midst of a luxurious and dissipated age, they preserved *two* houses in the capital, where the conversation was always moral at least, if not entertaining !

Dangle. Now, egad, I think the worst alteration is in the nicety of the audience. No double *entendre*, no smart innuendo admitted; even Vanbrugh and Congreve obliged to undergo a bungling reformation.

Sneer. Yes, and our prudery in this respect is just on a par with the artificial bashfulness of a courtezan, who increases the blush upon her cheek in exact proportion to the diminution of her modesty.

Dangle. Sneer can't even give the public a good word ! But what have we here? This seems a very odd——

Sneer. O, that's a comedy, on a very new plan; replete with wit and mirth, yet of a most serious moral ! You see it is called ' *The Reformed Housebreaker;*' where by the mere force of humour, *housebreaking* is put into so ridiculous a light, that if the piece has its proper run, I have no doubt but that bolts and bars will be entirely useless by the end of the season.

Dangle. Egad, this is new indeed !

Sneer. Yes; it is written by a particular friend of mine, who has discovered that the follies and foibles of society are subjects unworthy the notice of the Comic Muse, who should be taught to stoop only at the greater vices and blacker crimes of humanity:

gibbeting capital offences in five acts, and pillorying petty larcenies in two. In short, his idea is to dramatise the penal laws, and make the stage a court of ease to the Old Bailey.

Dangle. It is truly moral.

Enter SERVANT.

Serv. Sir Fretful Plagiary, sir.

Dangle. Beg him to walk up. [*Exit* SERVANT.] Now, Mrs. Dangle, Sir Fretful Plagiary is an author to your own taste.

Mrs. Dangle. I confess he is a favourite of mine, because everybody else abuses him.

Sneer. Very much to the credit of your charity, madam, if not of your judgment.

Dangle. But, egad, he allows no merit to any author but himself, that's the truth on't—though he's my friend.

Sneer. Never. He is as envious as an old maid verging on the desperation of six-and-thirty; and then the insidious humility with which he seduces you to give a free opinion on any of his works, can be exceeded only by the petulant arrogance with which he is sure to reject your observations.

Dangle. Very true, egad—though he's my friend.

Sneer. Then his affected contempt of all newspaper strictures; though, at the same time, he is the sorest man alive, and shrinks like scorched parchment from the fiery ordeal of true criticism; yet is he so covetous of popularity, that he had rather be abused than not mentioned at all.

Dangle. There's no denying it—though he's my friend.

Sneer. You have read the tragedy he has just finished, haven't you?

Dangle. O yes; he sent it to me yesterday.

Sneer. Well, and you think it execrable, don't you ?

Dangle. Why, between ourselves, egad, I must own —though he is my friend—that it is one of the most——He's here [*Aside.*]—finished and most admirable perform——

[*Sir Fretful without.*] Mr. Sneer with him, did you say ?

Enter Sir FRETFUL PLAGIARY.

Dangle. Ah, my dear friend ! Egad, we were just speaking of your tragedy. Admirable, Sir Fretful, admirable !

Sneer. You never did anything beyond it, Sir Fretful—never in your life.

Sir Fret. You make me extremely happy ; for without a compliment, my dear Sneer, there isn't a man in the world whose judgment I value as I do yours—and Mr. Dangle's.

Mrs. Dangle. They are only laughing at you, Sir Fretful ; for it was but just now that——

Dangle. Mrs. Dangle ! Ah, Sir Fretful, you know Mrs. Dangle. My friend Sneer was rallying just now. He knows how she admires you, and——

Sir Fret. O Lord, I am sure Mr. Sneer has more taste and sincerity than to——A d—d double-faced fellow !   [*Aside.*

Dangle. Yes, yes; Sneer will jest; but a better humoured——

Sir Fret. O, I know——

Dangle. He has a ready turn for ridicule; his wit costs him nothing.

Sir Fret. No, egad—or I should wonder how he came by it.   [*Aside.*

Mrs. Dangle. Because his jest is always at the expense of his friend.

Dangle. But, Sir Fretful, have you sent your play to the managers yet? or can I be of any service to you?

Sir Fret. No, no, I thank you; I believe the piece had sufficient recommendation with it. I thank you though. I sent it to the manager of Covent Garden Theatre this morning.

Sneer. I should have thought now, that it might have been cast (as the actors call it) better at Drury Lane?

Sir Fret. O lud! no; never send a play there while I live. Harkee! [*Whispers* SNEER.

Sneer. Writes himself! I know he does——

Sir Fret. I say nothing. I take away from no man's merit—am hurt at no man's good fortune. I say nothing. But this I will say, through all my knowledge of life, I have observed, that there is not a passion so strongly rooted in the human heart as envy!

Sneer. I believe you have reason for what you say, indeed.

Sir Fret. Besides; I can tell you it is not always so safe to leave a play in the hands of those who write themselves.

Sneer. What, they may steal from them, hey, my dear Plagiary?

Sir Fret. Steal! to be sure they may; and, egad, serve your best thoughts as gipsies do stolen children, disfigure them to make 'em pass for their own.

Sneer. But your present work is a sacrifice to Melpomene, and *he* you know never——

Sir Fret. That's no security. A dexterous plagiarist may do anything. Why, sir, for aught I know, he might take out some of the best things in my tragedy, and put them into his own comedy.

Sneer. That might be done, I dare be sworn.

Sir Fret. And then, if such a person gives you the least hint or assistance, he is devilish apt to take the merit of the whole——

Dangle. If it succeeds.

Sir Fret. Ay; but with regard to this piece, I think I can hit that gentleman, for I can safely swear he never read it.

Sneer. I'll tell you how you may hurt him more.

Sir Fret. How?

Sneer. Swear he wrote it.

Sir Fret. Plague on't now, Sneer, I shall take it ill. I believe you want to take away my character as an author.

Sneer. Then I am sure you ought to be very much obliged to me.

Sir Fret. Hey! sir!

Dangle. O you know, he never means what he says.

Sir Fret. Sincerely then, you do like the piece?

Sneer. Wonderfully!

Sir Fret. But come now, there must be something that you think might be mended, hey? Mr. Dangle, has nothing struck you?

Dangle. Why, faith, it is but an ungracious thing, for the most part, to——

Sir Fret. With most authors it is just so indeed; they are in general strangely tenacious! But, for my part, I am never so well pleased as when a judicious critic points out any defect to me; for what is the purpose of showing a work to a friend, if you don't mean to profit by his opinion?

Sneer. Very true. Why, then, though I seriously admire the piece upon the whole, yet there is one small objection; which, if you'll give me leave, I'll mention.

Sir Fret. Sir, you can't oblige me more.

Sneer. I think it wants incident.

Sir Fret. Good God! you surprise me! Wants incident!

Sneer. Yes; I own I think the incidents are too few.

Sir Fret. Good God! Believe me, Mr. Sneer, there is no person for whose judgment I have a more implicit deference. But I protest to you, Mr. Sneer, I am only apprehensive that the incidents are too crowded. My dear Dangle, how does it strike you?

Dangle. Really I can't agree with my friend Sneer. I think the plot quite sufficient; and the four first acts by many degrees the best I ever read or saw in my life. If I might venture to suggest anything, it is that the interest rather falls off in the fifth.

Sir Fret. Rises, I believe you mean, sir.

Dangle. No, I don't, upon my word.

Sir Fret. Yes, yes, you do, upon my soul; it certainly don't fall off, I assure you. No, no; it don't fall off.

Dangle. Now, Mrs. Dangle, didn't you say it struck you in the same light?

Mrs. Dangle. No, indeed, I did not. I did not see a fault in any part of the play, from the beginning to the end.

Sir Fret. Upon my soul, the women are the best judges after all!

Mrs. Dangle. Or, if I made any objection, I am sure it was to nothing in the piece; but that I was afraid it was, on the whole, a little too long.

Sir Fret. Pray, madam, do you speak as to duration of time; or do you mean that the story is tediously spun out?

Mrs. Dangle. O Lud! no. I speak only with reference to the usual length of acting plays.

Sir Fret. Then I am very happy—very happy indeed; because the play is a short play, a remarkably short play. I should not venture to differ with a lady on a point of taste; but, on these occasions, the watch, you know, is the critic.

Mrs. Dangle. Then, I suppose, it must have been Mr. Dangle's drawling manner of reading it to me.

Sir Fret. O, if Mr. Dangle read it, that's quite another affair! But I assure you, Mrs. Dangle, the first evening you can spare me three hours and a half, I'll undertake to read you the whole from beginning to end, with the prologue and epilogue, and allow time for the music between the acts.

Mrs. Dangle. I hope to see it on the stage next.

Dangle. Well, Sir Fretful, I wish you may be able to get rid as easily of the newspaper criticisms as you do of ours.

Sir Fret. The newspapers! Sir, they are the most villanous—licentious—abominable—infernal—Not that I ever read them. No, I make it a rule never to look into a newspaper.

Dangle. You are quite right; for it certainly must hurt an author of delicate feelings to see the liberties they take.

Sir Fret. No! quite the contrary; their abuse is, in fact, the best panegyric: I like it of all things. An author's reputation is only in danger from their support.

Sneer. Why that's true; and that attack, now, on you the other day——

Sir Fret. What? where?

Dangle. Ay, you mean in a paper of Thursday: it was completely ill-natured, to be sure.

Sir Fret. O, so much the better. Ha! ha! ha! I wou'dn't have it otherwise.

Dangle. Certainly it is only to be laughed at; for——

Sir Fret. You don't happen to recollect what the fellow said, do you?

Sneer. Pray, Dangle—Sir Fretful seems a little anxious——

Sir Fret. O Lud, no! Anxious, not I, not the least —I—But one may as well hear, you know.

Dangle. Sneer, do *you* recollect?—Make out something. [*Aside.*

Sneer. I will. [*To* DANGLE.] Yes, yes, I remember perfectly.

Sir Fret. Well, and pray now—not that it signifies —what might the gentleman say?

Sneer. Why, he roundly asserts that you have not the slightest invention or original genius whatever; though you are the greatest traducer of all other authors living.

Sir Fret. Ha! ha! ha! very good!

Sneer. That as to comedy, you have not one idea of your own, he believes, even in your common-place-book; where stray jokes and pilfered witticisms are kept with as much method as the ledger of the lost and stolen office.

Sir Fret. Ha! ha! ha! very pleasant!

Sneer. Nay, that you are so unlucky as not to have the skill even to *steal* with taste; but that you glean from the refuse of obscure volumes, where more judicious plagiarists have been before you; so that the body of your work is a composition of dregs and sediments, like a bad tavern's worst wine.

Sir Fret. Ha! ha!

Sneer. In your more serious efforts, he says, your bombast would be less intolerable, if the thoughts were ever suited to the expression; but the homeliness of the sentiment stares through the fantastic encumbrance of its fine language, like a clown in one of the new uniforms!

Sir Fret. Ha! ha!

Sneer. That your occasional tropes and flowers suit the general coarseness of your style, as tambour sprigs would a ground of linsey-woolsey; while your imitations of Shakspeare resemble the mimicry of Falstaff's page, and are about as near the standard of the original.

Sir Fret. Ha!——

Sneer. In short, that even the finest passages you steal are of no service to you; for the poverty of your own language prevents their assimilating; so that they lie on the surface like lumps of marl on a barren moor, encumbering what it is not in their power to fertilize!

Sir Fret. [*After great agitation.*] Now, another person would be vexed at this.

Sneer. Oh! but I wou'dn't have told you, only to divert you.

Sir Fret. I know it; I *am* diverted. Ha! ha! ha! not the least invention! Ha! ha! ha! very good! very good!

Sneer. Yes; no genius! Ha! ha! ha!

Dangle. A severe rogue! Ha! ha! ha! But you are quite right, Sir Fretful, never to read such nonsense.

Sir Fret. To be sure; for if there is anything to one's praise, it is a foolish vanity to be gratified at it; and if it is abuse, why one is always sure to hear of it from one d—d good-natured friend or another.

Enter SERVANT.

Serv. Sir, there is an Italian gentleman, with a

French interpreter, and three young ladies, and a dozen musicians, who say they are sent by Lady Rondeau and Mrs. Fuge.

Dangle. Gadso! they come by appointment. Dear Mrs. Dangle, do let them know I'll see them directly.

Mrs. Dangle. You know, Mr. Dangle, I sha'n't understand a word they say.

Dangle. But you hear there's an interpreter.

Mrs. Dangle. Well, I'll try to endure their complaisance till you come. [*Exit.*

Serv. And Mr. Puff, sir, has sent word that the last rehearsal is to be this morning, and that he'll call on you presently.

Dangle. That's true; I shall certainly be at home. [*Exit* SERVANT.] Now, Sir Fretful, if you have a mind to have justice done you in the way of answer, egad, Mr. Puff's your man.

Sir Fret. Pshaw! Sir, why should I wish to have it answered, when I tell you I am pleased at it?

Dangle. True, I had forgot that. But I hope you are not fretted at what Mr. Sneer——

Sir Fret. Z—ds! no, Mr. Dangle; don't I tell you these things never fret me in the least?

Dangle. Nay, I only thought——

Sir Fret. And let me tell you, Mr. Dangle, 'tis d—d affronting in you to suppose that I am hurt, when I tell you I am not.

Sneer. But why so warm, Sir Fretful?

Sir Fret. Gad's life! Mr. Sneer, you are as absurd as Dangle. How often must I repeat it to you, that nothing can vex me but your supposing it possible for me to mind the d—d nonsense you have been repeating to me! And let me tell you, if you continue to believe this, you must mean to insult me, gentlemen; and then your disrespect will affect me no more than the newspaper criticisms, and I shall treat it with exactly the same calm indifference and philosophic contempt; and so your servant.   [*Exit.*

Sneer. Ha! ha! ha! Poor Sir Fretful! Now will he go and vent his philosophy in anonymous abuse of all modern critics and authors. But, Dangle, you must get your friend Puff to take me to the rehearsal of his tragedy.

Dangle. I'll answer for't, he'll thank you for desiring it. But come and help me to judge of this musical family; they are recommended by people of conse-quence, I assure you.

Sneer. I am at your disposal the whole morning; but I thought you had been a decided critic in music, as well as in literature?

Dangle. So I am; but I have a bad ear. I'faith, Sneer, though, I am afraid we were a little too severe on Sir Fretful—though he is my friend.

Sneer. Why, 'tis certain, that unnecessarily to mortify the vanity of any writer is a cruelty which mere dul-ness never can deserve; but where a base and personal malignity usurps the place of literary emulation, the aggressor deserves neither quarter nor pity.

Dangle. That's true, egad!—though he's my friend!

SCENE II.

*A Drawing-room, Harpsichord, &c.   Italian Family,
French Interpreter,* Mrs. DANGLE *and* SERVANTS
discovered.

Interp. Je dis, madame, j'ai l'honneur to *introduce* et de vous demander votre protection pour le Signor Pas-ticcio Retornello et pour sa charmante famille.

Signor Past. Ah! Vosignoria, noi vi preghiamo di favoritevi colla vostra protezione.

1st Daugh. Vosignoria fatevi questi grazzie.

2nd Daugh. Si, signora.

Interp. Madame, *me interpret.* C'est-à-dire—in English—qu'ils vous prient de leur faire l'honneur——

Mrs. Dangle. I say again, gentlemen, I don't understand a word you say.

Signor Past. Questo signore spiegheró——

Interp. Oui, *me interpret.* Nous avons les lettres de recommendation pour Monsieur Dangle de——

Mrs. Dangle. Upon my word, sir, I don't understand you.

Signor Past. La Contessa Rondeau e nostra padrona.

3rd Daugh. Si, padre, et mi Ladi Fuge.

Interp. O! *me interpret.* Madame, ils disent—in English—qu'ils ont l'honneur d'être protégés de ces dames. *You understand?*

Mrs. Dangle. No, sir—no understand!

Enter DANGLE *and* SNEER.

Interp. Ah, voici Monsieur Dangle!

All Italians. A! Signor Dangle!

Mrs. Dangle. Mr. Dangle, here are two very civil gentlemen trying to make themselves understood, and I don't know which is the interpreter.

Dangle. Eh, bien!

Interp. Monsieur Dangle, le grand bruit de vos talents pour la critique, et de votre interêt avec Messieurs les Directeurs à tous les Théâtres——

Signor Past. Vosignoria flete si famoso par la vostra conoscensa, e vostra interessa colla le Direttore da——

Speaking together.

Dangle. Egad, I think the interpreter is the hardest to be understood of the two!

Sneer. Why I thought, Dangle, you had been an admirable linguist!

Dangle. So I am, if they would not talk so d—d fast.

Sneer. Well, I'll explain that—the less time we lose in hearing them the better—for that, I suppose is what they are brought here for.

> [SNEER *speaks to* Signor PASTICCIO ; *they sing trios,*
> *&c.,* DANGLE *beating out of time.* SERVANT *enters*
> *and whispers* DANGLE.

Dangle. Show him up. [*Exit* SERVANT.] Bravo! admirable! bravissimo! admirablissimo! Ah! Sneer! where will you find such as these voices in England?

Sneer. Not easily.

Dangle. But Puff is coming. Signor and little Signora's obligatissimo! Sposa Signora Danglena—Mrs. Dangle, shall I beg you to offer them some refreshments, and take their address in the next room.

> [*Exit* Mrs. DANGLE *with the Italians and*
> *Interpreter ceremoniously.*]

Re-enter SERVANT.

Serv. Mr. Puff, sir.

Dangle. My dear Puff !

Enter PUFF.

Puff. My dear Dangle, how is it with you?

Dangle. Mr. Sneer, give me leave to introduce Mr. Puff to you.

Puff. Mr. Sneer is this? Sir, he is a gentleman whom I have long panted for the honour of knowing— a gentleman whose critical talents and transcendent judgment——·

Sneer. Dear sir——

Dangle. Nay, don't be modest, Sneer. My friend
Puff only talks to you in the style of his profession.

Sneer. His profession!

Puff. Yes, sir; I make no secret of the trade I
follow. Among friends and brother authors, Dangle
knows I love to be frank on the subject, and to
advertise myself *vivâ voce.* I am, sir, a practitioner in
panegyric, or, to speak more plainly, a professor of the
art of puffing, at your service—or anybody else's.

Sneer. Sir, you are very obliging! I believe, Mr.
Puff, I have often admired your talents in the daily
prints.

Puff. Yes, sir, I flatter myself I do as much business
in that way as any six of the fraternity in town.
Devilish hard work all the summer, friend Dangle,
never worked harder! But, harkee, the winter managers were a little sore, I believe.

Dangle. No; I believe they took it all in good part.

Puff. Ay! then that must have been affectation in
them; for, egad, there were some of the attacks which
there was no laughing at.

Sneer. Ay, the humorous ones. But I should think,
Mr. Puff, that authors would in general be able to do
this sort of work for themselves.

Puff. Why, yes, but in a clumsy way; besides, we
look on that as an encroachment, and so take the
opposite side. I dare say, now, you conceive half the
very civil paragraphs and advertisements you see to be
written by the parties concerned, or their friends? No
such thing; nine out of ten manufactured by me in the
way of business.

Sneer. Indeed!

Puff. Even the auctioneers now—the auctioneers, I
say—though the rogues have lately got some credit for
their language—not an article of the merit theirs; take

them out of their pulpits, and they are as dull as cata-
logues! No, sir; 'twas I first enriched their style;
'twas I first taught them to crowd their advertisements
with panegyrical superlatives, each epithet rising above
the other, like the bidders in their own auction-rooms!
From me they learned to inlay their phraseology with
variegated chips of exotic metaphor; by me, too, their
inventive faculties were called forth—yes, sir, by me
they were instructed to clothe ideal walls with gra-
tuitous fruits; to insinuate obsequious rivulets into
visionary groves; to teach courteous shrubs to nod
their approbation of the grateful soil; or on emergencies to raise upstart oaks, where there never had
been an acorn; to create a delightful vicinage without the assistance of a neighbour; or fix the temple
of Hygeia in the fens of Lincolnshire!

Dangle. I am sure you have done them infinite
service; for now, when a gentleman is ruined, he parts
with his house with some credit.

Sneer. Service! If they had any gratitude, they
would erect a statue to him; they would figure him as
a presiding Mercury, the god of traffic and fiction, with
a hammer in his hand instead of a caduceus. But
pray, Mr. Puff, what first put you on exercising your
talents in this way?

Puff. Egad, sir, sheer necessity; the proper parent
of an art so nearly allied to invention. You must
know, Mr. Sneer, that from the first time I tried my
hand at an advertisement, my success was such, that
for some time after I led a most extraordinary life
indeed!

Sneer. How, pray?

Puff. Sir, I supported myself two years entirely by
my misfortunes.

Sneer. By your misfortunes?

Puff. Yes, sir, assisted by long sickness, and other occasional disorders; and a very comfortable living I had of it.

Sneer. From sickness and misfortunes! You practised as a doctor and an attorney at once?

Puff. No, egad; both maladies and miseries were my own.

Sneer. Hey! what the plague!

Dangle. 'Tis true, i'faith.

Puff. Harkee! By advertisements — 'To the charitable and humane!' and 'to those whom Providence hath blessed with affluence!'

Sneer. Oh, I understand you.

Puff. And, in truth, I deserved what I got; for I suppose never man went through such a series of calamities in the same space of time. Sir, I was five times made a bankrupt, and reduced from a state of affluence, by a train of unavoidable misfortunes; then, sir, though a very industrious tradesman, I was twice burnt out, and lost my little all both times. I lived upon those fires a month. I soon after was confined by a most excruciating disorder, and lost the use of my limbs: that told very well; for I had the case strongly attested, and went about to collect the subscriptions myself.

Dangle. Egad, I believe that was when you first called on me.

Puff. In November last? O, no; I was at that time a close prisoner in the Marshalsea, for a debt benevolently contracted to serve a friend. I was afterwards twice tapped for a dropsy, which declined into a very profitable consumption. I was then reduced to—O, no—then, I became a widow with six helpless children, after having had eleven husbands pressed, and being left every time eight months gone with child, and without money to get me into an hospital!

Sneer. And you bore all with patience, I make no doubt?

Puff. Why, yes; though I made some occasional attempts at *felo de se;* but as I did not find those *rash actions* answer, I left off killing myself very soon. Well, sir, at last, what with bankruptcies, fires, gouts, dropsies, imprisonments, and other valuable calamities, having got together a pretty handsome sum, I determined to quit a business which had always gone rather against my conscience, and in a more liberal way still to indulge my talents for fiction and embellishment, through my favourite channels of diurnal communication; and so, sir, you have my history.

Sneer. Most obligingly communicative indeed; and your confession, if published, might certainly serve the cause of true charity, by rescuing the most useful channels of appeal to benevolence from the cant of imposition. But surely, Mr. Puff, there is no great mystery in your present prefession?

Puff. Mystery, sir! I will take upon me to say the matter was never scientifically treated, nor reduced to rule before.

Sneer. Reduced to rule!

Puff. O lud, sir, you are very ignorant, I am afraid. Yes, sir, puffing is of various sorts; the principal are, the puff direct, the puff preliminary, the puff collateral, the puff collusive, and the puff oblique, or puff by implication. These all assume, as circumstances require, the various forms of letter to the editor, occasional anecdote, impartial critique, observation from correspondent, or advertisement from the party.

Sneer. The puff direct, I can conceive——

Puff. O yes, that's simple enough; for instance, a new comedy or farce is to be produced at one of the theatres (though, by-the-by, they don't bring out half what they ought to do), the author, suppose Mr. Smatter, or Mr. Dapper, or any particular friend of mine—very well; the day before it is to be performed, I write an account of the manner in which it was received; I have the plot from the author, and only add—characters strongly drawn—highly coloured—hand of a master—fund of genuine humour—mine of invention—neat dialogue—Attic salt. Then for the performance. Mr. Dodd was astonishingly great in the character of Sir Harry. That universal and judicious actor, Mr. Palmer, perhaps never appeared to more advantage than in the Colonel; but it is not in the power of language to do justice to Mr. King; indeed he more than merited those repeated bursts of applause which he drew from a most brilliant and judicious audience. As to the scenery, the miraculous powers of Mr. De Loutherbourg's pencil are universally acknowledged. In short, we are at a loss which to admire most, the unrivalled genius of the author, the great attention and liberality of the managers, the wonderful abilities of the painter, or the incredible exertions of all the performers.

Sneer. That's pretty well indeed, sir.

Puff. O, cool—quite cool—to what I sometimes do.

Sneer. And do you think there are any who are influenced by this?

Puff. O lud, yes, sir; the number of those who undergo the fatigue of judging for themselves is very small indeed.

Sneer. Well, sir, the puff preliminary?

Puff. O that, sir, does well in the form of a caution. In a matter of gallantry now—Sir Flimsy

Gossimer wishes to be well with Lady Fanny Fete. He applies to me. I open trenches for him with a paragraph in the Morning Post. It is recommended to the beautiful and accomplished Lady F four stars F dash E to be on her guard against that dangerous character, Sir F dash G; who, however pleasing and insinuating his manners may be, is certainly not remarkable for the *constancy of his attachments*—in Italics. Here, you see, Sir Flimsy Gossimer is introduced to the particular notice of Lady Fanny, who perhaps never thought of him before; she finds herself publicly cautioned to avoid him, which naturally makes her desirous of seeing him; the observation of their acquaintance causes a pretty kind of mutual embarrassment; this produces a sort of sympathy of interest, which, if Sir Flimsy is unable to improve effectually, he at least gains the credit of having their names mentioned together, by a particular set, and in a particular way; which nine times out of ten is the full accomplishment of modern gallantry.

Dangle. Egad, Sneer, you will be quite an adept in the business.

Puff. Now, sir, the puff collateral is much used as an appendage to advertisements, and may take the form of anecdote. Yesterday, as the celebrated George Bonmot was sauntering down St. James's Street, he met the lively Lady Mary Myrtle, coming out of the Park. 'Good God! Lady Mary, I'm surprised to meet you in a white jacket, for I expected never to have seen you but in a full-trimmed uniform and a light horseman's cap!' 'Heavens, George, where could you have learned that?' 'Why,' replied the wit, 'I just saw a print of you, in a new publication called the Camp Magazine, which, by-the-by, is a devilish clever thing, and is sold at No. 3, on the right hand of the way, two doors from the printing-office, the corner of Ivy Lane, Paternoster Row, price only one shilling! '

Sneer. Very ingenious indeed.

Puff. But the puff collusive is the newest of any; for it acts in the disguise of determined hostility. It is much used by bold booksellers and enterprising poets. An indignant correspondent observes, that the new poem called Beelzebub's Cotillion, or Proserpine's Fête Champêtre, is one of the most unjustifiable perform-ances he ever read. The severity with which certain characters are handled is quite shocking; and as there are many descriptions in it too warmly coloured for female delicacy, the shameful avidity with which this piece is bought by all people of fashion is a reproach on the taste of the times, and a disgrace to the delicacy of the age. Here you see the two strongest induce-ments are held forth; first, that nobody ought to read it; and secondly, that everybody buys it; on the strength of which the publisher boldly prints the tenth edition, before he had sold ten of the first; and then establishes it by threatening himself with the pillory, or absolutely indicting himself for scan. mag.

Dangle. Ha! ha! ha! 'gad, I know it is so.

Puff. As to the puff oblique, or puff by implication, it is too various and extensive to be illustrated by an instance; it attracts in titles and presumes in patents; it lurks in the limitation of a subscription, and invites in the assurance of crowd and incommodation at public places; it delights to draw forth concealed merit, with a most disinterested assiduity; and some-times wears a countenance of smiling censure and tender reproach. It has a wonderful memory for parliamentary debates, and will often give the whole speech of a favoured member with the most flatter-ing accuracy. But, above all, it is a great dealer in reports and suppositions. It has the earliest intelligence of intended preferments that will reflect *honour* on the *patrons;* and embryo promotions of modest gentlemen, who know nothing of the matter themselves. It can hint a riband for implied services in the air of a common report; and with the carelessness of a casual paragraph, suggest officers into commands, to which they have no pretension but their wishes. This, sir, is the last principal class of the art of puffing; an art which I hope you will now agree with me is of the highest dignity, yielding a tablature of benevolence and public spirit; befriending equally trade, gallantry, criticism, and politics: the applause of genius—the register of charity—the triumph of heroism—the self-defence of contractors—the fame of orators—and the gazette of ministers.

Sneer. Sir, I am completely a convert both to the importance and ingenuity of your profession; and now, sir, there is but one thing which can possibly increase my respect for you, and that is, your permitting me to be present this morning at the rehearsal of your new trage——

Puff. Hush, for heaven's sake! *My* tragedy! Egad, Dangle, I take this very ill: you know how apprehensive I am of being known to be the author.

Dangle. I'faith I would not have told; but it's in the papers, and your name at length in the Morning Chronicle.

Puff. Ah! those d—d editors never can keep a secret! Well, Mr. Sneer, no doubt you will do me great honour; I shall be infinitely happy; highly flattered——

Dangle. I believe it must be near the time; shall we go together?

Puff. No: it will not be yet this hour, for they are

always late at the theatre; besides, I must meet you there, for I have some little matters here to send to the papers, and a few paragraphs to scribble before I go. [*Looking at memorandum.*] Here is ' a conscientious Baker, on the Subject of the Army Bread;' and ' a Detester of visible Brick-work, in favour of the new-invented Stucco;' both in the style of Junius, and promised for to-morrow. The Thames navigation too is at a stand. Misomud or Anti-shoal must go to work again directly. Here too are some political memorandums; I see; ay.—To take Paul Jones, and get the Indiamen out of the Shannon; reinforce Byron; compel the Dutch to—so! I must do that in the evening papers, or reserve it for the Morning Herald; for I know that I have undertaken to-morrow, besides, to establish the unanimity of the fleet in the Public Advertiser, and to shoot Charles Fox in the Morning Post. So, egad, I ha'n't a moment to lose!

Dangle. Well! we'll meet in the Green Room.

[*Exeunt severally.*

ACT II.—SCENE I.

The Theatre.

Enter DANGLE, PUFF, *and* SNEER, *as before the Curtain.*

Puff. No, no, sir: what Shakespeare says of actors may be better applied to the purpose of plays; *they* ought to be ' the abstract and brief chronicles of the time.' Therefore when history, and particularly the history of our own country, furnishes anything like a case in point, to the time in which an author writes, if he knows his own interest, he will take advantage of it; so, sir, I call my tragedy the Spanish Armada, and have laid the scene before Tilbury Fort.

Sneer. A most happy thought, certainly!

Dangle. Egad it was—I told you so. But pray now, I don't understand how you have contrived to introduce any love into it.

Puff. Love! Oh, nothing so easy; for it is a received point among poets, that where history gives you a good heroic outline for a play, you may fill up with a little love at your own discretion; in doing which, nine times out of ten, you only make up a deficiency in the private history of the times. Now I rather think I have done this with some success.

Sneer. No scandal about Queen Elizabeth, I hope?

Puff. O lud! no, no. I only suppose the governor of Tilbury Fort's daughter to be in love with the son of the Spanish admiral.

Sneer. Oh, is that all!

Dangle. Excellent, i'faith! I see it at once. But won't this appear rather improbable?

Puff. To be sure it will; but, what the plague! a play is not to show occurrences that happen every day, but things just so strange, that though they never *did*, they might happen.

Sneer. Certainly nothing is unnatural, that is not physically impossible.

Puff. Very true; and for that matter, Don Ferolo Whiskerandos—for that's the lover's name—might have been over here in the train of the Spanish ambassador; or Tilburina—for that is the lady's name—might have been in love with him, from having heard his character, or seen his picture; or from knowing that he was the last man in the world she ought to be in love with—or for any other good female reason. However, sir, the fact is, that though she is but a knight's daughter, egad! she is in love like any princess!

Dangle. Poor young lady! I feel for her already! for I can conceive how great the conflict must be between her passion and her duty; her love for her country, and her love for Don Ferolo Whiskerandos!

Puff. O amazing! Her poor susceptible heart is swayed two and fro by contending passions, like——

Enter UNDER PROMPTER.

Under Promp. Sir, the scene is set, and everything is ready to begin, if you please.

Puff. Egad, then we'll lose no time.

Under Promp. Though, I believe, sir, you will find it very short, for all the performers have profited by the kind permission you granted them.

Puff. Hey! what?

Under Promp. You know, sir, you gave them leave to cut out or omit whatever they found heavy or unnecessary to the plot, and I must own they have taken very liberal advantage of your indulgence.

Puff. Well, well. They are in general very good judges, and I know I am luxuriant. Now, Mr. Hopkins, as soon as you please.

Under Promp. [*To the music.*] Gentlemen, will you play a few bars of something, just to——

Puff. Ay, that's right; for as we have the scenes and dresses, egad, we'll go to't, as if it was the first night's performance; but you need not mind stopping between the acts. [*Exit* UNDER PROMPTER. *Orchestra play, then the bell rings.*] Soh! stand clear, gentlemen. Now you know there will be a cry of down!

down! hats off! silence! Then up curtain, and let us see what our painters have done for us.

SCENE II.

The Curtain rises and discovers Tilbury Fort. Two Sentinels asleep.

Dangle. Tilbury Fort! very fine indeed!

Puff. Now, what do you think I open with?

Sneer. Faith, I can't guess——

Puff. A clock. Hark! [*Clock strikes.*] I open with a clock striking, to beget an awful attention in the audience; it also marks the time, which is four o'clock in the morning, and saves a description of the rising sun, and a great deal about gilding the eastern hemisphere.

Dangle. But pray, are the sentinels to be asleep?

Puff. Fast as watchmen.

Sneer. Isn't that odd though at such an alarming crisis?

Puff. To be sure it is, but smaller things must give way to a striking scene at the opening; that's a rule. And the case is, that two great men are coming to this very spot to begin the piece: now, it is not to be supposed they would open their lips, if these fellows were watching them; so, egad, I must either have sent them off their posts, or set them asleep.

Sneer. O, that accounts for it. But tell us, who are these coming?

Puff. These are they—Sir Walter Raleigh, and Sir Christopher Hatton. You'll know Sir Christopher by his turning out his toes—famous, you know, for his dancing. I like to preserve all the little traits of character. Now attend.

Enter Sir WALTER RALEIGH *and* Sir CHRISTOPHER
HATTON.

'*Sir Christ. H.* True, gallant Raleigh!'—

Dangle. What, they had been talking before?

Puff. O, yes; all the way as they came along. I
beg pardon, gentlemen [*to the actors*], but these are
particular friends of mine, whose remarks may be of
great service to us. Don't mind interrupting them
whenever anything strikes you.

[*To* SNEER *and* DANGLE.

'*Sir Christ. H.* True, gallant Raleigh!
'But O, thou champion of thy country's fame,
'There *is* a question which I yet must ask;
'A question which I never ask'd before—
'What mean these mighty armaments?
'This general muster? and this throng of chiefs?'

Sneer. Pray, Mr. Puff, how came Sir Christopher
Hatton never to ask that question before?

Puff. What, before the play began? How the
plague could he?

Dangle. That's true, i'faith!

Puff. But you will hear what he thinks of the
matter.

'*Sir Christ. H.* Alas! my noble friend, when I
behold
'Yon tented plains in martial symmetry
'Array'd; when I count o'er yon glittering lines
'Of crested warriors, where the proud steeds neigh,
'And valour-breathing trumpet's shrill appeal,
'Responsive vibrate on my list'ning ear;
'When virgin majesty herself I view,
'Like her protecting Pallas, veil'd in steel,

' With graceful confidence exhort to arms!
' When briefly all I hear or see bears stamp
' Of martial vigilance and stern defence,
' I cannot but surmise—forgive, my friend,
' If the conjecture's rash—I cannot but
' Surmise the state some danger apprehends!'

Sneer. A very cautious conjecture that.
Puff. Yes, that's his character; not to give an opinion but on secure grounds.   Now then.

' *Sir Walter R.* O, most accomplished Christopher '——

Puff. He calls him by his Christian name, to show that they are on the most familiar terms.

' *Sir Walter R.* O, most accomplish'd Christopher, I find
' Thy stanch sagacity still tracks the future,
' In the fresh print of the o'ertaken past.'

Puff. Figurative!

' *Sir Walter R.* Thy fears are just.
' *Sir Christ. H.* But where? whence? when? and what
' The danger is—methinks I fain would learn.
' *Sir Walter R.* You know, my friend, scarce two revolving suns,
' And three revolving moons, have closed their course,
' Since haughty Philip, in despite of peace,
' With hostile hand hath struck at England's trade.
' *Sir Christ. H.* I know it well.
' *Sir Walter R.* Philip, you know, is proud Iberia's king.
' *Sir Christ. H.* He is.
' *Sir Walter R.* His subjects in base bigotry

' And Catholic oppression held; while we,
' You know, the Protestant persuasion hold.
  ' *Sir Christ H.* We do.
  ' *Sir Walter R.* You know, beside, his boasted arma-
    ment,
' The famed Armada, by the Pope baptized,
' With purpose to invade these realms——
  ' *Sir Christ. H.*   Is sailed,
' Our last advices so report.
  ' *Sir Walter R.* While the Iberian admiral's chief
    hope,
' His darling son——
  ' *Sir Christ. H.*   Ferolo Whiskerandos hight——
  ' *Sir Walter R.* The same; by chance a pris'ner
    hath been ta'en,
' And in this fort of Tilbury——
  ' *Sir Christ. H.*   Is now
' Confined; 'tis true, and oft from yon tall turret's top
' I've mark'd the youthful Spaniard's haughty mien
' Unconquer'd, though in chains.
  ' *Sir Walter R.*   You also know——'

Dangle. Mr. Puff, as he *knows* all this, why does Sir
Walter go on telling him?

Puff. But the audience are not supposed to know
anything of the matter, are they?

Sneer. True; but I think you manage ill: for there
certainly appears no reason why Sir Walter should be
so communicative.

Puff. Fore gad, now, that is one of the most ungrateful observations I ever heard; for the less induce-
ment he has to tell all this, the more, I think, you
ought to be obliged to him; for I am sure you'd know
nothing of the matter without it.

Dangle. That's very true, upon my word.

Puff. But you will find he was *not* going on.

' *Sir Christ. H.* Enough, enough; 'tis plain—and I
        no more
' Am in amazement lost!——'

Puff. Here, now, you see, Sir Christopher did not in
fact ask any one question for his own information.

Sneer. No, indeed! his has been a most disinterested
curiosity!

Dangle. Really, I find, we are very much obliged to
them both.

Puff. To be sure you are. Now then for the commander-in-chief, the Earl of Leicester, who, you know,
was no favourite but of the queen. We left off, ' in
amazement lost!'

' *Sir Christ. H.*   Am in amazement lost.
' But see where noble Leicester comes! supreme
' In honours and command.
    ' *Sir Walter R.*   And yet, methinks,
' At such a time, so perilous, so fear'd,
' That staff might well become an abler grasp.
    ' *Sir Christ. H.* And so, by Heav'n! think I: but
        soft, he's here!'

Puff. Ay, they envy him.

Sneer. But who are these with him?

Puff. O! very valiant knights: one is the governor
of the fort, the other the master of the horse. And
now, I think, you shall hear some better language. I
was obliged to be plain and intelligible in the first
scene, because there was so much matter of fact in
it; but now, i'faith, you have trope, figure, and metaphor, as plenty as noun-substantives.

Enter Earl of Leicester, *the* Governor, *and others.*

' *Leicest.* How's this, my friends! is't thus your
    new-fledged zeal
' And plumed valour moulds in roosted sloth?
' Why dimly glimmers that heroic flame,
' Whose redd'ning blaze, by patriot spirit fed,
' Should be the beacon of a kindling realm?
' Can the quick current of a patriot heart
' Thus stagnate in a cold and weedy converse,
' Or freeze in tideless inactivity?
' No! rather let the fountain of your valour
' Spring through each stream of enterprise,
' Each petty channel of conducive daring,
' Till the full torrent of your foaming wrath
' O'erwhelm the flats of sunk hostility!'

Puff. There it is; followed up!

' *Sir Walter R.* No more! the fresh'ning breath of
    thy rebuke .
' Hath fill'd the swelling canvas of our souls!
' And thus, though fate should cut the cable of
                      [*All take hands.*]
' Our topmost hopes, in friendship's closing line
' We'll grapple with despair, and if we fall,
' We'll fall in Glory's wake!
  ' *Leicest.* There spoke old England's genius!
' Then, are we all resolved?
  ' *All.* We are—all resolved.
  ' *Leicest.* To conquer—or be free?
  ' *All.* To conquer, or be free.
  ' *Leicest.* All?
  ' *All.* All.'

Dangle. Nem. con. egad!

Puff. O yes; where they *do* agree on the stage their unanimity is wonderful.

' *Leicest.* Then, let's embrace—and now——'

Sneer. What the plague, is he going to pray?
Puff. Yes, hush! in great emergencies, there is nothing like a prayer.

' *Leicest.* O mighty Mars!'

Dangle. But why should he pray to Mars?
Puff. Hush!

' *Leicest.* If in thy homage bred,
' Each point of discipline I've still observed;
' Nor but by due promotion, and the right
' Of service, to the rank of major-general
' Have ris'n; assist thy votary now!
     ' *Govern.* Yet do not rise—hear me!
     ' *M. of Horse.* And me!
     ' *Knight.* And me!
     ' *Sir Water R.* And me!
     ' *Sir Christ. H.* And me!'

Puff. Now, pray all together.

' *All.* Behold thy votaries submissive beg,
' That thou wilt deign to grant them all they ask;
' Assist them to accomplish all their ends,
' And sanctify whatever means they use
' To gain them!'

Sneer. A very orthodox quintetto!
Puff. Vastly well, gentlemen. Is that well managed or not? Have you such a prayer as that on the stage?
Sneer. Not exactly.
Leicest. [*To* PUFF.]   But, sir, you hav'n't settled how we are to get off here.

Puff. You could not go off kneeling, could you?

Sir Walter R. [*To* Puff.] O no, sir; impossible!

Puff. It would have a good effect i'faith, if you could exeunt praying! yes, and would vary the established mode of springing off with a glance at the pit.

Sneer. O, never mind; so as you get them off, I'll answer for it the audience won't care how.

Puff. Well, then, repeat the last line standing, and go off the old way.

' *All.* And sanctify whatever means we use
' To gain them.' [*Exeunt.*

Dangle. Bravo! a fine exit.

Sneer. Well, really, Mr. Puff——

Puff. Stay a moment.

The Sentinels *get up.*

' 1*st Sent.* All this shall to Lord Burleigh's ear.
' 2*nd Sent.* 'Tis meet it should.' [*Exeunt* Sentinels.

Dangle. Hey! why I thought those fellows had been asleep?

Puff. Only a pretence; there's the art of it: they were spies of Lord Burleigh.

Sneer. But isn't it odd they were never taken notice of, not even by the commander-in-chief?

Puff. O lud, sir, if people who want to listen, or overhear, were not always connived at in a tragedy, there would be no carrying on any plot in the world.

Dangle. That's certain!

Puff. But take care, my dear Dangle; the morning gun is going to fire. [*Cannon fires.*

Dangle. Well, that will have a fine effect.

Puff. I think so, and helps to realize the scene. [*Cannon twice.*] What the plague! *three* morning

11—2

guns! there never is but one! ay, this is always the way at the theatre: give these fellows a good thing, and they never know when to have done with it. You have no more cannon to fire?

Promp. [*From within.*] No, sir.

Puff. Now, then, for soft music.

Sneer. Pray, what's that for?

Puff. It shows that Tilburina is coming; nothing introduces you a heroine like soft music. Here she comes.

Dangle. And her confidant, I suppose?

Puff. To be sure. Here they are—inconsolable to the minuet in Ariadne. [*Soft music.*

Enter Tilburina *and* Confidant.

' *Tilb.* Now has the whispering breath of gentle morn

' Bad Nature's voice and Nature's beauty rise;

' While orient Phœbus, with unborrow'd hues,

' Clothes the waked loveliness which all night slept

' In heav'nly drapery! Darkness is fled.

' Now flowers unfold their beauties to the sun,

' And, blushing, kiss the beam he sends to wake them—

' The striped carnation, and the guarded rose,

' The vulgar wallflower, and smart gillyflower,

' The polyanthus mean—the dapper daisy,

' Sweet William, and sweet marjoram—and all

' The tribe of single and of double pinks!

' Now, too, the feather'd warblers tune their notes

' Around, and charm the list'ning grove. The lark!

' The linnet! chaffinch! bullfinch! goldfinch! green finch!

' ——But O, to me no joy can they afford!

' Nor rose, nor wallflower, nor smart gillyflower,

' Nor polyanthus mean, nor dapper daisy,
' Nor William sweet, nor marjoram—nor lark,
' Linnet, nor all the finches of the grove !'

Puff. Your white handkerchief, madam.

Tilb. I thought, sir, I wasn't to use that till ' heart-rending woe.'

Puff. O yes, madam, at ' the finches of the grove,' if you please.

 ' *Tilb.*   Nor lark,
' Linnet, nor all the finches of the grove !'   [*Weeps.*

Puff. Vastly well, madam !
Dangle. Vastly well, indeed !

 ' *Tilb.* For, O, too sure, heart-rending woe is now
' The lot of wretched Tilburina !'

Dangle. Oh ! 'tis too much.
Sneer. Oh ! it is indeed.

 ' *Confid.* Be comforted, sweet lady ; for who knows,
' But Heav'n has yet some milk-white day in store?

 ' *Tilb.* Alas ! my gentle Nora,
' Thy tender youth as yet hath never mourn'd
' Love's fatal dart. Else wouldst thou know, that when
' The soul is sunk in comfortless despair,
' It cannot taste of merriment.'

Dangle. That's certain.

 ' *Confid.* But see where your stern father comes :
' It is not meet that he should find you thus.'

Puff. Hey, what the plague ! What a cut is here ! Why, what is become of the description of her first meeting with Don Whiskerandos ; his gallant behaviour in the sea fight ; and the simile of the canary bird ?

Tilb. Indeed, sir, you'll find they will not be missed.

Puff. Very well—very well!

Tilb. The cue, ma'am, if you please.

' *Confid.* It is not meet that he should find you thus.

' *Tilb.* Thou counsel'st right; but 'tis no easy task
' For barefaced grief to wear a mask of joy.'

Enter GOVERNOR.

' *Govern.* How's this! in tears?   O, Tilburina,
    shame!
' Is this a time for maudling tenderness,
' And Cupid's baby woes?   Hast thou not heard
' That haughty Spain's pope-consecrated fleet
' Advances to our shores, while England's fate,
' Like a clipp'd guinea, trembles in the scale?
    ' *Tilb.* Then is the crisis of *my* fate at hand!
' I see the fleet's approach—I see——'

Puff. Now, pray, gentlemen, mind. This is one of
the most useful figures we tragedy writers have, by
which a hero or heroine, in consideration of their being
often obliged to overlook things that *are* on the stage,
is allowed to hear and see a number of things that are
not.

Sneer. Yes; a kind of poetical second-sight.

Puff. Yes.   Now then, madam.

' *Tilb.*   I see their decks
' Are clear'd!   I see the signal made!
' The line is form'd! a cable's length asunder!
' I see the frigates station'd in the rear;
' And now, I hear the thunder of the guns!
' I hear the victor's shouts!   I also hear
' The vanquish'd groan! and now 'tis smoke—and now
' I see the loose sails shiver in the wind!
' I see——I see——what soon you'll see——

' *Govern.* Hold, daughter! peace! this love hath
    turn'd thy brain:
' The Spanish fleet thou *canst* not see; because
' ——It is not yet in sight!'

Dangle. Egad, though, the governor seems to make
no allowance for this poetical figure you talk of.

Puff. No, a plain matter-of-fact man; that's his
character.

' *Tilb.* But will you then refuse his offer?
' *Govern.* I must—I will—I can—I ought—I do.
' *Tilb.* Think what a noble price.
' *Govern.* No more; you urge in vain.
' *Tilb.* His liberty is all he asks.'

Sneer. All *who* asks, Mr. Puff? Who is——

Puff. Egad, sir, I can't tell: here has been such
cutting and slashing, I don't know where they have
got to myself.

Tilb. Indeed, sir, you will find it will connect very
well.

' ——And your reward secure.'

Puff. O, if they hadn't been so devilish free with
their cutting here, you would have found that ·Don
Whiskerandos has been tampering for his liberty, and
has persuaded Tilburina to make this proposal to her
father; and now, pray observe the conciseness with
which the argument is conducted. Egad, the *pro*
and *con.* goes as smart as hits in a fencing-match.
It is indeed a sort of small-sword logic, which we
have borrowed from the French.

' *Tilb.* A retreat in Spain!
' *Govern.* Outlawry here!
' *Tilb.* Your daughter's prayer!
' *Govern.* Your father's oath!

‘ *Tilb.* My lover!
‘ *Govern.* My country!
‘ *Tilb.* Tilburina!
‘ *Govern.* England!
‘ *Tilb.* A title!
‘ *Govern.* Honour!
‘ *Tilb.* A pension!
‘ *Govern.* Conscience!
‘ *Tilb.* A thousand pounds!
‘ *Govern.* Hah! thou hast touch’d me nearly!’

Puff. There you see; she threw in *Tilburina.*
Quick, parry carte with *England!* Hah! thrust in
tierce a title! parried by honour. Hah! a pension
over the arm! put by by conscience. Then flankonade
with a thousand pounds, and a palpable hit, egad!

‘ *Tilb.* Canst thou——
‘ Reject the *suppliant*, and the *daughter* too?
   ‘ *Govern.* No more; I would not hear thee plead in
      vain:
‘ The *father* softens; but the *governor*
‘ Is fix’d!’   [*Exit.*

Dangle. Ay, that antithesis of persons is a most
established figure.

‘ *Tilb.* ’Tis well, hence then, fond hopes, fond pas-
      sion, hence;
‘ Duty, behold I am all over thine——
   ‘ *Whiskerandos.* [*Without.*] Where is my love—
      my——
   ‘ *Tilb.* Ha!
‘ *Whiskerandos.* [*Entering.*] My beauteous enemy—’

Puff. O dear, ma’am, you must start a great deal
more than that: consider, you had just determined
in favour of duty; when, in a moment, the sound

of his voice revives your passion; overthrows your
resolution; destroys your obedience. If you don't
express all that in your start, you do nothing at all.

Tilb. Well, we'll try again!

Dangle. Speaking from within has always a fine
effect.

Sneer. Very.

' *Whiskerandos.* My conquering Tilburina! How!
    is't thus

' We meet? why are thy looks averse? what means

' That falling tear; that frown of boding woe?

' Hah! now indeed I am a prisoner!

' Yes, now I feel the galling weight of these

' Disgraceful chains; which, cruel Tilburina!

' Thy doting captive gloried in before.

' But thou art false, and Whiskerandos is undone!

    ' *Tilb.* O, no! how little dost thou know thy Til-
        burina!

    ' *Whiskerandos.* Art thou then true? Begone cares,
        doubts, and fears,

' I make you all a present to the winds;

' And if the winds reject you—try the waves.

Puff. The wind, you know, is the established receiver
of all stolen sighs, and cast-off griefs and apprehensions.

    ' *Tilb.* Yet we must part! stern duty seals our
        doom:

' Though here I call yon conscious clouds to witness,

' Could I pursue the bias of my soul,

' All friends, all right of parents, I'd disclaim,

' And thou, my Whiskerandos, shouldst be father

' And mother, brother, cousin, uncle, aunt,

' And friend to me!

    ' *Whiskerandos.* O, matchless excellence! And must
        we part?

' Well, if—we must—we must—and in that case
' The less is said the better.'

Puff. Hey day! here's a cut! What, are all the mutual protestations out?

Tilb. Now, pray, sir, don't interrupt us here; you ruin our feelings.

Puff. *Your* feelings! But z—ds, *my* feelings, ma'am!

Sneer. No; pray don't interrupt them.

' *Whiskerandos.* One last embrace.
' *Tilb.* Now, farewell, for ever!
' *Whiskerandos.* For ever!
' *Tilb.* Ay, for ever.'   [*Going.*

Puff. 'Sdeath and fury! Gad's life!—sir!—madam! if you go out without the parting look, you might as well dance out. Here, here!

Confid. But pray, sir, how am *I* to get off here?

Puff. You, pshaw! what the devil signifies how *you* get off! edge away at the top, or where you will [*Pushes the* CONFIDANT *off.*] Now, ma'am, you see——

Tilb. We understand you, sir.

                          ' Ay, for ever.
' *Both.* Ohh!'   [*Turning back, and exeunt.*
                    Scene closes.

Dangle. O, charming!

Puff. Hey! 'tis pretty well, I believe. You see I don't attempt to strike out anything new; but I take it I improve on the established modes.

Sneer. You do, indeed. But pray is not Queen Elizabeth to appear?

Puff. No, not at once; but she is to be talked of for ever; so that, egad, you'll think a hundred times that she is on the point of coming in.

Sneer. Hang it, I think it's a pity to keep *her* in the green room all the night.

Puff. O no, that always has a fine effect—it keeps up expectation.

Dangle. But are we not to have a battle?

Puff. Yes, yes, you will have a battle at last; but, egad, it's not to be by land, but by sea; and that is the only quite new thing in the piece.

Dangle. What, Drake at the Armada, hey?

Puff. Yes, i'faith—fire-ships and all; then we shall end with the procession. Hey! that will do, I think?

Sneer. No doubt on't.

Puff. Come, we must not lose time; so now for the under plot.

Sneer. What the plague, have you another plot?

Puff. O lord, yes; ever while you live have two plots to your tragedy. The grand point in managing them is only to let your under plot have as little connexion with your main plot as possible. I flatter myself nothing can be more distinct than mine; for as in my chief plot the characters are all great people, I have laid my under plot in low life; and as the former is to end in deep distress, I make the other end as happy as a farce. Now, Mr. Hopkins, as soon as you please.

Enter UNDER PROMPTER.

Under Promp. Sir, the carpenter says it is impossible you can go to the park scene yet.

Puff. The park scene; no. I mean the description scene here, in the wood.

Under Promp. Sir, the performers have cut it out.

Puff. Cut it out!

Under Promp. Yes, sir.

Puff. What! the whole account of Queen Elizabeth?

Under Promp. Yes, sir.

Puff. And the description of her horse and side-saddle?

Under Promp. Yes, sir.

Puff. So, so; this is very fine indeed. Mr. Hopkins, how the plague could you suffer this?

Hopkins. [*From within.*] Sir, indeed the pruning-knife——

Puff. The pruning-knife—z—ds! the axe! Why, here has been such lopping and topping, I sha'n't have the bare trunk of my play left presently. Very well, sir, the performers must do as they please; but, upon my soul, I'll print it, every word.

Sneer. That I would, indeed.

Puff. Very well, sir; then we must go on. Z—ds! I would not have parted with the description of the horse! Well, sir, go on. Sir, it was one of the finest and most laboured things. Very well, sir; let them go on; there you had him and his accoutrements from the bit to the crupper. Very well, sir; we must go to the park scene.

Under Promp. Sir, there is the point: the carpenters say, that unless there is some business put in here before the drop, they sha'n't have time to clear away the fort, or sink Gravesend and the river.

Puff. So! this is a pretty dilemma, truly! Gentlemen, you must excuse me; these fellows will never be ready, unless I go and look after them myself.

Sneer. O dear, sir, these little things will happen.

Puff. To cut out this scene! But I'll print it—egad, I'll print it every word!   [*Exeunt.*

•

ACT III.—SCENE I.

Before the Curtain.

Enter PUFF, SNEER, *and* DANGLE.

Puff. Well, we are ready; now then for the justices.

*Curtain rises—*JUSTICES, CONSTABLES, *&c., discovered.*

Sneer. This, I suppose, is a sort of senate scene.
Puff. To be sure; there has not been one yet.
Dangle. It is the under plot, isn't it?
Puff. Yes. What, gentlemen, do you mean to go at once to the discovery scene?
Justice. If you please, sir.
Puff. O, very well. Harkee, I don't choose to say anything more; but i'faith, they have mangled my play in a most shocking manner.
Dangle. It's a great pity!
Puff. Now, then, Mr. Justice, if you please.

' *Justice.* Are all the volunteers without?
' *Constable.*   They are.
' Some ten in fetters, and some twenty drunk.
   ' *Justice.* Attends the youth, whose most opprobrious
               fame
∶ And clear convicted crimes have stamped him soldier?
   ' *Constable.* He waits your pleasure; eager to repay
' The blest reprieve that sends him to the fields
' Of glory, there to raise his branded hand
' In honour's cause.
   ' *Justice.* 'Tis well—'tis justice arms him!
' O! may he now defend his country's laws

' With half the spirit he has broke them all!
' If 'tis your worships' pleasure, bid him enter.
  ' *Constable.* I fly, the herald of your will.'

                            [*Exit* CONSTABLE.

Puff. Quick, sir!

Sneer. But, Mr. Puff, I think not only the Justice, but the clown seems to talk in as high a style as the first hero among them.

Puff. Heaven forbid they should not, in a free country! Sir, I am not for making slavish distinctions, and giving all the fine language to the upper sort of people.

Dangle. That's very noble in you, indeed.

Enter JUSTICE'S LADY.

Puff. Now, pray mark this scene.

  ' *Lady.* Forgive this interruption, good my love;
' But as I just now passed a pris'ner youth,
' Whom rude hands hither lead, strange bodings seized
' My flutt'ring heart, and to myself I said,
' An if our *Tom* had lived, he'd surely been
' This stripling's height!
  ' *Justice.* Ha! sure some powerful sympathy directs
' Us both——

Enter SON *and* CONSTABLE.

  ' What is thy name?
  ' *Son.* My name's *Tom Jenkins*—*alias* have I none—
' Though orphan'd, and without a friend!
  ' *Justice.* Thy parents?
  ' *Son.* My father dwelt in Rochester—and was,
' As I have heard—a fishmonger—no more.'

Puff. What, sir, do you leave out the account of your birth, parentage, and education ?

Son. They have settled it so, sir, here.

Puff. Oh! oh!

' *Lady.* How loudly nature whispers to my heart!
' Had he no other name ?

' *Son.*   I've seen a bill
' Of his sign'd *Tomkins*, creditor.

  ' *Justice.* This does indeed confirm each circum-
      stance
' The gipsy told! Prepare!

  ' *Son.* I do.

  ' *Justice.* No orphan, nor without a friend art
      thou—
' *I* am thy father; *here's* thy mother; *there*
' Thy uncle—this thy first cousin, and those
' Are all your near relations!

  ' *Mother.* O ecstacy of bliss!

  ' *Son.* O most unlook'd for happiness!

  ' *Justice.* O wonderful event!'
                [*They faint alternately in each other's arms.*

Puff. There, you see relationship, like murder, will out.

  ' *Justice.* Now let's revive——else were this joy too
      much!
' But come—and we'll unfold the rest within ;
' And thou, my boy, must needs want rest and food.
' Hence may each orphan hope, as chance directs,
' To find a father—where he least expects!'   [*Exeunt.*

Puff. What do you think of that ?

Dangle. One of the finest discovery-scenes I ever saw. Why, this under plot would have made a tragedy itself.

Sneer. Ay, or a comedy either.

Puff. And keeps quite clear, you see, of the other.

Enter SCENEMEN, *taking away the seats.*

Puff. The scene remains, does it?

Sceneman. Yes, sir.

Puff. You are to leave one chair, you know. But it is always awkward in a tragedy to have you fellows coming in your playhouse liveries to remove things. I wish that could be managed better. So now for my mysterious yeoman.

Enter a BEEFEATER.

‘ *Beefeater.* Perdition catch my soul, but *I* do love
    thee.’

Sneer. Haven't I heard that line before?

Puff. No, I fancy not. Where, pray?

Dangle. Yes, I think there is something like it in Othello.

Puff. Gad! now you put me in mind on't, I believe there is: but that's of no consequence; all that can be said is, that two people happened to hit on the same thought; and Shakespeare made use of it first, that's all.

Sneer. Very true.

Puff. Now, sir, your soliloquy; but speak more to the pit, if you please; the soliloquy always to the pit —that's a rule.

‘ *Beefeater.* Though hopeless love finds comfort in
    despair,
‘ It never can endure a rival's bliss!
‘ But soft——I am observed.’   [*Exit* BEEFEATER.

Dangle. That's a very short soliloquy.

Puff. Yes; but it would have been a great deal longer if he had not been observed.

Sneer. A most sentimental Beefeater that, Mr. Puff.

Puff. Harkee; I would not have you be too sure that he *is* a Beefeater.

Sneer. What, a hero in disguise?

Puff. No matter; I only give you a hint. But now for my principal character. Here he comes—*Lord Burleigh* in person! Pray, gentlemen, step this way —softly. I only hope the Lord High Treasurer is perfect: if he is but perfect!

Enter BURLEIGH, *goes slowly to a chair, and sits.*

Sneer. Mr. Puff!

Puff. Hush! vastly well, sir! vastly well! a most interesting gravity!

Dangle. What, isn't he to speak at all?

Puff. Egad, I thought you'd ask me that. Yes, it is a very likely thing, that a minister in his situation, with the whole affairs of the nation on his head, should have time to talk! But hush! or you'll put him out.

Sneer. Put him out! how the plague can that be, if he's not going to say anything?

Puff. There's a reason! Why, his part is to *think;* and how the plague do you imagine he can *think* if you keep talking?

Dangle. That's very true, upon my word!

BURLEIGH *comes forward, shakes his head, and exit.*

Sneer. He is very perfect indeed. Now, pray what did he mean by that?

12

Puff. You don't take it?

Sneer. No, I don't, upon my soul.

Puff. Why, by that shake of the head, he gave you to understand that even though they had more justice in their cause, and wisdom in their measures, yet, if there was not a greater spirit shown on the part of the people, the country would at last fall a sacrifice to the hostile ambition of the Spanish monarchy.

Sneer. The devil! Did he mean all that by shaking his head?

Puff. Every word of it; if he shook his head as I taught him.

Dangle. Ah! there certainly is a vast deal to be done on the stage by dumb show and expression of face; and a judicious author knows how much he may trust to it.

Sneer. O, here are some of our old acquaintance.

Enter HATTON *and* RALEIGH.

' *Sir Christ. H. My* niece, and *your* niece too!

' By Heav'n! there's witchcraft in't. He could not else

' Have gain'd their hearts. But see where they approach;

' Some horrid purpose low'ring on their brows!

' *Sir Walter R.* Let us withdraw, and mark them.'

[*They withdraw.*

Sneer. What is all this?

Puff. Ah! here has been more pruning! But the fact is, these two young ladies are also in love with Don Whiskerandos. Now, gentlemen, this scene goes entirely for what we call *situation* and *stage effect,* by which the greatest applause may be obtained, without

the assistance of language, sentiment, or character :
pray mark !

Enter the Two NIECES.

' 1*st Niece.* Ellena here;
' She is his scorn as much as I ; that is
' Some comfort still !'

Puff. O dear, madam, you are not to say that to her
face ! *Aside,* ma'am, *aside.* The whole scene is to
be *aside.*

' 1*st Niece.* She is his scorn as much as I; that is
' Some comfort still !   [*Aside.*
' 2*nd Niece.* I know he prizes not Pollina's love;
' But Tilburina lords it o'er his heart.   [*Aside.*
' 1*st Niece.* But see the proud destroyer of my peace.
' Revenge is all the good I've left.   [*Aside.*
' 2*nd Niece.* He comes, the false disturber of my
quiet. ' Now, vengeance, do thy worst.   [*Aside.*

Enter WHISKERANDOS.

' O hateful liberty—if thus in vain
' I seek my Tilburina !
 ' *Both Nieces.* And ever shalt !

Sir CHRISTOPHER *and* Sir WALTER *come forward.*

' Hold ! we will avenge you.
' *Whiskerandos.* Hold *you*—or see your nieces bleed !'
  [*The two Nieces draw their two daggers to strike*
    WHISKERANDOS : *the two Uncles, at the instant,
    with their two swords drawn, catch their two
    Nieces' arms, and turn the points of their swords
    to* WHISKERANDOS, *who immediately draws two*

daggers, and holds them to the two Nieces' bosoms.]

Puff. There's situation for you! there's an heroic group! You see the ladies can't stab Whiskerandos: he durst not strike them, for fear of their uncles. The uncles durst not kill him, because of their nieces. I have them all at a dead lock! for every one of them is afraid to let go first.

Sneer. Why, then, they must stand there for ever.

Puff. So they would, if I hadn't a very fine contrivance for't. Now mind——

Enter BEEFEATER, *with his halberd.*

' *Beefeater.* In the queen's name, I charge you all
     to drop
' Your swords and daggers!'

                    [*They drop their swords and daggers.*
Sneer. That is a contrivance indeed.

Puff. Ay—in the queen's name.

' *Sir Christ. H.* Come, niece!
' *Sir Walter R.* Come, niece!

                    [*Exeunt, with the two Nieces.*
' *Whiskerandos.* What's he, who bids us thus renounce our guard?

' *Beefeater.* Thou must do more—renounce thy love!

' *Whiskerandos.* Thou liest, base Beefeater!

' *Beefeater.*   Ha! hell! the lie!
' By Heav'n, thou'st roused the lion in my heart!
' Off, yeoman's habit! base disguise! off! off!

          [*Discovers himself, by throwing off his upper dress,
            and appearing in a very fine waistcoat.*
' Am I a Beefeater now?
' Or beams my crest as terrible as when
' In Biscay's Bay I took thy captive sloop?'

Puff. There, egad! he comes out to be the very captain of the privateer who had taken Whiskerandos prisoner ; and was himself an old lover of Tilburina.

Dangle. Admirably managed, indeed.

Puff. Now, stand out of their way.

' *Whiskerandos.* I thank thee, fortune! that hast thus bestowed

' A weapon to chastise this insolent.

[*Takes up one of the swords.*

' *Beefeater.* I take thy challenge, Spaniard, and I thank thee,

' Fortune, too—!' [*Takes up the other sword.*

Dangle. That's excellently contrived! It seems as if the two uncles had left their swords on purpose for them.

Puff. No, egad, they could not help leaving them.

' *Whiskerandos.* Vengeance and Tilburina!

' *Beefeater.* Exactly so.

[*They fight, and after the usual number of wounds given,* WHISKERANDOS *falls.*

' *Whiskerandos.* O cursed parry! that last thrust in tierce

' Was fatal. Captain, thou hast fenced well!

' And Whiskerandos quits this bustling scene

' For all eter——

' *Beefeater.* —nity—He would have added, but stern death

' Cut short his being, and the noun at once!'

Puff. O, my dear sir, you are too slow: now mind me. Sir, shall I trouble you to die again?

' *Whiskerandos.* And Whiskerandos quits this bustling scene

' For all eter—

'*Beefeater.* —nity—He would have added——'

Puff. No, sir; that's not it.   Once more, if you please.

Whiskerandos. I wish, sir, you would practise this without me; I can't stay dying here all night.

Puff. Very well; we'll go over it by-and-by —— I must humour these gentlemen!

[*Exit* WHISKERANDOS.

'*Beefeater.* Farewell, brave Spaniard! and when
       next——'

Puff. Dear sir, you needn't speak that speech, as the body has walked off.

Beefeater. That's true, sir; then I'll join the fleet.

Puff. If you please.   [*Exit* BEEFEATER.]   Now, who comes on?

Enter GOVERNOR, *with his hair properly disordered.*

'*Govern.* A hemisphere of evil planets reign!
' And every planet sheds contagious frenzy!
' My Spanish prisoner is slain! my daughter,
' Meeting the dead corse borne along, has gone
' Distract!   [*A loud flourish of trumpets.*
       ' But hark! I am summon'd to the fort:
' Perhaps the fleets have met? amazing crisis!
' O Tilburina! from thy aged father's beard
' Thou'st pluck'd the few brown hairs which time had
       left!'   [*Exit* GOVERNOR.

Sneer. Poor gentleman!

Puff. Yes; and no one to blame but his daughter!

Dangle. And the planets——

Puff. True.   Now enter Tilburina!

Sneer. Egad, the business comes on quick here.

Puff. Yes, sir; now she comes in stark mad in white satin.

Sneer. Why in white satin?

Puff. O Lord, sir; when a heroine goes mad, she always goes into white satin; don't she, Dangle?

Dangle. Always; it's a rule.

Puff. Yes; here it is [*looking at the book*]. 'Enter Tilburina stark mad in white satin, and her confidant stark mad in white linen.'

Enter TILBURINA *and* CONFIDANT, *mad, according to custom.*

Sneer. But, what the deuce, is the confidant to be mad too?

Puff. To be sure she is: the confidant is always to do whatever her mistress does; weep when she weeps; smile when she smiles; go mad when she goes mad. Now, madam confidant; but keep your madness in the background, if you please.

' *Tilb.* The wind whistles——the moon rises——see,
' They have kill'd my squirrel in his cage!
' Is this a grasshopper? Ha! no; it is my
   Whiskerandos——you shall not keep him——
' I know you have him in your pocket——
' An oyster may be cross'd in love! Who says
' A whale's a bird? Ha! did you call, my love?
' —— He's here! He's there! He's everywhere!
' Ah me! He's nowhere!' [*Exit* TILBURINA.

Puff. There, do you ever desire to see anybody madder than that?

Sneer. Never, while I live!

Puff. You observed how she mangled the metre?

Dangle. Yes; egad, it was the first thing made me suspect she was out of her senses.

Sneer. And pray what becomes of her?

Puff. She is gone to throw herself into the sea, to be sure; and that brings us at once to the scene of action, and so to my catastrophe—my sea-fight, I mean.

Sneer. What you bring that in at last?

Puff. Yes, yes; you know my play is *called* the *Spanish Armada;* otherwise, egad, I have no occasion for the battle at all. Now then for my magnificence! my battle! my noise! and my procession! You are all ready?

PROMPTER *within.*

Yes, sir.

Puff. Is the Thames dressed?

Enter THAMES *with two Attendants.*

Thames. Here I am, sir.

Puff. Very well, indeed. See, gentlemen, there's a river for you! This is blending a little of the masque with my tragedy; a new fancy, you know, and very useful in my case; for as there *must be a procession*, I suppose Thames, and all his tributary rivers, to compliment Britannia with a fête in honour of the victory.

Sneer. But pray, who are these gentlemen in green with him?

Puff. Those? those are his banks.

Sneer. His banks?

Puff. Yes, one crowned with alders, and the other with a villa! You take the allusions? But hey! what the plague! you have got both your banks on one side. Here, sir, come round. Ever while you live, Thames, go between your banks. [*Bell rings.*] There, soh! now for't. Stand aside, my dear friends! away, Thames! [*Exit* THAMES *between his banks.*

[*Flourish of drums, trumpets, cannon, &c. &c. Scene*

changes to the sea, the fleets engage, the music plays ' Britons, strike home.' Spanish fleet destroyed by fireships, &c. English fleet advances, music plays ' Rule, Britannia.' The procession of all the English rivers, and their tributaries, with their emblems, &c. begins with Handel's water music, ends with a chorus, to the march in Judas Maccabæus. During this scene, Puff directs and applauds everything——then]

Puff. Well, pretty well; but not quite perfect; so, ladies and gentlemen, if you please, we'll rehearse this piece again to-morrow.   [*Curtain drops.*

PIZARRO:

A TRAGEDY.

ADVERTISEMENT.

As the two translations which have been published of Kotzebue's 'SPANIARDS IN PERU' have, I understand, been very generally read, the public are in possession of all the materials necessary to form a judgment on the merits and defects of the Play performed at Drury Lane Theatre.

DEDICATION.

To HER, whose approbation of this Drama, and whose peculiar delight in the applause it has received from the public, have been to me the highest gratification derived from its success—I dedicate this Play.

RICHARD BRINSLEY SHERIDAN.

PROLOGUE.

WRITTEN BY RICHARD BRINSLEY SHERIDAN.

SPOKEN BY MR. KING.

CHILL'D by rude gales, while yet reluctant May
Withholds the beauties of the vernal day;
As some fond maid, whom matron frowns reprove,
Suspends the smile her heart devotes to love;
The season's pleasures too delay their hour,
And Winter revels with protracted power:
Then blame not, critics, if, thus late, we bring
A winter Drama—but reproach—the Spring.
What prudent cit dares yet the season trust,
Bask in his whisky, and enjoy the dust?
Horsed in Cheapside, scarce yet the gayer spark
Achieves the Sunday triumph of the Park;
Scarce yet you see him, dreading to be late,
Scour the New-road, and dash thro' Grosvenor-gate—
Anxious—yet timorous too!—his steed to show,
The hack Bucephalus of Rotten-row.
Careless he seems, yet, vigilantly sly,
Woos the stray glance of ladies passing by,
While his off heel, insidiously aside,
Provokes the caper which he seems to chide.
Scarce rural Kensington due honour gains;
The vulgar verdure of her walk remains!
Where white-robed misses amble two by two,
Nodding to booted beaux—'How'do, how'do?'
With gen'rous questions that no answer wait,
'How vastly full! A'n't you come vastly late?

'I'n't it quite charming? When do you leave town?
'A'n't you quite tired? Pray, can we set you down?'
These suburb pleasures of a London May,
Imperfect yet, we hail the cold delay:
Should our Play please—and you're indulgent ever—
Be your decree—' 'Tis better late than never.'

DRAMATIS PERSONÆ,

AS ORIGINALLY ACTED AT DRURY LANE THEATRE, MAY 24, 1799.

Ataliba, King of Quito . . . . Mr. POWELL.
Rolla, ⎫ Commanders of his Army ⎧ Mr. KEMBLE.
Alonzo, ⎭ ⎨ Mr. C. KEMBLE.
Cora, Alonzo's Wife . . . . Mrs. JORDAN.
Pizarro, Leader of the Spaniards Mr. BARRYMORE.
Elvira, Pizarro's Mistress . . . Mrs. SIDDONS.
Almagro . . . . Mr. CAULFIELD.
Gonzalo, ⎫ ⎧ Mr. WENTWORTH.
Davilla, ⎬ Pizarro's Associates . ⎨ Mr. TRUEMAN.
Gomez, ⎭ ⎩ Mr. SURMONT.
Valverde, Pizarro's Secretary . . Mr. R. PALMER.
Las-Casas, a Spanish Ecclesiastic Mr. AICKIN.
An old blind Man . . . . . Mr. CORY.
Orozembo, an old Cacique : . . Mr. DOWTON.
A Boy . . . . Master CHATTERLEY
A Sentinel . . . . Mr. HOLLAND.
Attendant . . . . Mr. MADDOCKS.
Peruvian Officer . : . . . . Mr. ARCHER.

Soldiers, Messrs. FISHER, EVANS, CHIPPENDALE,
WEBB, &c. &c.

The Vocal Parts by Messrs. KELLY, SEDGWICK, DIGNUM
DANBY, &c.—Mrs. CROUCH, Miss DE CAMP, Miss
STEPHENS, Miss LEAK, Miss DUFOUR, &c.

PIZARRO.

ACT I.—SCENE I.

A magnificent Pavilion near PIZARRO'S *Tent—a View of the Spanish Camp in the background.* ELVIRA *is discovered sleeping under a canopy on one side of the pavilion.* VALVERDE *enters, gazes on* ELVIRA, *kneels, and attempts to kiss her hand;* ELVIRA *awakened, rises and looks at him with indignation.*

Elv. AUDACIOUS! Whence is thy privilege to interrupt the few moments of repose my harassed mind can snatch amid the tumults of this noisy camp? Shall I inform your master of this presumptuous treachery? Shall I disclose thee to Pizarro? hey!

Val. I am his servant, it is true—trusted by him— and I know him well; and therefore 'tis I ask, by what magic could Pizarro gain your heart; by what fatality still holds he your affection?

Elv. Hold! thou trusty secretary!

Val. Ignobly born! in mind and manners rude, ferocious, and unpolished, though cool and crafty if occasion need; in youth audacious—ill his first manhood—a licensed pirate—treating men as brutes—the world as booty; yet now the Spanish hero is he styled—the first of Spanish conquerors! and for a

warrior so accomplished, 'tis fit Elvira should leave
her noble family, her fame, her home, to share the
dangers, humours, and the crimes of such a lover as
Pizarro!

Elv. What! Valverde moralising! But grant I
am in error, what is my incentive? Passion, infatu-
ation, call it as you will; but what attaches thee to
this despised, unworthy leader? Base lucre is thy
object, mean fraud thy means. Could you gain me,
you only hope to win a higher interest in Pizarro. I
know you.

Val. On my soul, you wrong me; what else my
faults, I have none towards you: but indulge the scorn
and levity of your nature; do it while yet the time
permits; the gloomy hour, I fear, too soon approaches.

Elv. Valverde, a prophet too!

Val. Here me, Elvira. Shame from his late defeat,
and burning wishes for revenge, again have brought
Pizarro to Peru; but trust me, he over-rates his
strength, nor measures well the foe. Encamped in
a strange country, where terror cannot force, nor
corruption buy a single friend, what have we to hope?
The army murmuring at increasing hardships, while
Pizarro decorates with gaudy spoil the gay pavilion
of his luxury! each day diminishes our force.

Elv. But are you not the heirs of those that fall?

Val. Are gain and plunder then our only purpose?
Is this Elvira's heroism?

Elv. No, so save me, Heaven! I abhor the motive,
means, and end of your pursuits; but I will trust
none of you. In your whole army there is not one
of you that has a heart, or speaks ingenuously, aged
Las-Casas, and he alone, excepted.

Val. He! an enthusiast in the opposite and worse
extreme!

Elv. Oh! had I earlier known that virtuous man, how different might my lot have been!

Val. I will grant, Pizarro could not then so easily have duped you: forgive me, but at that event I still must wonder.

Elv. Hear me, Valverde. When first my virgin fancy waked to love, Pizarro was my country's idol. Self-taught, self-raised, and self-supported, he became a hero; and I was formed to be won by glory and renown. 'Tis known that when he left Panama in a slight vessel, his force was not a hundred men. Arrived in the island of Gallo, with his sword he drew a line upon the sands, and said, ' Pass, those who fear to die or conquer with their leader.' Thirteen alone remained, and at the head of these the warrior stood his ground. Even at the moment when my ears first caught this tale, my heart exclaimed, ' Pizarro is its lord!' What since I have perceived, or thought, or felt, you must have more worth to win the knowledge of.

Val. I press no further; still assured that while Alonzo de Molina, our general's former friend and pupil, leads the enemy, Pizarro never more will be a conqueror. [*Trumpets without.*

Elv. Silence! I hear him coming; look not perplexed. How mystery and fraud confound the countenance! Quick, put on an honest face, if thou canst.

Piz. [*Speaking without.*] Chain and secure him, I will examine him myself.

PIZARRO *enters.*

[VALVERDE *bows*—ELVIRA *laughs.*

Piz. Why dost thou smile, Elvira?

Elv. To laugh or weep without a reason, is one of the few privileges poor women have.

Piz. Elvira, I will know the cause, I am resolved!

Elv. I am glad of that, because I love resolution, and am resolved not to tell you. Now my resolution, I take it, is the better of the two, because it depends upon myself, and yours does not.

Piz. Psha! trifler!

Val. Elvira was laughing at my apprehensions that—

Piz. Apprehensions!

Val. Yes; that Alonzo's skill and genius should so have disciplined and informed the enemy, as to——

Piz. Alonzo! the traitor! How I once loved that man! His noble mother entrusted him, a boy, to my protection. At my table did he feast—in my tent did he repose. I had marked his early genius, and the valorous spirit that grew with it. Often I had talked to him of our first adventures—what storms we struggled with — what perils we surmounted! When landed with a slender host upon an unknown land—then, when I told how famine and fatigue, discord and toil, day by day, did thin our ranks; amid close-pressing enemies, how still undaunted I endured and dared; maintained my purpose and my power, in despite of growling mutiny or bold revolt, till with my faithful few remaining I became at last victorious! When, I say, of these things I spoke, the youth, Alonzo, with tears of wonder and delight, would throw him on my neck, and swear his soul's ambition owned no other leader.

Val. What could subdue attachment so begun?

Piz. Las-Casas. He it was, with fascinating craft and canting precepts of humanity, raised in Alonzo's mind a new enthusiasm, which forced him, as the stripling termed it, to forego his country's claims for those of human nature.

Val. Yes, the traitor left you, joined the Peruvians, and became thy enemy and Spain's.

Piz. But first with weariless remonstrance he sued to win me from my purpose, and untwine the sword from my determined grasp. Much he spoke of right, of justice, and humanity, calling the Peruvians our innocent and unoffending brethren.

Val. They!—Obdurate heathens!—They our brethren!

Piz. But when he found that the soft folly of the pleading tears he dropt upon my bosom fell on marble, he flew and joined the foe: then, profiting by the lessons he had gained in wronged Pizarro's school, the youth so disciplined and led his new allies, that soon he forced me—Ha! I burn with shame and fury while I own it!—in base retreat and foul discomfiture to quit the shore.

Val. But the hour of revenge is come.

Piz. It is; I am returned—my force is strengthened, and the audacious boy shall soon know that Pizarro lives, and has—a grateful recollection of the thanks he owes him.

Val. 'Tis doubted whether still Alonzo lives.

Piz. 'Tis certain that he does; one of his armourbearers is just made prisoner: twelve thousand is their force, as he reports, led by Alonzo and Peruvian Rolla. This day they make a solemn sacrifice on their ungodly altars. We must profit by their security, and attack them unprepared; the sacrificers shall become the victims.

Elv. Wretched innocents! And their own blood shall bedew their altars!

Piz. Right. [*Trumpets without.*] Elvira, retire!

Elv. Why should I retire?

Piz. Because men are to meet here, and on manly business.

Elv. O, men! men! ungrateful and perverse! O, woman! still affectionate though wronged! The beings to whose eyes you turn for animation, hope, and rapture, through the days of mirth and revelry; and on whose bosoms in the hour of sore calamity you seek for rest and consolation; *them,* when the pompous follies of your mean ambition are the question, you treat as playthings or as slaves! I shall not retire.

Piz. Remain then; and, if thou canst, be silent.

Elv. They only babble who practise not reflection; I shall think; and thought is silence.

Piz. Ha! there's somewhat in her manner lately—

[PIZARRO *looks sternly and suspiciously towards* ELVIRA, *who meets him with a commanding and unaltered eye.*

Enter LAS-CASAS, ALMAGRO, GONZALO, DAVILLA, *Officers and Soldiers. Trumpets without.*

Las-Cas. Pizarro, we attend your summons.

Piz. Welcome, venerable father—my friends, most welcome. Friends and fellow-soldiers, at length the hour is arrived, which to Pizarro's hopes presents the full reward of our undaunted enterprise and long-enduring toils. Confident in security, this day the foe devotes to solemn sacrifice; if with bold surprise we strike on their solemnity—trust to your leader's word —we shall not fail.

Alm. Too long inactive have we been mouldering on the coast; our stores exhausted, and our soldiers murmuring. Battle! battle! then death to the armed, and chains for the defenceless.

Dav. Death to the whole Peruvian race!

Las-Cas. Merciful Heaven!

Alm. Yes, general, the attack, and instantly! Then shall Alonzo, basking at his ease, soon cease to scoff our suffering and scorn our force.

Las-Cas. Alonzo! scorn and presumption are not in his nature.

Alm. 'Tis fit Las-Casas should defend his pupil.

Piz. Speak not of the traitor; or hear his name but as the bloody summons to assault and vengeance. It appears we are agreed?

Alm. and Dav. We are.

Gon. All! Battle! battle!

Las-Cas. Is then the dreadful measure of your cruelty not yet complete? Battle! gracious Heaven! Against whom? Against a king, in whose mild bosom your atrocious injuries even yet have not excited hate! but who, insulted or victorious, still sues for peace. Against a people who never wronged the living being their Creator formed; a people, who, children of innocence! received you as cherished guests with eager hospitality and confiding kindness. Generously and freely did they share with you their comforts, their treasures, and their homes; you repaid them by fraud, oppression, and dishonour. These eyes have witnessed all I speak—as gods you were received: as fiends have you acted.

Piz. Las-Casas!

Las-Cas. Pizarro, hear me! Hear me, chieftains! And thou, All-powerful! whose thunders can shiver into sand the adamantine rock—whose lightnings can pierce to the core of the rived and quaking earth. Oh! let thy power give effect to thy servant's words, as thy spirit gives courage to his will! Do not, I implore you, chieftains—countrymen—do not, I implore you, renew the foul barbarities which your insatiate avarice has inflicted on this wretched, unoffending race! But hush, my sighs—fall not, drops of useless sorrow!—heart-breaking anguish, choke not my utterance. All I entreat is, send me once more to those you *call* your enemies. Oh! let me be the messenger of penitence from you. I shall return with blessings and with peace from them. Elvira, you weep! Alas! and does this dreadful crisis move no heart but thine?

Alm. Because there are no women here but she and thou.

Piz. Close this idle war of words; time flies, and our opportunity will be lost. Chieftains, are ye for instant battle?

Alm. We are.

Las-Cas. Oh, men of blood! [*Kneels.*] God! thou hast anointed me thy servant—not to curse, but to bless my countrymen; yet now my blessing on their force were blasphemy against thy goodness. [*Rises.*] No! I curse your purpose, homicides! I curse the bond of blood by which you are united. May fell division, infamy, and rout defeat your projects and rebuke your hopes! On you, and on your children, be the peril of the innocent blood which shall be shed this day! I leave you, and for ever! No longer shall these aged eyes be scared by the horrors they have witnessed. In caves, in forests, will I hide myself; with tigers and with savage beasts will I commune; and when at length we meet again before the blessed tribunal of that Deity, whose mild doctrines and whose mercies ye have this day renounced, then shall *you* feel the agony and grief of soul which tear the bosom of your accuser now!   [*Going.*

Elv. Las-Casas! Oh! take me with thee, Las-Casas.

Las-Cas. Stay! lost, abused lady! I alone am useless here. Perhaps thy loveliness may persuade to pity, where reason and religion plead in vain. Oh! save thy innocent fellow-creatures if thou canst; then shall thy frailty be redeemed, and thou wilt share the mercy thou bestowest. [*Exit.*

Piz. How, Elvira! wouldst thou leave me?

Elv. I am bewildered, grown terrified! Your inhumanity—and that good Las-Casas—oh! he appeared to me just now something more than heavenly; and you! ye all looked worse than earthly.

Piz. Compassion sometimes becomes a beauty.

Elv. Humanity always becomes a conqueror.

Alm. Well! Heaven be praised, we are rid of the old moralist.

Gon. I hope he'll join his preaching pupil, Alonzo.

Piz. Now to prepare our muster and our march. At mid-day is the hour of the sacrifice. Consulting with our guides, the route of your divisions shall be given to each commander. If we surprise, we conquer; and if we conquer, the gates of Quito will be open to us.

Alm. And Pizarro then be monarch of Peru.

Piz. Not so fast, ambition for a time must take counsel from discretion. Ataliba must still hold the shadow of a sceptre in his hand;—Pizarro still appear dependent upon Spain; while the pledge of future peace, his daughter's hand, secures the proud succession to the crown I seek.

Alm. This is best. In Pizarro's plans observe the statesman's wisdom guides the warrior's valour.

Val. [*To* ELVIRA.] You mark, Elvira?

Elv. O, yes, this is best—this is excellent.

Piz. You seem offended. Elvira still retains my heart. Think, a sceptre waves me on.

Elv. Offended? No!—Thou know'st thy glory is my idol; and this will be most glorious, most just and honourable.

Piz. What mean you?

Elv. Oh! nothing—mere woman's prattle—a jealous whim, perhaps; but let it not impede the royal hero's course. [*Trumpets without.*] The call of arms invites you. Away! away! you, his brave, his worthy fellow-warriors.

Piz. And go you not with me?

Elv. Undoubtedly! I needs must be the first to hail the future monarch of Peru.

Enter GOMEZ.

Alm. How, Gomez! what bring'st thou?

Gom. On yonder hill, among the palm-trees, we have surprised an old cacique; escape by flight he could not, and we seized him and his attendant unresisting; yet his lips breathe naught but bitterness and scorn.

Piz. Drag him before us.

[GOMEZ *leaves the tent, and returns, conducting*
　　　OROZEMBO *and Attendant, in chains, guarded.*
What art thou, stranger?

Oro. First tell me which among you is the captain of this band of robbers.

Piz. Ha!

Alm. Madman! Tear out his tongue, or else——

Oro. Thou'lt hear some truth.

Dav. [*Showing his poniard.*] Shall I not plunge this into his heart?

Oro. [*To* PIZARRO.] Does your army boast many such heroes as this?

Piz. Audacious! This insolence has sealed thy doom.

Die thou shalt, gray-headed ruffian. But first confess what thou knowest.

Oro. I know that which thou has just assured me of—that I shall die.

Piz. Less audacity perhaps might have preserved thy life.

Oro. My life is as a withered tree; it is not worth preserving.

Piz. Hear me, old man. Even now we march against the Peruvian army. We know there is a secret path that leads to your stronghold among the rocks; guide us to that, and name thy reward. If wealth be thy wish——

Oro. Ha! ha! ha! ha!

Piz. Dost thou despise my offer?

Oro. Thee and thy offer! Wealth! I have the wealth of two dear gallant sons; I have stored in heaven the riches which repay good actions here; and still my chiefest treasure do I bear about me.

Piz. What is that? Inform me.

Oro. I will, for it never can be thine—the treasure of a pure, unsullied conscience.

Piz. I believe there is no other Peruvian who dares speak as thou dost.

Oro. Would I could believe there is no other Spaniard who dares act as thou dost.

Gon. Obdurate Pagan! How numerous is your army?

Oro. Count the leaves of yonder forest.

Alm. Which is the weakest part of your camp?

Oro. It has no weak part, on every side 'tis fortified by justice.

Piz. Where have you concealed your wives and your children?

Oro. In the hearts of their husbands and their fathers.

Piz. Know'st thou Alonzo?

Oro. Know him! Alonzo! Know him! Our nation's benefactor! The guardian angel of Peru!

Piz. By what has he merited that title?

Oro. By not resembling thee.

Alm. Who is this Rolla, joined with Alonzo in command?

Oro. I will answer that; for I love to hear and to repeat the hero's name. Rolla, the kinsman of the king, is the idol of our army; in war a tiger, chafed by the hunter's spear; in peace more gentle than the unweaned lamb. Cora was once betrothed to him; but finding she preferred Alonzo, he resigned his claim, and, I fear, his peace, to friendship and to Cora's happiness; yet still he loves her with a pure and holy fire.

Piz. Romantic savage! I shall meet this Rolla soon.

Oro. Thou hadst better not! The terrors of his noble eye would strike thee dead.

Dav. Silence, or tremble!

Oro. Beardless robber! I never yet have trembled before God, why should I tremble before man? Why before thee, thou less than man!

Dav. Another word, audacious heathen, and I strike!

Oro. Strike, Christian! Then boast among thy fellows—I too have murdered a Peruvian!

Dav. Hell and vengeance seize thee!   [*Stabs him.*

Piz. Hold!

Dav. Couldst thou longer have endured his insults?

Piz. And therefore should he die untortured?

Oro. True! Observe, young man, your unthinking rashness has saved me from the rack; and you yourself have lost the opportunity of a useful lesson; you might have seen with what cruelty vengeance would have inflicted torments, and with what patience virtue would have borne them.

Elv. [*Supporting* OROZEMBO's *head upon her bosom.*]
Oh! ye are monsters all. Look up, thou martyred
innocent; look up once more, and bless me ere thou
diest. God! how I pity thee!

Oro. Pity me! Me! so near my happiness! Bless
thee, lady! Spaniards—Heaven turn your hearts,
and pardon you as I do.

[OROZEMBO *is borne off dying.*

Piz. Away! Davilla! If thus rash a second time——

Dav. Forgive the hasty indignation which——

Piz. No more; unbind that trembling wretch; let
him depart; 'tis well he should report the mercy which
we show to insolent defiance. Hark! our troops are
moving.

Attend. [*On passing* ELVIRA.] If through your
gentle means my master's poor remains might be
preserved from insult——

Elv. I understand you.

Attend. His sons may yet thank your charity, if not
avenge their father's fate. [*Exit.*

Piz. What says the slave?

Elv. A parting word to thank you for your mercy.

Piz. Our guard and guides approach. [*Soldiers
march through the tents.*] Follow me, friends, each
shall have his post assigned, and ere Peruvia's god
shall sink beneath the main, the Spanish banner,
bathed in blood, shall float above the walls of van-
quished Quito. [*Exeunt.*

Manent ELVIRA *and* VALVERDE.

Val. Is it now presumption that my hopes gain
strength with the increasing horrors which I see appal
Elvira's soul?

Elv. I am mad with terror and remorse! Would I could fly these dreadful scenes!

Val. Might not Valverde's true attachment be thy refuge?

Elv. What wouldst thou do to save or to avenge me?

Val. I dare do all thy injuries may demand; a word, and he lies bleeding at your feet.

Elv. Perhaps we will speak again of this. Now leave me.   [*Exit* VALVERDE.

Elv. [*Alone.*] No! not this revenge; no! not this instrument. Fie, Elvira! even for a moment to counsel with this unworthy traitor! Can a wretch, false to a confiding master, be true to any pledge of love or honour? Pizarro will abandon me: yes; me, who, for his sake, have sacrificed—oh, God! what have I not sacrificed for him? yet, curbing the avenging pride that swells this bosom, I still will further try him. Oh, men! ye who, wearied by the fond fidelity of virtuous love, seek in the wanton's flattery a new delight, oh, ye may insult and leave the hearts to which your faith was pledged, and, stifling self-reproach, may fear no other peril; because such hearts, howe'er you injure and desert them, have yet the proud retreat of an unspotted fame, of unreproaching conscience. But beware the desperate libertine who forsakes the creature whom his arts have first deprived of all natural protection, of all self-consolation! What has he left her? Despair and vengeance!   [*Exit.*

ACT II.—SCENE I.

A Bank surrounded by a wild Wood, and Rocks. CORA,
sitting on the root of a tree, is playing with her Child.
ALONZO *hangs over them with delight and cheerfulness.*

Cora. Now confess, does he resemble thee, or not?

Alon. Indeed he is liker thee; thy rosy softness, thy
smiling gentleness.

Cora. But his auburn hair, the colour of his eyes,
Alonzo. O! my lord's image, and my heart's adored!
[*Pressing the Child to her bosom.*

Alon. The little daring urchin robs me, I doubt,
of some portion of thy love, my Cora. At least he
shares caresses, which till his birth were only mine.

Cora. Oh no, Alonzo! a mother's love for her sweet
babe is not a stealth from the dear father's store; it
is a new delight that turns with quickened gratitude
to Him, the author of her augmented bliss.

Alon. Could Cora think me serious?

Cora. I am sure he will speak soon: then will be
the last of the three holydays allowed by Nature's
sanction to the fond anxious mother's heart.

Alon. What are those three?

Cora. The ecstacy of his birth I pass; that in part
is selfish: but when first the white blossoms of his
teeth appear, breaking the crimson buds that did in-
case them; that is a day of joy: next, when from his
father's arms he runs without support, and clings,
laughing and delighted, to his mother's knee, that is
the mother's heart's next holyday: and sweeter still

14—2

the third, whene'er his little stammering tongue shall utter the grateful sound of father! mother! O! that is the dearest joy of all!

Alon. Beloved Cora!

Cora. Oh! my Alonzo! daily, hourly, do I pour thanks to Heaven for the dear blessing I possess in him and thee.

Alon. To Heaven and Rolla!

Cora. Yes, to Heaven and Rolla: and art thou not grateful to them too, Alonzo? art thou not happy?

Alon. Can Cora ask that question?

Cora. Why then of late so restless on thy couch? Why to my waking, watching ear so often does the stillness of the night betray thy struggling sighs?

Alon. Must not I fight against my country, against my brethren?

Cora. Do they not seek our destruction; and are not all men brethren?

Alon. Should they prove victorious?

Cora. I will fly, and meet thee in the mountains?

Alon. Fly, with thy infant, Cora?

Cora. What! think you a mother, when she runs from danger, can feel the weight of her child?

Alon. Cora, my beloved, do you wish to set my heart at rest?

Cora. Oh yes! yes! yes!

Alon. Hasten then to the concealment in the mountains; where all our matrons and virgins, and our warrior's offspring, are allotted to await the issue of the war. Cora will not alone resist her husband's, her sisters', and her monarch's wish.

Cora. Alonzo, I cannot leave you. Oh! how in every moment's absence would my fancy paint you, wounded, alone, abandoned! No, no, I cannot leave you.

Alon. Rolla will be with me.

Cora. Yes, while the battle rages, and where' it rages most, brave Rolla will be found. He may revenge, but cannot save thee.' To follow danger, he will leave even thee. But I have sworn never to forsake thee but with life. Dear, dear Alonzo! can you wish that I should break my vow?

Alon. Then be it so. Oh! excellence in all that's great and lovely, in courage, gentleness, and truth; my pride, my content, my all! Can there on this earth be fools who seek for happiness, and pass by love in the pursuit?

Cora. Alonzo, I cannot thank you: silence is the gratitude of true affection: who seeks to follow it by sound will miss the track. [*Shout without.*] Does the king approach?

Alon. No, 'tis the general placing the guard that will surround the temple during the sacrifice. 'Tis Rolla comes, the first and best of heroes.

[*Trumpets sound.*

ROLLA.

Rol. [*As entering.*] Then place them on the hill fronting the Spanish camp. [*Enters.*]

Cora. Rolla! my friend, my brother!

Alon. Rolla! my friend, my benefactor! how can our lives repay the obligations which we owe you?

Rol. Pass them in peace and bliss. Let Rolla witness it, he is overpaid.

Cora. Look on this child. He is the life-blood of my heart; but if ever he loves or reveres thee less than his own father, his mother's hate fall on him!

Rol. Oh, no more! What sacrifice have I made to merit gratitude? The object of my love was Cora's happiness. I see her happy. Is not my object gained, and am I not rewarded? Now, Cora, listen to a friend's advice. You must away; you must seek the sacred caverns, the unprofaned recess, whither, after this day's sacrifice, our matrons, and e'en the Virgins of the Sun, retire.

Cora. Not secure with Alonzo and with thee, Rolla?

Rol. We have heard Pizarro's plan is to surprise us. Thy presence, Cora, cannot aid, but may impede our efforts.

Cora. Impede!

Rol. Yes, yes. Thou know'st how tenderly we love thee; we, thy husband and thy friend. Art thou near us? our thoughts, our valour—vengeance will not be our own. No advantage will be pursued that leads us from the spot where thou art placed; no succour will be given but for thy protection. The faithful lover dares not be all himself amid the war, until he knows that the beloved of his soul is absent from the peril of the fight.

Alon. Thanks to my friend! 'tis this I would have urged.

Cora. This timid excess of love, producing fear instead of valour, flatters, but does not convince me: the wife is incredulous.

Rol. And is the mother unbelieving too?

Cora. No more. Do with me as you please. My friend, my husband! place me where you will.

Alon. My adored! we thank you both. [*March without.*] Hark! the king approaches to the sacrifice. You, Rolla, spoke of rumours of surprise. A servant of mine, I hear, is missing; whether surprised or treacherous, I know not.

Rol. It matters not. We are everywhere prepared.

Come, Cora, upon the altar 'mid the rocks thou'lt implore a blessing on our cause. The pious supplication of the trembling wife, and mother's heart, rises to the throne of mercy, the most resistless prayer of human homage. [*Exeunt.*

SCENE II.

The Temple of the Sun: it represents the magnificence of Peruvian idolatry: in the centre is the altar. A solemn march. The Warriors and King enter on one side of the Temple. ROLLA, ALONZO, and CORA, on the other.

Ata. Welcome, Alonzo! [*To* ROLLA.] Kinsman, thy hand. [*To* CORA.] Blessed be the object of the happy mother's love.

Cora. May the sun bless the father of his people!

Ata. In the welfare of his children lives the happiness of their king. Friends, what is the temper of our soldiers?

Rol. Such as becomes the cause which they support; their cry is, Victory or death! our king! our country! and our God!

Ata. Thou, Rolla, in the hour of peril, hast been wont to animate the spirit of their leaders, ere we proceed to consecrate the banners which thy valour knows so well to guard.

Rol. Yet never was the hour of peril near, when to inspire them words were so little needed. My brave associates—partners of my toil, my feelings, and my fame! can Rolla's words add vigour to the virtuous energies which inspire your hearts? No! You have judged, as I have, the foulness of the crafty plea by

which these bold invaders would delude you. Your
generous spirit has compared, as mine has, the motives
which, in a war like this, can animate their minds,
and ours. They, by a strange frenzy driven, fight for
power, for plunder, and extended rule: we, for our
country, our altars, and our homes. They follow an
adventurer whom they fear, and obey a power which
they hate: we serve a monarch whom we love—a God
whom we adore. Whene'er they move in anger,
desolation tracks their progress! Where'er they pause
in amity, affliction mourns their friendship. They
boast they come but to improve our state, enlarge our
thoughts, and free us from the yoke of error! 'Yes:
they will give enlightened freedom to our minds, who
are themselves the slaves of passion, avarice, and
pride. They offer us their protection. Yes, such
protection as vultures give to lambs—covering and
devouring them! They call on us to barter all of
good we have inherited and proved, for the desperate
chance of something better which they promise. Be
our plain answer this: The throne we honour is the
people's choice; the laws we reverence are our brave
fathers' legacy; the faith we follow teaches us to live
in bonds of charity with all mankind, and die with
hope of bliss beyond the grave. Tell your invaders
this, and tell them too, we seek no change; and, least
of all, such change as they would bring us.
                    [*Loud shouts of the soldiery.*
Ata. [*Embracing* ROLLA.] Now, holy friends, ever
mindful of these sacred truths, begin the sacrifice. [*A
solemn procession commences from the recess of the
temple above the altar. The Priests and Virgins of the
Sun arrange themselves on either side. The High-priest
approaches the altar, and the solemnity begins. The
invocation of the High-priest is followed by the choruses*

of the Priests and Virgins. Fire from above lights upon the altar. The whole assembly rise, and join in the thanksgiving.] Our offering is accepted. Now to arms, my friends; prepare for battle.

Enter ORANO.

Ora. The enemy!

Ata. How near?

Ora. From the hill's brow, e'en now as I o'erlooked their force, suddenly I perceived the whole in motion; with eager haste they march towards our deserted camp, as if apprised of this most solemn sacrifice.

Rol. They must be met before they reach it.

Ata. And you, my daughters, with your dear children, away to the appointed place of safety.

Cora. Oh, Alonzo! [*Embracing him.*

Alon. We shall meet again.

Cora. Bless us once more, ere you leave us.

Alon. Heaven protect and bless thee, my beloved; and thee, my innocent!

Ata. Haste, haste! each moment is precious!

Cora. Farewell, Alonzo! Remember thy life is mine.

Rol. Not one farewell to Rolla?

Cora. [*Giving him her hand.*] Farewell! The God of war be with you; but, bring me back Alonzo.
[*Exit with the child.*

Ata. [*Draws his sword.*] Now, my brethren, my sons, my friends, I know your valour. Should ill success assail us, be despair the last feeling of your hearts. If successful, let mercy be the first. Alonzo, to you I give to defend the narrow passage of the mountains. On the right of the wood be Rolla's station. For me, straight forwards will I march to meet them, and fight until I see my people saved, or they behold their monarch fall. Be the word of battle—God! and our native land.   [*A march. Exeunt.*

SCENE III.

The Wood between the Temple and the Camp.

Enter ROLLA *and* ALONZO.

Rol. Here, my friend, we separate—soon, I trust, to meet again in triumph.

Alon. Or perhaps we part to meet no more. Rolla, a moment's pause; we are yet before our army's strength; one earnest word at parting.

Rol. There is in language now no word but battle.

Alon. Yes, one word more—Cora!

Rol. Cora! speak!

Alon. The next hour brings us——

Rol. Death or victory!

Alon. It may be victory to one—death to the other.

Rol. Or both may fall.

Alon. If so, my wife and child I bequeath to the protection of Heaven and my king. But should I only fall, Rolla, be thou my heir.

Rol. How?

Alon. Be Cora thy wife; be thou a father to my child.

Rol. Rouse thee, Alonzo! Banish these timid fancies.

Alon. Rolla! I have tried in vain, and cannot fly from the foreboding which oppresses me; thou know'st it will not shake me in the fight; but give me the promise I exact.

Rol. If it be Cora's will—Yes, I promise. [*Gives his hand.*]

Alon. Tell her it was my last wish; and bear to her and to my son my last blessing.

Rol. I will. Now then to our posts, and let our swords speak for us.   [*They draw their swords.*

Alon. For the king and Cora!

Rol. For Cora and the king !

[*Exeunt different ways. Alarms without.*

SCENE IV.

A view of the Peruvian Camp, with a distant View of a Peruvian Village. Trees growing from a rocky Eminence on one Side. Alarms continue.

Enter an OLD BLIND MAN *and a* BOY.

O. Man. Have none returned to the camp ?

Boy. One messenger alone. From the temple they all marched to meet the foe.

O. Man. Hark, I hear the din of battle. O! had I still retained my sight, I might now have grasped a sword, and died a soldier's death ! Are we quite alone ?

Boy. Yes ! I hope my father will be safe.

O. Man. He will do his duty. I am more anxious for thee, my child.

Boy. I can stay with you, dear grandfather:

O. Man: But, should the enemy come, they will drag thee from me, my boy.

Boy: Impossible, grandfather ; for they will see at once that you are old and blind, and cannot do without me.

O. Man. Poor child ! you little know the hearts of

these inhuman men. [*Discharge of cannon heard.*] Hark! the noise is near. I hear the dreadful roaring of the fiery engines of these cruel strangers. [*Shouts at a distance.*] At every shout, with involuntary haste I clench my hand, and fancy still it grasps a sword! Alas! I can only serve my country by my prayers. Heaven preserve the Inca and his gallant soldiers!

Boy. O father! there are soldiers running——

O. Man. Spaniards, boy?

Boy. No, Peruvians!

O. Man. How! And flying from the field! It cannot be.

Enter two Peruvian Soldiers.

O speak to them, boy! Whence come you? How goes the battle?

Sold. We may not stop; we are sent for the reserve behind the hill. The day's against us.

[*Exeunt Soldiers.*

O. Man. Quick, then, quick!

Boy. I see the points of lances glittering in the light.

O: Man. Those are Peruvians. Do they bend this way?

Enter a Peruvian Soldier.

Boy. Soldier, speak to my blind father.

Sold. I am sent to tell the helpless father to retreat among the rocks; all will be lost, I fear. The king is wounded.

O. Man. Quick, boy! Lead me to the hill, where thou may'st view the plain. [*Alarms.*

Enter ATALIBA, *wounded, with* ORANO, *Officers, and Soldiers.*

Ata. My wound is bound; believe me, the hurt is nothing. I may return to the fight.

Ora. Pardon your servant; but the allotted priest who attends the sacred banner has pronounced that the Inca's blood once shed, no blessing can await the day until he leave the field.

Ata. Hard restraint! O, my poor brave soldiers! Hard that I may no longer be a witness of their valour. But haste you; return to your comrades. I will not keep one soldier from his post. Go, and avenge your fallen brethren. [*Exeunt* ORANO, *Officers, and Soldiers.*] I will not repine; my own fate is the last anxiety of my heart. It is for you, my people, that I feel and fear. [OLD MAN *and* BOY *advance.*

O. Man. Did I not hear the voice of an unfortunate? Who is it complains thus?

Ata. One almost by hope forsaken.

O. Man. Is the king alive?

Ata. The king still lives.

O. Man. Then thou art not forsaken! Ataliba protects the meanest of his subjects.

Ata. And who shall protect Ataliba?

O. Man. The immortal Powers, that protect the just. The virtues of our monarch alike secure to him the affection of his people and the benign regard of Heaven.

Ata. How impious, had I murmured! How wondrous, thou supreme Disposer, are thy acts! Even in this moment, which I had thought the bitterest trial of mortal suffering, thou hast infused the sweetest sensation of my life—it is the assurance of my people's love.

Boy. [*Turning forward.*] O, father! Stranger! see those hideous men that rush upon us yonder!

Ata. Ha! Spaniards! And I, Ataliba, ill-fated fugitive, without a sword even to try the ransom of a monarch life.

Enter DAVILLA, ALMAGRO, *and Spanish Soldiers.*

Dav. 'Tis he—our hopes are answered—I know him well—it is the king!

Alm. Away! Follow with your prize. Avoid those Peruvians, though in flight. This way we may regain our line.

[*Exeunt* DAVILLA, ALMAGRO, *and Soldiers,
with* ATALIBA *prisoner.*

O. Man. The king! Wretched old man, that could not see his gracious form! Boy, would thou hadst led me to the reach of those ruffians' swords!

Boy. Father! all our countrymen are flying here for refuge.

O. Man. No—to the rescue of their king—they never will desert him. [*Alarms without.*

*Enter Peruvian Officers and Soldiers flying across the
stage;* ORANO *following.*

Ora. Hold, I charge you! Rolla calls you.

Officer. We cannot combat with their dreadful engines.

Enter ROLLA.

Rol. Hold! recreants! cowards! What, fear ye death, and fear not shame? By my soul's fury, I cleave to the earth the first of you that stirs, or plunge your dastard swords into your leader's heart, that he no more may witness your disgrace. Where is the king?

Ora. From this old man and boy I learn that the detachment of the enemy, which you observed so suddenly to quit the field, have succeeded in surprising him; they are yet in sight.

Rol. And bear the Inca off a prisoner? Hear this, ye base, disloyal rout! Look there! The dust you see hangs on the bloody Spaniards' track, dragging with ruffian taunts your king, your father. Ataliba in bondage! Now fly, and seek your own vile safety, if you can.

O. Man. Bless the voice of Rolla, and bless the stroke I once lamented, but which now spares these extinguished eyes the shame of seeing the pale trembling wretches who dare not follow Rolla though to save their king!

Rol. Shrink ye from the thunder of the foe, and fall ye not at this rebuke? Oh! had ye each but one drop of the loyal blood which gushes to waste through the brave heart of this sightless veteran! Eternal shame pursue you, if you desert me now! But do; alone I go—alone, to die with glory by my monarch's side!

Soldiers. Rolla! we'll follow thee.

[*Trumpets sound;* ROLLA *rushes out, followed by* ORANO, *Officers and Soldiers.*

O. Man. O godlike Rolla! And thou sun, send from thy clouds avenging lightning to his aid! Haste, my boy; ascend some height, and tell to my impatient terror what thou seest.

Boy. I can climb this rock, and the tree above [*Ascends a rock, and from thence into the tree.*] O now I see them; now—yes—and the Spaniards turning by the steep.

O. Man. Rolla follows them?

Boy. He does; he does; he moves like an arrow! now he waves his arm to our soldiers. [*Report of cannon heard.*] Now there is fire and smoke.

O. Man. Yes, fire is the weapon of those fiends.

Boy. The wind blows off the smoke: they are all mixed together.

O. Man. Seest thou the king?

Boy. Yes; Rolla is near him! His sword sheds fire as he strikes!

O. Man. Bless thee, Rolla! Spare not the monsters.

Boy. Father! father! the Spaniards fly! O, now I see the king embracing Rolla.
[*Waving his cap for joy. Shouts of victory, flourish of trumpets, &c.*

O. Man. [*Falls on his knees.*] Fountain of life! how can my exhausted breath bear to thee thanks for this one moment of my life! My boy, come down, and let me kiss thee; my strength is gone!
[*The* Boy *having run to the* Old Man.

Boy. Let me help you, father. You tremble so——

O. Man. 'Tis with transport, boy!
[Boy *leads the* Old Man *off. Shouts, Flourish, &c.*

Enter Ataliba, Rolla, *and Peruvian Officers and Soldiers.*

Ata. In the name of my people, the saviour of whose sovereign you have this day been, accept this emblem of his gratitude. [*Giving* Rolla *his sun of diamonds.*] The tear that falls upon it may for a moment dim its lustre, yet does it not impair the value of the gift.

Rol. It was the hand of Heaven, not mine, that saved my king.

Enter Peruvian Officer, and Soldiers.

Rol. Now, soldier, from Alonzo?

Off. Alonzo's genius soon repaired the panic which early broke our ranks; but I fear we have to mourn Alonzo's loss: his eager spirit urged him too far in the pursuit?

Ata. How! Alonzo slain?

1st Sold. I saw him fall.

2nd Sold. Trust me, I beheld him up again and fighting; he was then surrounded and disarmed.

Ata. O! victory, dearly purchased!

Rol. O, Cora! who shall tell thee this?

Ata. Rolla, our friend is lost; our native country saved! Our private sorrows must yield to the public claim for triumph. Now go we to fulfil the first, the most sacred duty which belongs to victory; to dry the widowed and the orphaned tear of those whose brave protectors have perished in their country's cause.

[*Triumphant march, and exeunt.*

ACT III.—SCENE I.

A wild Retreat among stupendous Rocks. CORA *and her Child, with other Wives and Children of the Peruvian Warriors, are scattered about the scene in groups. They sing alternately stanzas expressive of their situation, with a Chorus, in which all join.*

1st Peruv. Wom. Zuluga, seest thou nothing yet?

Zul. Yes, two Peruvian soldiers; one on the hill, the other entering the thicket in the vale.

2nd Peruv. Wom. One more has passed. He comes, but pale and terrified.

Cora. My heart will start from my bosom.

Enter a Peruvian Soldier, panting for breath.

Wom. Well! joy or death?

Sold. The battle is against us. The king is wounded, and a prisoner.

Wom. Despair and misery!

Cora. [*In a faint voice.*] And Alonzo?

Sold. I have not seen him.

1st Wom. Oh! whither must we fly?

2nd Wom. Deeper into the forest.

Cora. I shall not move.

Another Peruvian Soldier. [*Without.*] Victory! victory! [*He enters hastily.*] Rejoice! rejoice! We are victorious!

Wom. [*Springing up.*] Welcome, welcome, thou messenger of joy: but the king!

Sold. He leads the brave warriors, who approach.

[*The triumphal march of the army is heard at a distance. The Women and Children join in a strain expressive of anxiety and exultation. The Warriors enter singing the Song of Victory, in which all join. The King and* ROLLA *follow, and are met with rapturous and affectionate respect.* CORA, *during this scene, with her Child in her arms, runs through the ranks searching and inquiring for* ALONZO.

Ata. Thanks, thanks, my children! I am well: believe it; the blood once stopped, my wound was nothing. [CORA *at length approaches* ROLLA, *who ap-*

pears to have been mournfully avoiding her.] Where is Alonzo? ROLLA *turns away in silence.*

Cora. [*Falling at the King's feet.*] Give me my husband; give this child his father.

Ata. I grieve that Alonzo is not here.

Cora. Hoped you to find him?

Ata. Most anxiously.

Cora. Ataliba! is he not dead?

Ata. No! the gods will have heard our prayers.

Cora. Is he not dead, Ataliba?

Ata. He lives—in my heart.

Cora. Oh, king! torture me not thus! speak out, is this child fatherless?

Ata. Dearest Cora! do not thus dash aside the little hope that still remains.

Cora. The little hope! yet still there is hope! Speak to me, Rolla: you are the friend of truth.

Rol. Alonzo has not been found.

Cora. Not found! What mean you? Will not you, Rolla, tell me truth? Oh! let me not hear the thunder rolling at a distance; let the bolt fall and crush my brain at once. Say not that he is not found: say at once that he is dead.

Rol. Then should I say false.

Cora. False! Blessings on thee for that word! But snatch me from this terrible suspense. Lift up thy little hands, my child; perhaps thy ignorance may plead better than thy mother's agony.

Rol. Alonzo is taken prisoner.

Cora. Prisoner! And by the Spaniards? Pizarro's prisoner? Then he is dead.

Ata. Hope better; the richest ransom which our realm can yield a herald shall this instant bear.

Peruv. Wom. Oh! for Alonzo's ransom; our gold, our gems! all!——Here, dear Cora,—here! here!

15—2

[*The Peruvian Women eagerly tear off all their ornaments, and run and take them from their children, to offer them to* Cora.

Ata. Yes, for Alonzo's ransom they would give all! I thank thee, Father, who hast given me such hearts to rule over!

Cora. Now one boon more, beloved monarch. Let me go with the herald.

Ata. Remember, Cora, thou art not a wife only, but a mother too; hazard not your own honour, and the safety of your infant. Among these barbarians the sight of thy youth, thy loveliness, and innocence, would but rivet faster your Alonzo's chains, and rack his heart with added fears for thee. Wait, Cora, the return of the herald.

Cora. Teach me how to live till then.

Ata. Now we go to offer to the gods thanks for our victory, and prayers for our Alonzo's safety.

[*March and procession. Exeunt omnes.*

SCENE II.

The Wood.

Enter Cora *and Child.*

Cora. Mild innocence, what will become of thee?

Enter Rolla.

Rol. Cora, I attend thy summons at the appointed spot.

Cora. Oh, my child, my boy! hast thou still a father?

Rol. Cora, can thy child be fatherless, while Rolla lives?

Cora. Will he not soon want a mother too? For canst thou think I will survive Alonzo's loss?

Rol. Yes! for his child's sake. Yes, as thou didst love Alonzo, Cora, listen to Alonzo's friend.

Cora. You bid me listen to the world. Who was not Alonzo's friend?

Rol. His parting words——

Cora. His parting words! [*Wildly.*] Oh, speak!

Rol. Consigned to me two precious trusts—his blessing to his son, and a last request to thee.

Cora. His last request! his last! Oh, name it!

Rol. If I fall, said he—(and sad forebodings shook him while he spoke)—promise to take my Cora for thy wife; be thou a father to my child. I pledged my word to him, and we parted. Observe me, Cora, I repeat this only, as my faith to do so was given to Alonzo; for myself, I neither cherish claim nor hope.

Cora. Ha! does my reason fail me, or what is this horrid light that presses on my brain? Oh, Alonzo! It may be thou hast fallen a victim to thine own guileless heart; hadst thou been silent, hadst thou not made a fatal legacy of these wretched charms——

Rol. Cora! what hateful suspicion has possessed thy mind?

Cora. Yes, yes, 'tis clear; his spirit was ensnared; he was led to the fatal spot, where mortal valour could not front a host of murderers. He fell; in vain did he exclaim for help to Rolla. At a distance you looked on and smiled: you could have saved him—could—but did not.

Rol. Oh, glorious sun! can I have deserved this? Cora, rather bid me strike this sword into my heart.

Cora. No!—live! live for love!—for that love

thou seekest; whose blossoms are to shoot from the
bleeding grave of thy betrayed and slaughtered friend!
But thou hast borne to me the last words of my
Alonzo! now hear mine.   Sooner shall this boy draw
poison from this tortured breast—sooner would I link
me to the pallid corse of the meanest wretch that
perished with Alonzo, than he call Rolla father—than
I call Rolla husband!

Rol. Yet call me what I am—thy friend, thy protector!

Cora. [*Distractedly.*]   Away! I have no protector
but my God!   With this child in my arms I will
hasten to the field of slaughter: there with these
hands will I turn up to the light every mangled body;
seeking, howe'er by death disfigured, the sweet smile
of my Alonzo: with fearful cries I will shriek out his
name till my veins snap!   If the smallest spark of
life remain, he will know the voice of his Cora, open
for a moment his unshrouded eyes, and bless me with a
last look.   But if we find him not, Oh! then, my boy,
we will to the Spanish camp; that look of thine will
win me passage through a thousand swords.   They
too are men.   Is there a heart that could drive back
the wife that seeks her bleeding husband; or the
innocent babe that cries for his imprisoned father.   No,
no, my child, everywhere we shall be safe.   A
wretched mother, bearing a poor orphan in her arms,
has Nature's passport through the world.   Yes, yes,
my son, we'll go and seek thy father.

[*Exit with the Child.*

Rol. [*After a pause of agitation.*]   Could I have
merited one breath of thy reproaches, Cora, I should
be the wretch I think I was not formed to be.   Her
safety must be my present purpose; then to convince
her she has wronged me!   [*Exit.*

SCENE III.

Pizarro's Tent.

PIZARRO, *traversing the scene in gloomy and furious agitation.*

Well, capricious idol, Fortune, be my ruin thy work and boast. To myself I will still be true. Yet ere I fall, grant me thy smile to prosper in one act of vengeance, and be that smile Alonzo's death.

Enter ELVIRA.

Who's there? who dares intrude? Why does my guard neglect their duty?

Elv. Your guard did what they could; but they knew their duty better than to enforce authority, when I refused obedience.

Piz. And what is it you desire?

Elv. To see how a hero bears misfortune. Thou, Pizarro, art not now collected—not thyself.

Piz. Wouldst thou I should rejoice that the spears of the enemy, led by accursed Alonzo, have pierced the bravest hearts of my followers?

Elv. No! I would have thee cold and dark as the night that follows the departed storm; still and sullen as the awful pause that precedes Nature's convulsion: yet I would have thee feel assured that a new morning shall arise, when the warrior's spirit shall stalk forth; nor fear the future, nor lament the past.

Piz. Woman! Elvira! Why had not all my men hearts like thine?

Elv. Then would thy brows have this day worn the crown of Quito.

Piz. Oh! hope fails me while that scourge of my life and fame, Alonzo, leads the enemy.

Elv. Pizarro, I am come to probe the hero farther: not now his courage, but his magnanimity. Alonzo is your prisoner.

Piz. How!

Elv. 'Tis certain; Valverde saw him even now dragged in chains within your camp. I chose to bring you the intelligence myself.

Piz. Bless thee, Elvira, for the news! Alonzo in my power! then I am the conqueror; the victory is mine!

Elv. Pizarro, this is savage and unmanly triumph. Believe me, you raise impatience in my mind to see the man whose valour, and whose genius, awe Pizarro; whose misfortunes are Pizarro's triumph; whose bondage is Pizarro's safety.

Piz. Guard! [*Enter Guard.*] Drag here the Spanish prisoner, Alonzo! Quick, bring the traitor here.   [*Exit Guar .*

Elv. What shall be his fate?

Piz. Death! death! in lingering torments! protracted to the last stretch that burning vengeance can devise, and fainting life sustain.

Elv. Shame on thee! Wilt thou have it said that the Peruvians found Pizarro could not conquer till Alonzo felt that he could murder?

Piz. Be it said, I care not. His fate is sealed.

Elv. Follow then thy will: but mark me; if basely thou dost shed the blood of this brave youth, Elvira's lost to thee for ever.

Piz. Why this interest for a stranger? What is Alonzo's fate to thee!

Elv. His fate! nothing! thy glory, everything! Think'st thou I could love thee stript of fame, of honour, and a just renown? Know me better.

Piz. Thou shouldst have known me better. Thou shouldst have known, that, once provoked to hate, I am for ever fixed in vengeance. [ALONZO *is brought in, in chains, guarded.* ELVIRA *observes him with attention and admiration.*] Welcome, welcome, Don Alonzo de Molina; 'tis long since we have met: thy mended looks should speak a life of rural indolence. How is it that amid the toils and cares of war thou dost preserve the healthful bloom of careless ease? Tell me thy secret?

Alon. Thou wilt not profit by it. Whate'er the toils or cares of war, peace still is here. [*Putting his hand to his heart.*]

Piz. Sarcastic boy!

Elv. Thou art answered rightly. Why sport with the unfortunate?

Piz. And thou art wedded too, I hear; ay, and the father of a lovely boy—the heir, no doubt, of all his father's loyalty, of all his mother's faith.

Alon. The heir, I trust, of all his father's scorn of fraud, oppression, and hypocrisy—the heir, I hope, of all his mother's virtue, gentleness, and truth—the heir, I am sure, to all Pizarro's hate.

Piz. Really! Now do I feel for this poor orphan; for fatherless to-morrow's sun shall see that child. Alonzo, thy hours are numbered.

Elv. Pizarro; no.

Piz. Hence; or dread my anger.

Elv. I will not hence; nor do I dread thy anger.

Alon. Generous loveliness! spare thy unavailing pity. Seek not to thwart the tiger with his prey beneath his fangs.

Piz. Audacious rebel! Thou a renegado from thy monarch and thy God!

Alon. 'Tis false.

Piz. Art thou not, tell me, a deserter from thy country's legions; and, with vile heathens leagued, hast thou not warred against thy native land?

Alon. No! Deserter I am none! I was not born among robbers! pirates! murderers! When those legions, lured by the abhorred lust of gold, and by thy foul ambition urged, forgot the honour of Castilians, and forsook the duties of humanity, they deserted me. I have not warred against my native land, but against those who have usurped its power. The banners of my country, when first I followed arms beneath them, were justice, faith, and mercy. If these are beaten down and trampled under foot, I have no country, nor exists the power entitled to reproach me with revolt.

Piz. The power to judge and punish thee at least exists.

Alon. Where are my judges?

Piz. Thou wouldst appeal to the war council?

Alon. If the good Las-Casas have yet a seat there, yes; if not, I appeal to Heaven!

Piz. And to impose upon the folly of Las-Casas, what would be the excuses of thy treason?

Elv. The folly of Las-Casas! Such, doubtless, his mild precepts seem to thy hard-hearted wisdom! O would I might have lived as I will die, a sharer in the follies of Las-Casas!

Alon. To him I should not need to urge the foul barbarities which drove me from your side; but I would gently lead him by the hand through all the lovely fields of Quito; there, in many a spot where late was barrenness and waste, I would show him how

now the opening blossom, blade, or perfumed bud, sweet,
bashful pledges of delicious harvest, wafting their incense to the ripening sun, give cheerful promise to the
hope of industry. This, I would say, is my work!
Next I should tell how hurtful customs and super-
stitions, strange and sullen, would often scatter and
dismay the credulous minds of these deluded innocents;
and then would I point out to him where now, in
clustered villages, they live like brethren, social and
confiding, while through the burning day Content sits
basking on the cheek of Toil, till laughing Pastime
leads them to the hour of rest—this too is mine! And
prouder yet, at that still pause between exertion and
repose, belonging not to pastime, labour, or to rest, but
unto Him who sanctions and ordains them all, I would
show him many an eye, and many a hand, by gentleness from error won, raised in pure devotion to the
true and only God!—this too I could tell him is Alonzo's
work! Then would Las-Casas clasp me in his aged
arms; from his uplifted eyes a tear of gracious thank-
fulness would fall upon my head, and that one blessed
drop would be to me at once this world's best proof
that I had acted rightly here, and surest hope of my
Creator's mercy and reward hereafter.

Elv. Happy, virtuous Alonzo! And thou, Pizarro,
wouldst appal with fear of death a man who thinks
and acts as he does!

Piz. Daring, obstinate enthusiast! But know the
pious blessing of thy preceptor's tears does not await
thee here; he has fled like thee—like thee, no doubt, to
join the foes of Spain. The perilous trial of the next
reward you hope is nearer than perhaps you've
thought; for, by my country's wrongs, and by mine
own, to-morrow's sun shall see thy death.

Elv. Hold! Pizarro—hear me. If not always

justly, at least act always greatly. Name not thy
country's wrongs: 'tis plain they have no share in thy
resentment. Thy fury 'gainst this youth is private hate
and deadly personal revenge; if this be so—and even
now thy detected conscience in that look avows it—
profane not the name of justice or thy country's cause,
but let him arm, and bid him to the field on equal
terms.

Piz. Officious advocate for treason—peace! Bear
him hence; he knows his sentence.

Alon. Thy revenge is eager, and I'm thankful for it;
to me thy haste is mercy. For thee, sweet pleader in
misfortune's cause, accept my parting thanks. This
camp is not thy proper sphere. Wert thou among
yon savages, as they are called, thou'dst find com-
panions more congenial to thy heart.

Piz. Yes; she shall bear the tidings of thy death
to Cora.

Alon. Inhuman man! that pang, at least, might have
been spared me; but thy malice shall not shake my
constancy. I go to death; many shall bless, and none
will curse my memory. Thou still wilt live, and still
wilt be—Pizarro.   [*Exit, guarded.*

Elv. Now, by the indignant scorn that burns upon
my cheek, my soul is shamed and sickened at the
meanness of thy vengeance.

Piz. What has thy romantic folly aimed at? He
is mine enemy, and in my power.

Elv. He is in your power, and therefore is no more
an enemy. Pizarro, I demand not of thee virtue; I
ask not from thee nobleness of mind; I require only
just dealing to the fame thou hast acquired; be not the
assassin of thine own renown. How often have you
sworn, that the sacrifice which thy wondrous valour's
high report had won you from subdued Elvira, was the

proudest triumph of your fame! Thou knowest I bear
a mind not cast in the common mould—not formed for
tame, sequestered love—content mid household cares to
prattle to an idle offspring, and wait the dull delight
of an obscure lover's kindness—no! my heart was
framed to look up with awe and homage to the
object it adored; my ears to own no music but the
thrilling records of his praise; my lips to scorn all
babbling but the tales of his achievements; my brain
to turn giddy with delight, reading the applauding
tributes of his monarch's and his country's gratitude;
my every faculty to throb with transport, while I heard
the shouts of acclamation which announced the coming
of my hero; my whole soul to love him with devotion,
with enthusiasm! to see no other object—to own no
other tie, but to make him my world! Thus to love is
at least no common weakness. Pizarro! was not such
my love for thee?

Piz. It was, Elvira!

Elv. Then do not make me hateful to myself, by
tearing off the mask at once, baring the hideous im-
posture that has undone me! Do not an act which,
howe'er thy present power may gloss it to the world,
will make thee hateful to all future ages, accursed and
scorned by posterity.

Piz. And should posterity applaud my deeds, think'st
thou my mouldering bones would rattle then with transport in my tomb? This is renown for visionary boys
to dream of. I understand it not. The fame I value
shall uplift my living estimation, o'erbear with popular
support the envy of my foes, advance my purposes, and
aid my power.

Elv. Each word thou speakest, each moment that
I hear thee, dispels the fatal mist through which I've
judged thee. Thou man of mighty name, but little

soul, I see thou wert not born to feel what genuine
fame and glory are: go! prefer the flattery of thy
own fleeting day to the bright circle of a deathless
name: go! prefer to stare upon the grain of sand on
which you trample, to musing on the starred canopy
above thee. Fame, the sovereign deity of proud ambition, is not to be worshipped so: who seeks alone for
living homage, stands a mean canvasser in her temple's
porch, wooing promiscuously from the fickle breath
of every wretch that passes the brittle tribute of his
praise. He dares not approach the sacred altar; no
noble sacrifice of his is placed there, nor ever shall his
worshipped image, fixed above, claim for his memory a
glorious immortality.

Piz. Elvira, leave me.

Elv. Pizarro, you no longer love me.

Piz. It is not so, Elvira. But what might I not
suspect; this wondrous interest for a stranger! Take
back thy reproach.

Elv. No, Pizarro; as yet I am not lost to you; one
string still remains, and binds me to your fate. Do
not, I conjure you; do not, for thine own sake, tear it
asunder; shed not Alonzo's blood!

Piz. My resolution's fixed.

Elv. Even though that moment lost you Elvira for
ever?

Piz. Even so.

Elv. Pizarro, if not to honour, if not to humanity,
yet listen to affection; bear some memory of the sacri-
fices I have made for thy sake. Have I not for thee
quitted my parents, my friends, my fame, my native
land? When escaping, did I not risk in rushing to
thy arms to bury myself in the bosom of the deep?
Have I not shared all thy perils, heavy storms at sea,
and frightful 'scapes on shore? Even on this dreadful

day, amid the rout of battle, who remained firm and constant at Pizarro's side? Who presented her bosom as his shield to the assailing foe?

Piz. 'Tis truly spoken all. In love thou art thy sex's miracle; in war the soldier's pattern; and therefore my whole heart and half my acquisitions are thy right.

Elv. Convince me I possess the first; I exchange all title to the latter for mercy to Alonzo.

Piz. No more! Had I intended to prolong his doom, each word thou utterest now would hasten on his fate.

Elv. Alonzo then at morn will die?

Piz. Think'st thou yon sun will set? As surely at his rising shall Alonzo die.

Elv. Then be it done; the string is cracked; sundered for ever. But mark me; thou hast heretofore had cause, 'tis true, to doubt my resolution, howe'er offended: but mark me now, the lips which, cold and jeering, barbing revenge with rancorous mockery, can insult a fallen enemy, shall never more receive the pledge of love: the arm which, unshaken by its bloody purpose, shall assign to needless torture the victim who avows his heart, never more shall press the hand of faith! Pizarro, scorn not my words; beware you slight them not!' I feel how noble are the motives which now animate my thoughts; who could not feel as I do, I condemn—who, feeling so, yet would not act as I shall, I despise!

Piz. [*After a pause, looking at her with an affected smile of contempt.*] I have heard thee, Elvira, and know well the noble motives which inspire thee; fit advocate in virtue's cause! Believe me, I pity thy tender feelings for the youth Alonzo! He dies at sunrise! [*Exit.*

Elv. 'Tis well! 'tis just I should be humbled. I had forgot myself, and in the cause of innocence assumed the tone of virtue. 'Twas fit I should be rebuked, and by Pizarro. Fall, fall, ye few reluctant drops of weakness, the last these eyes shall ever shed. How a woman can love, Pizarro, thou hast known too well; how she can hate, thou hast yet to learn. Yes, thou undaunted! thou, whom yet no mortal hazard has appalled! thou, who on Panama's brow didst make alliance with the raving elements, that tore the silence of that horrid night; when thou didst follow, as thy pioneer, the crashing thunder's drift, and stalking o'er the trembling earth, didst plant thy banner by the red volcano's mouth! Thou, who when battling on the sea, and thy brave ship was blown to splinters, wast seen, as thou didst bestride a fragment of the smoking wreck, to wave thy glittering sword above thy head, as thou wouldst defy the world in that extremity! Come, fearless man, now meet the last and fellest peril of thy life, meet, and survive, an injured woman's fury, if thou canst.　　　　　　　　　　　　　　[*Exit.*

ACT IV.—SCENE I.

A Dungeon in the Rock, near the Spanish Camp. Alonzo *in Chains. A Sentinel walking near the Entrance.*

Alon. For the last time I have beheld the shadowed ocean close upon the light. For the last time, through my cleft dungeon's roof, I now behold the quivering

lustre of the stars. For the last time, O sun! and
soon the hour I shall behold thy rising, and thy level
beams melting the pale mists of morn to glittering
dewdrops. Then comes my death, and in the
morning of my day I fall, which —— No, Alonzo,
date not the life which thou hast run by the mean
reckoning of the hours and days which thou hast
breathed: a life spent worthily should be measured
by a nobler line—by deeds, not years; then wouldst
thou murmur not, but bless the Providence which, in
so short a span, made thee the instrument of wide
and spreading blessings to the helpless and oppressed!
Though sinking in decrepit age, he prematurely falls,
whose memory records no benefit conferred by him
on man. They only have lived long, who have lived
virtuously.

Enter a Soldier, shows the SENTINEL *a passport, who
withdraws.*

Alon. What bear you there?

Sold. These refreshments I was ordered to leave in
your dungeon.

Alon. By whom ordered?

Sold. By the lady Elvira: she will be here herself
before the dawn.

Alon. Bear back to her my humblest thanks; and
take thou the refreshments, friend—I need them not.

Sold. I have served under you, Don Alonzo. Pardon my saying, that my heart pities you. [*Exit.*

Alon. In Pizarro's camp, to pity the unfortunate,
no doubt requires forgiveness. [*Looking out.*] Surely,
even now, thin streaks of glimmering light steal on
the darkness of the east. If so, my life is but one
hour more. I will not watch the coming dawn; but

in the darkness of my cell, my last prayer to thee, Power Supreme! shall be for my wife and child! Grant them to dwell in innocence and peace; grant health and purity of mind—all else is worthless.

[*Enters the cavern.*

Sent. Who's there? answer quickly! who's there?

Rol. A friar, come to visit your prisoner.

ROLLA *enters, disguised as a monk.*

Rol. Inform me, friend; is not Alonzo, the Spanish prisoner, confined in this dungeon?

Sent. He is.

Rol. I must speak with him.

Sent. You must not.

Rol. He is my friend.

Sent. Not if he were your brother.

Rol. What is to be his fate?

Sent. He dies at sunrise.

Rol. Ha! then I am come in time.

Sent. Just—to witness his death.

Rol. Soldier, I must speak with him.

Sent. Back, back. It is impossible!

Rol. I do entreat you but for one moment!

Sent. You entreat in vain; my orders are most strict.

Rol. Even now, I saw a messenger go hence.

Sent. He brought a pass, which we are all accustomed to obey.

Rol. Look on this wedge of massive gold; look on these precious gems. In thy own land they will be wealth for thee and thine, beyond thy hope or wish. Take them; they are thine. Let me but pass one minute with Alonzo.

Sent. Away ! wouldst thou corrupt me ! Me ! an old Castilian ! I know my duty better.

Rol. Soldier ! hast thou a wife ?

Sent. I have.

Rol. Hast thou children ?

Sent. Four—honest, lively boys.

Rol. Where didst thou leave them ?

Sent. In my native village; even in the cot where myself was born.

Rol. Dost thou love thy children and thy wife ?

Sent. Do I love them ! God knows my heart: I do.

Rol. Soldier ! imagine thou wert doomed to die a cruel death in this strange land. What would be thy last request ?

Sent. That some of my comrades should carry my dying blessing to my wife and children.

Rol. Oh ! but if that comrade was at thy prison gate, and should there be told, Thy fellow-soldier dies at sunrise—yet thou shalt not for a moment see him, nor shalt thou bear his dying blessing to his poor children or his wretched wife—what wouldst thou think of him, who thus could drive thy comrade from the door ?

Sent. How !

Rol. Alonzo has a wife and child; I am come but to receive for her and for her babe the last blessing of my friend.

Sent. Go in. *[Retires.*

Rol. Oh ! holy nature ! thou dost never plead in vain. There is not, of our earth, a creature bearing form and life, human or savage—native of the forest wild or giddy air—around whose parent bosom thou hast not a cord entwined of power to tie them to their offspring's claims, and at thy will to draw them back to thee. On iron pinions borne, the blood-stained vulture cleaves the storm; yet is the plumage closest to her heart soft as the cygnet's down, and o'er her unshelled brood the murmuring ring-dove sits not more gently! Yes, now he is beyond the porch, barring the outer gate! Alonzo! Alonzo! my friend! Ha! in gentle sleep! Alonzo!—rise!

Alon. How! Is my hour elapsed? Well [*returning from the recess*], I am ready.

Rol. Alonzo, know me.

Alon. What voice is that?

Rol. 'Tis Rolla's.

Alon. Rolla!—my friend! [*Embraces him.*] Heavens! how couldst thou pass the guard? Did this habit——

Rol. There is not a moment to be lost in words; this disguise I tore from the dead body of a friar, as I passed our field of battle; it has gained me entrance to thy dungeon; now take it thou, and fly.

Alon. And Rolla——

Rol. Will remain here in thy place.

Alon. And die for me! No! Rather eternal tortures rack me.

Rol. I shall not die, Alonzo. It is thy life Pizarro seeks, not Rolla's; and from my prison soon will thy arm deliver me; or, should it be otherwise, I am as a blighted plantain standing alone amid the sandy desert—nothing seeks or lives beneath my shelter. Thou art a husband, and a father; the being of a lovely wife and helpless infant hangs upon thy life. Go!—go! Alonzo!—go! to save, not thyself, but Cora, and thy child!

Alon. Urge me not thus, my friend. I had prepared to die in peace.

Rol. To die in peace! devoting her you've sworn to live for—to madness, misery, and death! For, be assured, the state I left her in forbids all hope, but from thy quick return.

Alon. Oh, God!

Rol. If thou art yet irresolute, Alonzo—now heed me well. I think thou hast not known that Rolla ever pledged his word, and shrunk from its fulfilment. And by the heart of truth I swear, if thou art proudly obstinate to deny thy friend the transport of preserving Cora's life, in thee, no power that sways the will of man shall stir me hence; and thou'lt but have the desperate triumph of seeing Rolla perish by thy side, with the assured conviction that Cora and thy child are lost for ever.

Alon. Oh! Rolla! you distract me!

Rol. A moment's further pause, and all is lost. The dawn approaches. Fear not for me. I will treat with Pizarro as for surrender and submission. I shall gain time, doubt not; while thou, with a chosen band, passing the secret way, mayst at night return, release thy friend, and bear him back in triumph. Yes; hasten, dear Alonzo! Even now I hear the frantic Cora call thee! Haste!—haste!—haste!

Alon. Rolla, I fear your friendship drives me from honour, and from right.

Rol. Did Rolla ever counsel dishonour to his friend?

Alon. Oh! my preserver! [*Embraces him.*

Rol. I feel thy warm tears dropping on my cheek. Go! I am rewarded. [*Throws the Friar's garment over Alonzo.*] There! conceal thy face; and, that they may not clank, hold fast thy chains. Now, God be with thee!

Alon. At night we meet again. Then, so aid me Heaven! I return to save or perish with thee! [*Exit.*

Rol. [*Alone.*] He has passed the outer porch. He is safe! He will soon embrace his wife and child!

Now, Cora, didst thou not wrong me? This is the
first time throughout my life I ever deceived man.
Forgive me, God of truth! if I am wrong. Alonzo
flatters himself that we shall meet again. Yes. There!
[*lifting his hands to heaven*] assuredly, we shall meet
again:—there possess in peace the joys of everlasting
love and friendship—on earth, imperfect and em-
bittered. I will retire, lest the guard return before
Alonzo may have passed their lines.

[Retires into the Recess.

Enter ELVIRA.

Elv. No; not Pizarro's brutal taunts; not the
glowing admiration which I feel for this noble youth,
shall raise an interest in my harassed bosom which
honour would not sanction. If he reject the vengeance
my heart has sworn against the tyrant, whose death
alone can save this land, yet shall the delight be
mine to restore him to his Cora's arms, to his dear
child, and to the unoffending people, whom his virtues
guide, and valour guards. Alonzo, come forth!

Enter ROLLA.

Ha! Who art thou? Where is Alonzo?

Rol. Alonzo's fled.

Elv. Fled!

Rol. Yes; and he must not be pursued. Pardon
this roughness [*seizing her hand*], but a moment's
precious to Alonzo's flight.

Elv. What if I call the guard?

Rol. Do so—Alonzo still gains time.

Elv. What if thus I free myself? [*Shows a dagger.*

Rol. Strike it to my heart. Still, with the convulsive grasp of death, I'll hold thee fast.

Elv. Release me; I give my faith, I neither will alarm the guard nor cause pursuit.

Rol. At once I trust thy word. A feeling boldness in those eyes assures me that thy soul is noble.

Elv. What is thy name? Speak freely. By my order the guard is removed beyond the outer porch.

Rol. My name is Rolla.

Elv. The Peruvian leader?

Rol. I was so yesterday. To-day, the Spaniard's captive.

Elv. And friendship for Alonzo moved thee to this act?

Rol. Alonzo is my friend. I am prepared to die for him. Yet is the cause a motive stronger far than friendship.

Elv. One only passion else could urge such generous rashness.

Rol. And that is——

Elv. Love?

Rol. True!

Elv. Gallant, ingenuous Rolla! Know that my purpose here was thine; and were I to save thy friend——

Rol. How! a woman blessed with gentleness and courage, and yet not Cora!

Elv. Does Rolla think so meanly of all female hearts?

Rol. Not so; you are worse and better than we are!

Elv. Were I to save thee, Rolla, from the tyrant's vengeance—restore thee to thy native land—and thy native land to peace—wouldst thou not rank Elvira with the good?

Rol. To judge the action, I must know the means.

Elv. Take this dagger.

Rol. How to be used?

Elv. I will conduct thee to the tent where fell Pizarro sleeps. The scourge of innocence, the terror of thy race, the fiend that desolates thy afflicted country.

Rol. Have you not been injured by Pizarro ?

Elv. Deeply as scorn and insult can infuse their deadly venom.

Rol. And you ask that I shall murder him in his sleep !

Elv. Would he not have murdered Alonzo in his chains ? He that sleeps, and he that's bound, are equally defenceless. Hear me, Rolla; so may I prosper in this perilous act, as searching my full heart, I have put by all rancorous motive of private vengeance there, and feel that I advance to my dread purpose in the cause of human nature, and at the call of sacred justice.

Rol. The God of justice sanctifies no evil as a step towards good. Great actions cannot be achieved by wicked means.

Elv. Then, Peruvian ! since thou dost feel so coldly for thy country's wrongs, this hand, though it revolt my soul, shall strike the blow.

Rol. Then is thy destruction certain, and for Peru thou perishest ! Give me the dagger !

Elv. Now follow me; but first—and dreadful is the hard necessity—you must strike down the guard.

Rol. The soldier who was on duty here ?

Elv. Yes, him; else, seeing thee, the alarm will be instant.

Rol. And I must stab that soldier as I pass ? Take back thy dagger.

Elv. Rolla !

Rol. That soldier, mark me, is a man. All are not men that bear the human form. He refused my prayers, refused my gold, denying to admit me, till his own feelings bribed him. For my nation's safety I would not harm that man!

Elv. Then he must with us. I will answer for his safety.

Rol. Be that plainly understood between us; for, whate'er betide our enterprise, I will not risk a hair of that man's head, to save my heart-strings from consuming fire. [*Exeunt.*

SCENE II.

The Inside of PIZARRO'S *Tent.* PIZARRO *on a Couch, in disturbed sleep.*

Piz. [*In his sleep.*] No mercy, traitor. Now at his heart! Stand off there, you; let me see him bleed! Ha! ha! ha! Let me hear that groan again.

Enter ROLLA *and* ELVIRA.

Elv. There. Now, lose not a moment.

Rol. You must leave me now. This scene of blood fits not a woman's presence.

Elv. But a moment's pause may——

Rol. Go! Retire to your own tent, and return not here; I will come to you. Be thou not known in this business, I implore you.

Elv. I will withdraw the guard that waits.
[*Exit* ELVIRA.

Rol. Now have I in my power the accursed destroyer of my country's peace; yet tranquilly he rests. God! can this man sleep?

Piz. [*In his sleep.*] Away! away! Hideous fiends! Tear not my bosom thus!

Rol. No; I was in error, the balm of sweet repose he never more can know. Look here, ambition's fools. Ye, by whose inhuman pride the bleeding sacrifice of nations is held as nothing—behold the rest of the guilty. He is at my mercy, and one blow! No; my heart and hand refuse the act. Rolla cannot be an assassin! Yet Elvira must be saved. [*Approaches the couch.*] Pizarro! awake!

Piz. [*Starts up.*] Who?—Guard!——

Rol. Speak not; another word is thy death. Call not for aid; this arm will be swifter than thy guard.

Piz. Who art thou? and what is thy will?

Rol. I am thine enemy, Peruvian Rolla! Thy death is not my will, or I could have slain thee sleeping.

Piz. Speak, what else?

Rol. Now thou art at my mercy, answer me. Did a Peruvian ever yet wrong or injure thee, or any of thy nation? Didst thou, or any of thy nation, ever yet show mercy to a Peruvian in your power? Now shalt thou feel—and if thou hast a heart, thou'lt feel it keenly—a Peruvian's vengeance! *Drops the dagger at his feet.*] There!

Piz. Is it possible!   [*Walks aside confounded.*

Rol. Can Pizarro be surprised at this? I thought forgiveness of injuries had been the Christian's precept. Thou seest, at least, it is the Peruvian's practice.

Piz. Rolla, thou hast indeed surprised—subdued me.
          [*Walks again aside as in irresolute thought.*

Re-enter ELVIRA [*not seeing* PIZARRO.]

Elv. Is it done? Is he dead? [*Sees* PIZARRO.] How! still living! Then I am lost! And for you, wretched Peruvians, mercy is no more! Oh, Rolla! treacherous, or cowardly?

Piz. How, can it be that——

Rol. Away! Elvira speaks she knows not what. Leave me [*to* ELVIRA], I conjure you, with Pizarro.

Elv. How! Rolla, dost thou think I shall retract, or that I meanly will deny, that in thy hand I placed a poniard to be plunged into that tyrant's heart? No; my sole regret is, that I trusted to thy weakness, and did not strike the blow myself. Too soon thou'lt learn that mercy to that man is direct cruelty to all thy race.

Piz. Guard! quick! a guard, to seize this frantic woman.

Elv. Yes, a guard; I call them too! And soon I know they'll lead me to my death: But think not, Pizarro, the fury of thy flashing eyes shall awe me for a moment. Nor think that woman's anger, or the feelings of an injured heart, prompted me to this design—no! Had I been only influenced so, thus failing, shame and remorse would weigh me down. But though defeated and destroyed, as now I am, such is the greatness of the cause that urged me, I shall perish glorying in the attempt, and my last breath of life shall speak the proud avowal of my purpose—to have rescued millions of innocents from the bloodthirsty tyranny of one—by ridding the insulted world of thee.

Rol. Had the act been noble as the motive, Rolla would not have shrunk from its performance.

Enter Guards.

Piz. Seize this discovered fiend, who sought to kill your leader.

Elv. Touch me not, at the peril of your souls; I am your prisoner, and will follow you. But thou,

their triumphant leader, shalt hear me. Yet, first—
for thee, Rolla, accept my forgiveness: even had I
been the victim of thy nobleness of heart, I should
have admired thee for it. But 'twas myself provoked
my doom. Thou wouldst have shielded me. Let not
thy contempt follow me to the grave. Didst thou
but know the spell-like arts by which this hypocrite
first undermined the virtue of a guileless heart! how,
even in the pious sanctuary wherein I dwelt, by corruption and by fraud, he practised upon those in
whom I most confided, till my distempered fancy led
me, step by step, into the abyss of guilt——

Piz. Why am I not obeyed? Tear her hence!

Elv. 'Tis past; but didst thou know my story,
Rolla, thou wouldst pity me.

Rol. From my soul I do pity thee!

Piz. Villains! drag her to the dungeon! Prepare
the torture instantly.

Elv. Soldiers—but a moment more. 'Tis to applaud your general. It is to tell the astonished world,
that, for once, Pizarro's sentence is an act of justice:
yes, rack me with the sharpest tortures that ever
agonized the human frame, it will be justice. Yes,
bid the minions of thy fury wrench forth the sinews
of those arms that have caressed, and even have
defended thee! Bid them pour burning metal into
the bleeding cases of these eyes, that so oft—oh, God!
—have hung with love and homage on thy looks;
then approach me bound on the abhorred wheel;
there glut thy savage eyes with the convulsive spasms
of that dishonoured bosom, which was once thy pillow!
Yet will I bear it all; for it will be justice, all!
And when thou shalt bid them tear me to my death,
hoping that thy unshrinking ears may at last be
feasted with the music of my cries, I will not utter one

shriek or groan, but to the last gasp my body's patience shall deride thy vengeance, as my soul defies thy power.

Piz. [*Endeavouring to conceal his agitation.*] Hearest thou the wretch whose hands were even now prepared for murder?

Rol. Yes! and if her accusation's false, thou wilt not shrink from hearing her: if true, thy barbarity cannot make her suffer the pangs thy conscience will inflict on thee.

Elv. And now, farewell, world! Rolla, farewell! Farewell, thou condemned of Heaven! [*to* PIZARRO] for repentance and remorse, I know, will never touch thy heart. We shall meet again. Ha! be it thy horror here to know that we shall meet hereafter! And when thy parting hour approaches, hark to the knell, whose dreadful beat will strike to thy despairing soul. Then will vibrate on thy ear the curses of the cloistered saint from whom you stole me. Then the last shrieks which burst from my mother's breaking heart, as she died, appealing to her God against the seducer of her child! Then the blood-stifled groan of my murdered brother—murdered by thee, fell monster!—seeking atonement for his sister's ruined honour. I hear them now! To me the recollection's madness! At such an hour—what will it be to thee?

Piz. A moment's more delay, and at the peril of your lives——

Elv. I have spoken; and the last mortal frailty of my heart is past. And now, with an undaunted spirit and unshaken firmness, I go to meet my destiny. That I could not live nobly, has been Pizarro's act: that I will die nobly, shall be my own. [*Exit, guarded.*

Piz. Rolla, I would not thou, a warrior, valiant and renowned, shouldst credit the vile tales of this frantic, woman.　The cause of all this fury—O! a wanton passion for the rebel youth Alonzo, now my prisoner.

Rol. Alonzo is not now thy prisoner.

Piz. How!

Rol. I came to rescue him—to deceive his guard. I have succeeded; I remain thy prisoner.

Piz. Alonzo fled! Is then the vengeance dearest to my heart never to be gratified?

Rol. Dismiss such passions from thy heart, then thou'lt consult its peace.

Piz. I can face all enemies that dare confront me— I cannot war against my nature.

Rol. Then, Pizarro, ask not to be deemed a hero. To triumph o'er ourselves is the only conquest where fortune makes no claim. In battle, chance may snatch the laurel from thee, or chance may place it on thy brow; but in a contest with yourself, be resolute, and the virtuous impulse must be the victor.

Piz. Peruvian! thou shalt not find me to thee ungrateful or ungenerous. Return to your country-men. You are at liberty.

Rol. Thou dost act in this as honour and as duty bid thee.

Piz. I cannot but admire thee, Rolla. I would we might be friends.

Rol. Farewell. Pity Elvira! Become the friend of virtue, and thou wilt be mine.　　　　　　[*Exit.*

Piz. Ambition! tell me what is the phantom I have followed? Where is the one delight which it has made my own? My fame is the mark of envy—my love the dupe of treachery—my glory eclipsed by the boy I taught—my revenge defeated and rebuked by the rude honour of a savage foe, before whose native dignity of soul I have sunk confounded and subdued. I would I could retrace my steps—I cannot. Would I could evade my own reflections. No!——thought and memory are my hell.   [*Exit.*

———————

ACT V.—SCENE I.

A thick Forest. In the background, a Hut, almost covered by Boughs of Trees. A dreadful Storm, with Thunder and Lightning. CORA has covered her Child on a Bed of Leaves and Moss. Her whole appearance is wild and distracted.

Cora. O Nature! thou hast not the strength of love. My anxious spirit is untired in its march; my wearied, shivering frame sinks under it. And for thee, my boy, when faint beneath thy lovely burden, could I refuse to give thy slumbers that poor bed of rest! O my child! were I assured thy father breathes no more, how quickly would I lay me down by thy dear side!—but down—down for ever. [*Thunder and lightning.*] I ask thee not, unpitying storm! to abate thy rage, in mercy to poor Cora's misery; nor while thy thunders spare his slumbers will I disturb my sleeping cherub. Though Heaven knows I wish to hear the voice of life, and feel that life is near me. But I will endure all while what I have of reason holds.

SONG.

Yes, yes, be merciless, thou Tempest dire;
  Unaw'd, unshelter'd, I thy fury brave:
I'll bare my bosom to thy forked fire,
  Let it but guide me to Alonzo's grave!

O'er his pale corse then, while thy lightnings glare,
I'll press his clay-cold lips, and perish there.

But thou wilt wake again, my boy,
Again thou'lt rise to life and joy—
  Thy father never!——
Thy laughing eyes will meet the light,
Unconscious that eternal night
  Veils his for ever.

On yon green bed of moss there lies my child,
  Oh! safer lies from these chill'd arms apart;
He sleeps, sweet lamb! nor heeds the tempest wild,
  Oh! sweeter sleeps, than near this breaking heart.

Alas! my babe, if thou wouldst peaceful rest,
Thy cradle must not be thy mother's breast.

Yet, thou wilt wake again, my boy,
Again thou'lt rise to life and joy—
  Thy father never!——
Thy laughing eyes will meet the light,
Unconscious that eternal night
  Veils his for ever.

                  [*Thunder and lightning.*
Still, still implacable! unfeeling elements! yet still
dost thou sleep, my smiling innocent! O death!
when wilt thou grant to this babe's mother such repose? Sure I may shield thee better from the storm;
my veil may——
    [*While she is wrapping her mantle and her veil
      over him,* ALONZO's *voice is heard at a great
      distance.*
Alon. Cora!
Cora. Ha! [*Rises.*]
Alon. [*Again.*] Cora!

Cora. O my heart! Sweet Heaven, deceive me not! Is it not Alonzo's voice?

Alon. [*Nearer.*] Cora!

Cora. It is—it is Alonzo!

Alon. [*Nearer still.*] Cora! my beloved!——

Cora. Alonzo! Here!—here!—Alonzo!

[*Runs out.*

Enter two Spanish Soldiers.

1st Sold. I tell you we are near our out-posts, and the word we heard just now was the countersign.

2nd Sold. Well, in our escape from the enemy, to have discovered their secret passage through the rocks, will prove a lucky chance to us; Pizarro will reward us.

1st Sold. This way. The sun, though clouded, is on our left. [*Perceives the Child.*] What have we here? A child! as I'm a soldier.

2nd Sold. 'Tis a sweet little babe. Now would it be a great charity to take this infant from its pagan mother's power.

1st Sold. It would so. I have one at home shall play with it. Come along.

[*Takes the Child. Exeunt.*

Re-enter CORA with ALONZO.

Cora. [*Speaking without.*] This way, dear Alonzo. Now am I right—there—there—under that tree. Was it possible the instinct of a mother's heart could mistake the spot? Now will you look at him as he sleeps, or shall I bring him waking with his full blue laughing eyes to welcome you at once? Yes, yes. Stand thou there. I'll snatch him from his rosy slumber, blushing like the perfumed morn.

[*She runs up to the spot, and finding only the mantle and veil, which she tears from the ground, and the Child gone, shrieks, and stands in speechless agony.*]

Alon. [*Running to her.*] Cora!—my heart's beloved!

Cora. He is gone?

Alon. Eternal God!

Cora. He is gone!—my child! my child!

Alon. Where did you leave him ?

Cora. [*Dashing herself on the spot.*] Here!

Alon. Be calm, beloved Cora; he has waked and crept to a little distance; we shall find him. Are you assured this was the spot you left him in ?

Cora. Did not these hands make that bed and shelter for him?—and is not this the veil that covered him ?

Alon. Here is a hut yet unobserved.

Cora. Ha ! yes, yes! there lives the savage that has robbed me of my child. [*Beats at the door, exclaiming*] Give me back my child—restore to me my boy !

Enter Las-Casas *from the Hut.*

Las-Cas. Who calls me from my wretched solitude ?

Cora. Give me back my child ! [*Goes into the Hut, and calls*] Fernando !

Alon. Almighty powers ! do my eyes deceive me ? Las-Casas !

Las-Cas. Alonzo, my beloved young friend !

Alon. My revered instructor !   [*Embracing.*

Cora. [*Returned.*] Will you embrace this man before he restores my boy ?

Alon. Alas, my friend, in what a moment of misery do we meet !

Cora. Yet his look is goodness and humanity.

Good old man, have compassion on a wretched mother, and I will be your servant while I live. But do not, for pity's sake—do not say you have him not—do not say you have not seen him—do not say you have not seen him!   [*Runs into the wood.*

Las-Cas. What can this mean ?

Alon. She is my wife. Just rescued from the Spaniards' prison, I learned she had fled to this wild forest. Hearing my voice, she left the child, and flew to meet me; he was left sleeping under yonder tree.

Las-Cas. How! did you leave him ?——

      [Cora *returns.*

Cora. O, you are right! right! unnatural mother that I was—I left my child—I forsook my innocent— but I will fly to the earth's brink but I will find him.

      [*Runs out.*

Alon. Forgive me, Las-Casas, I must follow her: for at night I attempt brave Rolla's rescue.

Las-Cas. I will not leave thee, Alonzo; you must try to lead her to the right—that way lies your camp. Wait not my infirm steps. I follow thee, my friend.

      [*Exeunt.*

SCENE II.

The Outpost of the Spanish Camp. The background wild and rocky, with a Torrent falling down the Precipice, over which a Bridge is formed by a felled Tree. Trumpets sound without.

Almagro. [*Without.*] Bear him along; his story must be false. [*Entering.*]

Rolla, *in Chains, brought in by Soldiers.*

Rol. False! Rolla utter falsehood! I would I

17—2

had thee in a desert with thy troops around thee; and I, but with my sword in this unshackled hand!

[*Trumpets without.*

Alm. Is it to be credited that Rolla, the renowned Peruvian hero, should be detected like a spy, skulking through our camp?

Rol. Skulking!

Alm. But answer to the general—he is here.

Enter PIZARRO.

Piz. What do I see! Rolla!

Rol. O! to thy surprise, no doubt.

Piz. And bound too!

Rol. So fast, thou need'st not fear approaching me.

Alm. The guards surprised him passing our out-post.

Piz. Release him instantly. Believe me, I regret this insult.

Rol. You feel then as you ought.

Piz. Nor can I brook to see a warrior of Rolla's fame disarmed. Accept this, though it has been thy enemy's. [*Gives a sword.*] The Spaniards know the courtesy that's due to valour.

Rol. And the Peruvian how to forget offence.

Piz. May not Rolla and Pizarro cease to be foes?

Rol. When the sea divides us; yes! May I now depart?

Piz. Freely.

Rol. And shall I not again be intercepted?

Piz. No! let the word be given that Rolla passes freely.

Enter DAVILLA *and Soldiers, with the Child.*

Dav. Here are two soldiers, captived yesterday, who have escaped from the Peruvian hold, and by the secret way we have so long endeavoured to discover.

Piz. Silence, imprudent!   Seest thou not——?

[*Pointing to* Rolla.

Dav. In their way, they found a Peruvian child, who seems——

Piz. What is the imp to me?   Bid them toss it into the sea.

Rol. Gracious heavens! it is Alonzo's child! give it to me.

Piz. Ha! Alonzo's child!   Welcome, thou pretty hostage.   Now Alonzo is again my prisoner!

Rol. Thou wilt not keep the infant from its mother?

Piz. Will I not!   What, when I shall meet Alonzo in the heat of the victorious fight, think'st thou I shall not have a check upon the valour of his heart, when he is reminded that a word of mine is this child's death?

Rol. I do not understand you.

Piz. My vengeance has a long arrear of hate to settle with Alonzo! and this pledge may help to settle the account.

Rol. Man! man!   Art thou a man?   Couldst thou hurt that innocent?   By Heaven! it's smiling in thy face.

Piz. Tell me, does it resemble Cora?

Rol. Pizarro! thou hast set my heart on fire.   If thou dost harm that child, think not his blood will sink into the barren sand.   No! faithful to the eager hope that now trembles in this indignant heart, 'twill rise to the common God of nature and humanity, and cry aloud for vengeance on his accursed destroyer's head.

Piz. Be that peril mine.

Rol. [*Throwing himself at his feet.*]   Behold me at thy feet.   Me, Rolla! me, the preserver of thy life! Me, that have never yet bent or bowed before created man!   In humble agony I sue to you, prostrate I implore you; but spare that child, and I will be your slave.

Piz. Rolla! still art thou free to go, this boy remains with me.

Rol. Then was this sword Heaven's gift, not thine! [*Seizes the Child.*] Who moves one step to follow me, dies upon the spot.   [*Exit, with the Child.*

Piz. Pursue him instantly; but spare his life. [*Exeunt* ALMAGRO *and Soldiers.*] With what fury he defends himself! Ha! he fells them to the ground; and now——

Enter ALMAGRO.

Alm. Three of your brave soldiers are already victims to your command to spare this madman's life; and if he once gains the thicket——

Piz. Spare him no longer. [*Exit* ALMAGRO.] Their guns must reach him; he'll yet escape; holloa to those horse; the Peruvian sees them; and now he turns among the rocks; then is his retreat cut off.

> [ROLLA *crosses the wooden bridge over the cataract,
>   pursued by the soldiers—they fire at him—a shot
>   strikes him.* PIZARRO *exclaims*——

Piz. Now! quick! quick! seize the child!——

> [ROLLA *tears from the rock the tree which supports
>   the bridge, and retreats by the background bear-
>   ing off the Child.*

Re-enter ALMAGRO.

Alm. By hell! he has escaped! and with the child unhurt.

Dav. No; he bears his death with him. Believe me, I saw him struck upon the side.

Piz. But the child is saved. Alonzo's child! Oh! the furies of disappointed vengeance!

Alm. Away with the revenge of words; let us to deeds. Forget not we have acquired the knowledge of the secret pass, which through the rocky cavern's gloom brings you at once to the stronghold, where are lodged their women and their treasures.

Piz. Right, Almagro! Swift as thy thought draw forth a daring and a chosen band. I will not wait for numbers. Stay, Almagro! Valverde is informed Elvira dies to-day?

Alm. He is; and one request alone she——

Piz. I'll hear of none.

Alm. The boon is small; 'tis but the noviciate habit which you first beheld her in; she wishes not to suffer in the gaudy trappings, which remind her of her shame.

Piz. Well, do as thou wilt; but tell Valverde, at our return, as his life shall answer it, to let me hear that she is dead.   [*Exeunt, severally.*

SCENE III.

ATALIBA'S *Tent.*

Enter ATALIBA, *followed by* CORA *and* ALONZO.

Cora. Oh! Avoid me not, Ataliba! To whom, but her king, is the wretched mother to address her griefs? The gods refuse to hear my prayers! Did not my Alonzo fight for you? And will not my sweet boy, if thou'lt but restore him to me, one day fight thy battles too?

Alon. Oh! my suffering love, my poor heart-broken

Cora! you but wound our sovereign's feeling soul, and not relieve thy own.

Cor. Is he our sovereign, and has he not the power to give me back my child?

Ata. When I reward desert, or can relieve my people, I feel what is the real glory of a king; when I hear them suffer, and cannot aid them, I mourn the impotence of all mortal power.

[*Voices behind.*] Rolla! Rolla! Rolla!

Enter ROLLA, *bleeding, with the Child, followed by Peruvian Soldiers.*

Rol. Thy child!

 [*Gives the Child into* CORA'S *arms and falls.*

Cora. Oh God! there's blood upon him!

Rol. 'Tis my blood, Cora!

Alon. Rolla, thou diest!

Rol. For thee, and Cora.   [*Dies.*

Enter ORANO.

Ora. Treachery has revealed our asylum in the rocks. Even now the foe assails the peaceful band retired for protection there.

Alon. Lose not a moment! Swords be quick! Your wives and children cry to you. Bear our loved hero's body in the van. 'Twill raise the fury of our men to madness. Now, fell Pizarro, the death of one of us is near! Away! Be the word of assault, Revenge and Rolla!   [*Exeunt. Charge.*

SCENE IV.

A romantic part of the Recess among the Rocks. Alarms.
Women are seen flying, pursued by the Spanish
Soldiers. The Peruvian Soldiers drive the Spaniards
back from the Field. The Fight is continued on the
Heights.

Enter PIZARRO, ALMAGRO, VALVERDE, *and Spanish*
Soldiers.

Piz. Well! if surrounded, we must perish in the
centre of them. Where do Rolla and Alonzo hide
their heads?

Enter ALONZO, ORANO, *and Peruvians.*

Alon. Alonzo answers thee, and Alonzo's sword
shall speak for Rolla.
Piz. Thou know'st the advantage of thy numbers.
Thou dar'st not singly face Pizarro.
Alon. Peruvians, stir not a man! Be this contest
only ours.
Piz. Spaniards! observe ye the same.   [*Charge.*
        [*They fight.* ALONZO's *shield is broken, and*
            he is beat down.]
Piz. Now, traitor, to thy heart!
    [*At this moment* ELVIRA *enters, habited as when*
        PIZARRO *first beheld her.* PIZARRO, *appalled,*
        staggers back. ALONZO *renews the fight, and*
        slays him. Loud shouts from the Peruvians.

ATALIBA *enters, and embraces* ALONZO.

Ata. My brave Alonzo!

Alm. Alonzo, we submit.   Spare us! We will em-
bark, and leave the coast.

Val. Elvira will confess I saved her life ; she has
saved thine.

Alon. Fear not.   You are safe.

[Spaniards lay down their arms.

Elv. Valverde speaks the truth ; nor could he think
to meet me here: An awful impulse which my soul
could not resist impelled me hither.

Alon. Noble Elvira; my preserver! How can I
speak what I, Ataliba, and his rescued country owe
to thee? If amid this grateful nation thou wouldst
remain——

Elv. Alonzo, no! the destination of my future life
is fixed.   Humbled in penitence, I will endeavour to
atone the guilty errors, which, however masked by
shallow cheerfulness, have long consumed my secret
heart.   When, by my sufferings purified, and penitence sincere, my soul shall dare address the throne of
mercy in behalf of others ; for thee, Alonzo, for thy
Cora, and thy child; for thee, thou virtuous monarch,
and the innocent race you reign over, shall Elvira's
prayers address the God of nature.   Valverde, you
have preserved my life.   Cherish humanity ; avoid the
foul examples thou hast viewed.   Spaniards returning
to your native home, assure your rulers they mistake
the road to glory or to power.   Tell them, that the
pursuits of avarice, conquest, and ambition, never yet
made a people happy, or a nation great.

[Casts a look of agony on the dead body of Pizarro
as she passes, and exit.

Flourish of trumpets.

[Valverde, Almagro, *and Spanish Soldiers,*

exeunt, bearing off PIZARRO'S *body. On a signal from* ALONZO, *flourish of music.*

Alon. Ataliba! think not I wish to check the voice of triumph, when I entreat we first may pay the tribute due to our loved Rolla's memory.

[*A solemn march. Procession of Peruvian Soldiers, bearing* ROLLA'S *body on a bier, surrounded by military trophies. The Priests and Priestesses attending chant a dirge over the bier.* ALONZO *and* CORA *kneel on either side of it, and kiss* ROLLA'S *hands in silent agony. In the looks of the King, and of all present, the triumph of the day is lost, in mourning for the fallen hero.*

[*The curtain slowly descends.*

EPILOGUE.

WRITTEN BY THE HON. WILLIAM LAMB.

SPOKEN BY MRS. JORDAN.

Ere yet Suspense has still'd its throbbing fear,
Or Melancholy wiped the grateful tear,
While e'en the miseries of a sinking state,
A monarch's danger, and a nation's fate,
Command not now your eyes with grief to flow,
Lost in a trembling mother's nearer woe;
What moral lay shall Poetry rehearse,
Or how shall Elocution pour the verse
So sweetly, that its music shall repay
The loved illusion, which it drives away?
Mine is the task, to rigid custom due,
To me ungrateful, as 'tis harsh to you,
To mar the work the tragic scene has wrought,
To rouse the mind that broods in pensive thought,
To scare Reflection, which, in absent dreams,
Still lingers musing on the recent themes;
Attention, ere with contemplation tired,
To turn from all that pleased, from all that fired;
To weaken lessons strongly now impress'd,
And chill the interest glowing in the breast—
Mine is the task; and be it mine to spare
The souls that pant, the griefs they see, to share;
Let me with no unhallow'd jest deride
The sigh, that sweet Compassion owns with pride—

The sigh of Comfort, to Affliction dear,
That Kindness heaves, and Virtue loves to hear.
E'en gay Thalia will not now refuse
This gentle homage to her sister-muse.
    O ye, who listen to the plaintive strain,
With strange enjoyment, and with rapturous pain,
Who erst have felt the Stranger's lone despair,
And Haller's settled, sad, remorseful care,
Does Rolla's pure affection less excite
The inexpressive anguish of delight?
Do Cora's fears, which beat without control,
With less solicitude engross the soul?
Ah, no! your minds with kindred zeal approve
Maternal feeling, and heroic love.
You must approve: where man exists below,
In temperate climes, or midst drear wastes of snow,
Or where the solar fires incessant flame,
Thy laws, all-powerful Nature, are the same:
Vainly the sophist boasts, he can explain
The causes of thy universal reign—
More vainly would his cold presumptuous art
Disprove thy general empire o'er the heart:
A voice proclaims thee, that we must believe,
A voice, that surely speaks not to deceive;
That voice poor Cora heard, and closely press'd
Her darling infant to her fearful breast;
Distracted dared the bloody field to tread,
And sought Alonzo through the heaps of dead,
Eager to catch the music of his breath,
Though faltering in the agonies of death,
To touch his lips, though pale and cold, once more,
And clasp his bosom, though it stream'd with gore;
That voice too Rolla heard, and greatly brave,
His Cora's dearest treasure died to save;

Gave to the hopeless parent's arms her child;
Beheld her transports, and expiring smiled.
That voice we hear.   Oh! be its will obey'd!
'Tis Valour's impulse, and 'tis Virtue's aid—
It prompts to all Benevolence admires,
To all that heav'nly Piety inspires,
To all that Praise repeats through lengthen'd years,
That Honour sanctifies, and Time reveres.

VERSES

TO THE

MEMORY OF GARRICK.

SPOKEN AS A MONODY, AT THE THEATRE ROYAL IN DRURY LANE.

.

18—2

VERSES

TO THE

MEMORY OF GARRICK.

IF dying excellence deserves a tear,
If fond remembrance still is cherish'd here,
Can we persist to bid your sorrows flow
For fabled suff'rers, and delusive woe?
Or with quaint smiles dismiss the plaintive strain,
Point the quick jest—indulge the comic vein—
Ere yet to buried Roscius we assign
One kind regret, one tributary line!
   His fame requires we act a tenderer part:
His memory claims the tear you gave his art!
   The general voice, the meed of mournful verse,
The splendid sorrows that adorn'd his hearse,
The throng that mourn'd as their dead favourite pass'd,
The graced respect that claim'd him to the last,
While Shakespeare's image from its hallow'd base
Seem'd to prescribe the grave, and point the place,
Nor these, nor all the sad regrets that flow
From fond fidelity's domestic woe,
So much are Garrick's praise, so much his due,
As on this spot, one tear bestow'd by you.
   Amid the hearts which seek ingenuous fame,
Our toil attempts the most precarious claim!
To him, whose mimic pencil wins the prize,
Obedient Fame immortal wreaths supplies:

Whate'er of wonder Reynolds now may raise,
Raphael still boasts contemporary praise:
Each dazzling light and gaudier bloom subdued,
With undiminish'd awe his works are viewed:
E'en Beauty's portrait wears a softer prime,
Touch'd by the tender hand of mellowing Time.

The patient Sculptor owns an humbler part,
A ruder toil, and more mechanic art;
Content with slow and timorous stroke to trace
The lingering line, and mould the tardy grace:
But once achieved, though barbarous wreck o'erthrow
The sacred fane, and lay its glories low,
Yet shall the sculptured ruin rise to day,
Graced by defect, and worshipp'd in decay;
Th' enduring record bears the artist's name,
Demands his honours, and asserts his fame.

Superior hopes the Poet's bosom fire;
O proud distinction of the sacred lyre!
Wide as th' inspiring Phœbus darts his ray,
Diffusive splendour gilds his votary's lay.
Whether the song heroic woes rehearse,
With epic grandeur, and the pomp of verse;
Or, fondly gay, with unambitious guile,
Attempt no prize but favouring beauty's smile;
Or bear dejected to the lonely grove
The soft despair of unprevailing love—
Whate'er the theme, through every age and clime
Congenial passions meet th' according rhyme;
The pride of glory—pity's sigh sincere—
Youth's earliest blush, and beauty's virgin tear.

Such is their meed, their honours thus secure,
Whose arts yield objects, and whose works endure.
The Actor, only, shrinks from Time's award;
Feeble tradition is his memory's guard;

By whose faint breath his merits must abide,
Unvouch'd by proof, to substance unallied !
E'en matchless Garrick's art, to heav'n resign'd,
No fix'd effect, no model leaves behind !
    The grace of action, the adapted mien,
Faithful as nature to the varied scene ;
Th' expressive glance, whose subtle comment draws
Entranced attention, and a mute applause ;
Gesture that marks, with force and feeling fraught,
A sense in silence, and a will in thought ;
Harmonious speech, whose pure and liquid tone
Gives verse a music, scarce confess'd its own ;
As light from gems assumes a brighter ray,
And clothed with orient hues, transcends the day !
Passion's wild break, and frowns that awe the sense,
And every charm of gentler eloquence—
All perishable ! like th' electric fire,
But strike the frame, and as they strike expire ;
Incense too pure a bodied flame to bear,
Its fragrance charms the sense, and blends with air.
    Where then, while sunk in cold decay he lies,
And pale eclipse for ever veils those eyes,
Where is the blest memorial that ensures
Our Garrick's fame? whose is the trust ?   'Tis yours.
    And O ! by every charm his art essay'd
To soothe your cares !—by every grief allay'd !
By the hush'd wonder which his accents drew !
By his last parting tear, repaid by you !
By all those thoughts, which, many a distant night,
Shall mark his memory with a sad delight !
Still in your hearts' dear record bear his name ;
Cherish the keen regret that lifts his fame ;
To you it is bequeath'd, assert the trust,
And to his worth—'tis all you can—be just.

What more is due from sanctifying Time,
To cheerful wit, and many a favour'd rhyme,
O'er his graced urn shall bloom, a deathless wreath,
Whose blossom'd sweets shall deck the mask beneath:
For these, when Sculpture's votive toil shall rear
The due memorial of a loss so dear,
O loveliest mourner, gentle Muse! be thine
The pleasing woe to guard the laurell'd shrine.
As Fancy, oft by Superstition led
To roam the mansion of the sainted dead,
Has view'd, by shadowy eve's unfaithful gloom,
A weeping cherub on a martyr's tomb,
So thou, sweet Muse, hang o'er his sculptured bier,
With patient woe, that loves the lingering tear;
With thoughts that mourn, nor yet desire relief;
With meek regret, and fond enduring grief;
With looks that speak.   He never shall return!
Chilling thy tender bosom, clasp his urn;
And with soft sighs disperse th' irreverend dust
Which Time may strew upon his sacred bust.

THE

CAMP :

A MUSICAL ENTERTAINMENT.

PROLOGUE.

WRITTEN BY RICHARD TICKELL, ESQ.

The stage is still the mirror of the day,
Where fashion's forms in bright succession play:
True to its end, what image can it yield,
In times like these, but the embattled field?
What juster semblance than the glittering plains
of village warriors, and heroic swains!
Invasions, battles, now fill rumour's breath,
From camp to fleets, from Plymouth to Coxheath.
Through every rank some panic terror spread,
And each in various phrase express their dread.
At 'Change no vulgar patriot passions fright
The firm and philosophic—Israelite!
Ask him his hopes, ' 'Tis all de same to me!
' I fix my wishes by my policy.
' I'll do you *Keppel;* or increase *De Barters.*'
You will, ' I'll underwrite *de Duc de Chartres.*'
Miss Tittup, gasping from her stiff French stays,
' Why if these French should come, we'll have French
        plays:
' Upon my word, I wish these wars would cease!'
Settling her tucker, while she sighs for peace.
With wilder throbs the glutton's bosom beats,
Anxious and trembling for West India fleets:
Sir Gobble Greenfat felt, in pangs of death,
The ruling passion taint his parting breath:
Search in the latest as in all the past,
' Oh! save my turtle, *Keppel!*' was his last.

No pang like this the macaroni racks,
Calmly he dates the downfall of *Almack's.*
' As Gad's my judge, I shall be glad to see
' Our Paris friends here—for variety.
' The clubs are poor; let them their Louis bring,
' Th' invasion would be rather a good thing.'
Perish such fears! what can our arms oppose,
When female warriors join our martial beaux?
Fierce from the toilet the plumed bands appear;
Miss struts a major, ma'am a brigadier:
A spruce Bonduca simpers in the rear.
Unusual watch her *femmes-de-chambre* keep;
Militia phantoms haunt her in her sleep:
She starts, she wakes, she quivers, kneels and prays.
' Side-saddle my horse! ah, lace my stays!
' Soft, 'twas but a dream! my fears are vain,
' And Lady Minikin's herself again.'
Yet hold, nor let false ridicule profane
These fair associates of the embattled plain:
Victorious wreaths their efforts justly claim,
Whose praise is triumph, and whose smiles are fame.

DRAMATIS PERSONÆ,

AS ORIGINALLY ACTED AT DRURY LANE THEATRE, OCT. 15, 1778.

Gage . . . . . . Mr. PARSONS.
O'Daub . . . . . Mr. MOODY.
Sergeant Drill . . . Mr. BANNISTER.
William . . . . . Mr. WEBSTER.
Bouillard . . . . . Mr. BADDELEY.
Commander-in-Chief . Mr. FARREN.
Sir Harry Bouquet . . Mr. DODD.

Officers, Recruits, &c., &c.

Nell . . . . Mrs. WRIGHTEN.
Lady Sash . . . . . Miss FARREN.
Lady Plume · . . . Mrs. ROBINSON.
Lady Gorget . . . . Mrs. CUYLER.
Nancy . . . . . . Miss WALPOLE.

Countrywomen, &c., &c.

THE CAMP.

ACT I.—SCENE I.

The Road near the Camp.

Enter OLD MAN.

Old Man.   COME along, neighbours, come along ; we shall be too late for the sutlers' market.

Enter SECOND MAN.

2nd Man. Put on, put on, neighbours.   Here, Robin, where are you, boy ?

Robin [*behind.*] I'm coming, feather, as soon as I can get the colt up ; for the plaguy beast is down again, and mother and chickens are all in the slough.

O. Man. Why, is the colt down again.   You graceless dog, help your mother up.   Oh, neighbour Farrow has helped her up, I see.

Enter OLD WOMAN.

O. Woman. Husband, as sure as you are alive, that rogue of a boy drove the colt in the dirt for the purpose, and down we came with such a wang——

O. Man. What a mercy it is the chickens escaped !
Come, put on, neighbours.

Enter ROBIN *and Colt.*

Robin. Why, feather, how could I help it? The colt has not had an eye in his head these eight years.

O. Woman. O, here comes our kinswoman and her daughter——

Enter MISS.

Bless me, child! you are in such a heat, you'll quite spoil your complexion.

Miss. Lord, neighbours, you hurry one so.

2nd Woman. Put on, put on; make haste, we shall be too late. O dear, here comes Nell, and she'll scold us all for cheating the soldiers.

3rd Woman. D——n that wench, she won't cheat herself, nor let other honest people do it, if she can help it; and she says she likes a soldier so well she would sell them goods for nothing.

2nd Man. Come, neighbours, now we shall see what bargains your daughter will make at the Camp.

2nd Woman. Ay, ay, soldiers are testy customers. They won't buy of the ugly ones. O, here Nell comes.

Enter NELL.

Nell. Why, how now? what you are consulting how you shall cheat the poor soldiers; for shame! for shame! how can you use the poor fellows so?—a parcel of unfeeling wretches! Poor fellows, that risk their lives to defend your property, and yet you make it your study to defraud them.

O. Woman. It's very hard, Nell, you won't let us have a little picking among 'em. What is it to you what we do?

Nell. Yes, it is to me. I never will bear to see a

soldier cheated, with my eyes open. I love a soldier, and will always stand by them.

Miss. Mind your own business, Nell.

Nell. What's that you say, Miss Minx? Here's a wench dressed out: the poor soldiers are forced to pay for all this finery, you impudent slut you.

2nd Man. Why, Nell, if you go on at this rate we'll tell his worship, Mr. Gage, of you; he's an exciseman, and a great friend to us poor folks.

Nell. What's that you say, Master Grinder? Come forward, you sneaking, snivelling sot you. I think your tricks are pretty well known. Wasn't you caught soaking eggs in lime and water to make them pass for new ones? and did not you sit in the stocks for robbing the squire's rookery to make your pigeon pies?

2nd Woman. Well, well, we'll tell Mr. Gage, and then what will he say to you?

Nell. Tell Mr. Gage, will you? He's a pretty protector indeed; he's a disgrace to his Majesty's inkhorn: while he seizes with one hand, he smuggles with the other. Why, no longer ago than last summer, he was a broken attorney at Rochester, and came down here, and bought this place with his vote, and now he is both a smuggler and contractor. O' my conscience, if I had the management of affairs, I would severely punish all such fellows, who would be so base as to cheat a poor soldier.

2nd Woman. If his worship was here, you dare not say so. Here he comes—here he comes. Now you'll change your note.

Nell. Will I? you shall see if I do. No, no; I'll tell him my mind: that's always my way.

Enter GAGE.

All. Ah ! Mr. Gage.

Gage. Hey day ! what's the matter ? What the plague, is there a civil war broke out among you ?

1st Woman. Why, Mr. Gage, Nell here has been scolding us for cheating the soldiers.

2nd Woman. Yes, and says you encourage us in it.

Gage. Encourage you ! to be sure I do, in the way of trade.

All. Ay, in the way of trade.

1st Woman. Yes, and she has been rating the poor girl, and says I dress her up thus only to make the better bargains.

Gage. And ecod you're in the right of it ; your mother is a sensible old woman. Well said, dame ; put plenty in your baskets, and sell your wares at the sign of your daughter's face.

1st Woman. Ay, ay, so I say.

Gage. Right. Soldiers are testy customers, and this is the market where the prettiest will always make the best bargains.

All. Very true, very true.

Gage. To be sure. I hate to see an awkward gawky come sneaking into the market, with her d—d half-price countenance, and is never able to get scarce double the value of her best goods.

Nell. I can hold no longer. Are you not ashamed, you who are a contractor, and has the honour to carry his Majesty's inkhorn at your button-hole, to teach these poor wretches all your court tricks ? I'll tell you what : if I was to sit on a court-martial against such a fellow as you, you should have your deserts, from the pilfering sutler to the head contractor ; you should have the cat o' nine tails, and be forced to run the gauntlet, from Coxheath to Warley Common, that you should.

1st Man. How durst you talk so saucily to his worship?

Nell. Hold your tongue, or I'll throttle you, you sheep-biter. [*Collaring him.*

1st Man. O Lord, your worship! if you don't put her under arrest, she'll choke me.

Gage. [*Aside.*] Come, Nell, hold your tongue, and I'll give you a pound of smuggled hyson, and throw you a silk handkerchief into the bargain.

Nell. Here's a rogue! Bear witness, neighbours, he has offered me a bribe: a pound of tea. No, sir, take your pitiful present, and know that I am not to be bribed to screen your villanies by influence and corruption. [*Throws it at him.*

Gage. Don't mind her; she's mad, she talks treason. Away with you! I'll put everybody under an arrest that stays to listen to her.

All. Ay, ay, she's mad. Come along; we shall be too late for market. [GAGE *drives them off.*

Gage. Here, Nell, will you take the tea?
[*Offers it to her.*

Nell. No, sir, I won't.

Gage. Well, then, I will. [*Puts it in his pocket.*

AIR.

Nell. Now coaxing, caressing,
  Now wheedling, distressing,
As fortune delights to exalt or confound
  Her smile or her frown
  Sets them up, knocks them down;
Turning, turning, turning as the wheel goes round.

O fie, Mr. Gage!
Quit the tricks of the age;
Scorn the slaves that to fortune, false fortune, are bound,
    Their cringes and bows,
    Protections and vows,
Turning, turning, &c.

[*Exit* NELL.

Gage. Foolish girl, not to accept a bribe, and follow the example of her betters. But who have we here?

Enter O'DAUB.

O'Daub. Ah, my little Gage! To be sure, I am not in luck. I will not want an interpreter to show me the views about here; and by my shoul, I'll force you to accept my offer.

Gage. Why, what's your errand?

O'Daub. Why, upon my conscience, a very dangerous one; Jack the Painter's job was a fool to it. I am come to take the Camp.

Gage. The devil you are!

O'Daub. Ay, and must bring it away with me in my pocket, too.

Gage. Indeed!

O'Daub. Ay, here's my military chest; these are my colours, you know.

Gage. O, I guess your errand.

O'Daub. Then, faith, it's a very foolish one. You must know, I got so much credit at the *féte champêtre* there, that little Roscius recommended me to the managers of Drury Lane, and so now I am a sort of deputy superintendent under Mr. Lanternberg, the great painter; that as soon as he executes a thing, I always design it after him, my jewel; so I'm going to take a side front view of it.

Gage. What, then, they are going to introduce the Camp on the stage, I suppose.

O'Daub. To be sure you have hit it. Coxheath by candlelight, my jewel.

Gage. And will that answer?

O'Daub. O, to be sure it will answer, when a jontleman can have a warm seat, and see the whole tote of it for two thirteens, and be comfortable into the bargain. Why it has cost me above three guineas already, and I came the cheapest way too; for three of us went halves in the Maidstone Dilly, my dear.

Gage. Well, and how do you like the prospect?

O'Daub. Upon my shoul, my jewel, I don't know what to make on't, so I am come to be a little farther off, that I may have a nearer view of it. I think it looks like my cousin O'Doiley's great bleach-yard in the county of Antrim. [BOUILLARD *sings without.*] Tunder and wounds! what outlandish creature is this coming here?

Gage. O, that is Monsieur Bouillard, the sutler.

O'Daub. Then perhaps he can help me to a bit of something to eat, for I feel a sort of craving in my stomach after my journey.

Gage. Why, he's a very honest fellow, and will be happy in obliging you. Oh, here he comes.

Enter BOUILLARD.

Bouil. Ah! begar, Monsieur Gage, I am glad I have found you; begar, I have been through Berkshire, Suffolk, and Yorkshire, and could not find you.

O'Daub. Through Berkshire, Suffolk, and Yorkshire. What the devil does he mean?

Gage. Oh, he means through the regiments.

Bouil. Begar, Monsieur Gage, I must depend on

you for supply. I have got one, two, tree brigade dinners bespoke, besides the fat alderman and his lady from London.

Gage. Then you must send out a party of cooks to forage at Maidstone.

Bouil. Parbleu, Monsieur Gage, I must look to you; for begar, I have got nothing in de house to eat.

O'Daub. Then the devil burn me if I come to dine with you, honey.

Bouil. O, sire, I have got every ting for you and Monsieur Gage. You shall have any ting you like in von moment!

O'Daub. Ah, ha! I tank you, honey. But pray now, Mr. Blaud, if your own countrymen were to come over here, would not you be a little puzzled to know which side to be on?

Bouil. Puzzled! Parbleu, Monsieur, I do assure you I love de English ver well, and vill never leave dem vile dey are victorious; and I do love mine own countrymen very well; but depend on it, Monsieur Gage, I vill always stay with de strongest.

Gage. You see, Mr. O'Daub, my friend, Monsieur Bouillard, is divested of all national prejudice, I assure you.

Bouil. Prejudice! begar, I have too much honour ever to leave de English while dey do vin de battle. But, Monsieur Gage, vill you bring your friend, and taste my vine? I have got every ting for you and your friend. I assure you, Monsieur Gage, I vill never forsake de English, so long as dey are victorious; but if mine own countrymen were to come, and make de English run, I would run a little way with dem; and if mine own countrymen were likely to overtake dem, I would stop short, bow to them, and say, how do you do, my ver good countrymen? By gar, I shall be ver glad to see you both ; so come along ; but depend on mine honour, Monsieur Gage, I vill never leave de English vile dey do vin de battle.   No, never, never !

[*Exit singing.*

Gage. Well said, Monsieur Bouillard.

O'Daub. Your sarvant, Mr Blaud ; though, faith, to do him justice, he has forgot the fashion of his country ; for when he is determined to be a rogue he is honest enough to own it.   But pray, what connection have you with the sutlers ?   You are no victualler here, are you ?

Gage. Not absolutely a victualler, but I deal in various articles.

O'Daub. Indeed.

Gage. Yes, but no business is done here only by contract.

O'Daub. A contractor !   Why, what the devil, you are not risen to such preferment as that sure ?   I never knew you was able to furnish any contract.

Gaye. Nothing more easy ; the circumstance depends upon the quantity, not the quality.   I got on very well lately, but at first it brought me in several confounded scrapes.

O'Daub. As how ?

Gage. Why, I undertook to serve a regiment with hair powder.

O'Daub. Hair powder !   What, and you sent them flour, I suppose ?

Gage. Flour ! no, no ; I should have saved nothing by that : I went to the fountain head—the pit, and gave them a plentiful stock of lime.

O'Daub. Lime ! brick and mortar lime ?

Gage. Yes, brick and mortar lime.

O'Daub. And, what the plague, was not the cheat found out ?

Gage. Why at first it answered the purpose very well : while the weather was fine it did charmingly ; but one field-day they were all caught in a fine soaking shower ; the smoke ran along the lines ; ecod their heads were all slack'd in an instant, and by the time they returned to the camp, d—e if all their heads were not as smooth as an old half-crown.

O'Daub. A very cross accident indeed.

Gage. Yes, I stood a near chance of being tied up to the halberts ; but I excused myself by saying they looked only like raw recruits before, but now they appeared like old veterans of service.

O'Daub. But you lost your contract, I suppose ?

Gage. Yes, but I soon got another ; a shaving contract to a company of Grenadiers.

O'Daub. 'Faith, I never knew you practised that business.

Gage. Never handled a razor in all my life : I shave by deputy ; hired Sam Sickle down from London ; an excellent hand! handles a razor like a scythe : he'll mow you down a regiment of beards in the beating a *réveille.*

O'Daub. Upon my conscience, a pretty way this of working at second-hand. I wish myself could do a little by proxy.

Gage. But come, what say you for something to eat, and a glass of my friend Bouillard's wine, and drink his Majesty's health ?

O'Daub. With all my heart, my dear, and to the two camps, if you will.

Gage. Two ! what two do you mean ?

O'Daub. Why, the one at Coxheath, and the other at Drury Lane. [*Exeunt.*

SCENE II.

A Grove near the Camp.

Enter Two Countrymen.

1st Coun. I tell you I will certainly list; I ha' made up my mind on't.

2nd Coun. Well, well, I'll say no more.

1st Coun. Besides, the camp lies so convenient, I mayn't have such another opportunity.

2nd Coun. Why, it's main jolly to be sure, and all that so fair. Now, if I were to list, I should like hugely to belong to a regiment of horse, and here is one of the grandest troop com'd lately. I see'd two of the officers, mighty delicate looking gentlemen; they were dress'd quite different from the others; their jackets, indeed, are pretty much the same; but then they wear a sort of petticoat, as 'twere, with a large hat and feather, and a mortal sight of hair. I suppose now they are some of your outlandish troops; your foreign Hessians, or such like.

1st Coun. Ay, like enough. Here comes the sergeant. Ecod, he can sing louder than his own drum. Zooks! see how brave they march. Well, walking is a mighty dull way of going, after all.

Enter Sergeant, Drummer, Recruits, *&c.*

SONG.—SERGEANT.

Great Cæsar, once renown'd in fame,
For a mighty arm, and a laurel brow,
With his *veni, vidi, vici,* came,
And he conquer'd the world with his row, dow, dow.

Chorus. Row, dow, dow; row, dow, dow;
And he conquer'd the world, &c.

Then should our vaunting enemies come,
      And winds and waves their cause allow,
By freedom's flag we'll beat our drum,
And they'll fly from the sound of our row, dow, dow.
        Row, dow, dow, &c.

Then come, my lads, our bounty share,
    While honest hearts British valour avow;
In freedom's cause to camp repair,
And follow the beat of my row, dow, dow.
        Row, dow, dow, &c.

Serg. Come, my lads, now is your time to serve the king, and make men of yourselves. Well, my lad, what do you say?

2nd Coun. I canno' leave my farm.

Serg. Your farm! what, would you plough and sow for the hungry Frenchmen to come and reap? Come, my lads! let your fields lie fallow this year, and I'll ensure you double crops ever after. Why now, here's a fellow made for a soldier: there's a leg for a spatterdash, with an eye like the king of Prussia.

1st Coun. Ay, but, sergeant, I hanna' the air.

Serg. The air! O, we'll soon learn you that; why now, here's little Ralph; there's a fellow for you: he has not been listed a fortnight, and see what a presence—there's dignity! O, there is nothing like the drill for grace!

1st Coun. Sergeant, I'm your man.

2nd Coun. And so am I.

Serg. That's right, my lads; this is much better than to be dragged away like a slave, or be scratched off the church door for the militia. Now you have present pay, and the bounty-money into the bargain. But come, my lads, let me ask you a few questions, and then the business is done.

TRIO.

Serg.	Yet ere you're permitted to list with me, Answer me straight twice questions three.
1st Coun.	No lies, master sergeant, we'll tell unto you; For though we be poor lads, we're honest and true.
Serg.	First, can you drink well?
1st Coun.	Cheerly, cheerly.
Serg.	Each man a gallon?
2nd Coun.	Nearly, nearly.
Serg.	Love a sweet wench too?
Both.	Dearly, dearly.
Serg.	The answer is honest, bold, and fair; So drink to the king, for his soldiers you are.
Chorus.	The answer is honest, &c.
Serg.	When bullets are whizzing around your head, You'll boldly march on wherever you're led?
2nd Coun.	To death we'll rush forward without delay, If, good master sergeant, you'll show us the way.
Serg.	Next, you can swear well?
2nd Coun.	Bluffly, bluffly.
Serg.	Handle a Frenchman?
1st Coun.	Roughly, roughly.
Serg.	Frown at a cannon?
Both.	Gruffly, gruffly.
Serg.	The answers are honest, bold, and fair; So drink to the king, for his soldiers you are.
Chorus.	The answers are honest, &c. Huzza! huzza! huzza!

Enter NELL.

Nell. Well said, my lads. I am glad to see so many good hearts in the country. O, but was not you saying one of your recruits knows me?

Serg. O yes, Nell, a lad from Suffolk. Hark ye, where's the Suffolk boy, as we call him? O, here he comes!

Enter NANCY.

Nancy. Ah, sergeant, did you not begin to think you had lost me? But come, will you leave me a few minutes with Nelly?

Serg. With all my heart. Come, my lads, let's to the Heart of Oak, where we'll drink his Majesty's health.

[*Exit singing, The answer, &c., and two huzzas.*
Nancy. Why, Nelly, don't you know me?

Nell. Know you! egad, I do not know whether I do or not; sure it can't be—and yet, sure it is Nancy Granger?

Nancy. It is her, my dear Nelly, who kisses you now with the truest sense of gratitude for your former kindness and friendship.

Nell. My dear girl. Odso! I must take care of my reputation. But what in the name of fancy brings you here, and in this dress, child?

Nancy. How can you ask me that question, Nelly? You are no stranger to the love William and I have for each other; a few days would have united us for ever, had not cruel fate separated us; the regiment being ordered to march immediately, no resource was then left but my flying from my father's house. I procured a dress from one of our neighbour's sons, and that love which induced me to forsake my sex still supports me under every affliction. Fortunately, on my way I met the sergeant, and after some entreaty was enlisted, and equipped as you see. What think you, Nell, does not my dress become me?

Nell. Yes, indeed, I think you make a smart little soldier.

Nancy. Why, indeed I am rather under size; but I fancy, in action I could do more real execution than those who look bigger, and talk louder. But tell me, my dear Nelly, where is William? I long to see him. Does he ever speak of his poor Nancy? Sure he cannot be faithless?

Nell. Why, really, Nancy, I have some doubts.

Nancy. Heavens! is it possible?

Nell. Ah, my poor little soldier, I only did it to try your affection. Your William is true, and worthy of your love.

Nancy. You have made a greater shock on my spirits than even an army of Frenchmen could have done.

AIR.

When war's alarms enticed my Willy from me,
  My poor heart with grief did sigh;
Each fond remembrance brought fresh sorrow on me;
  I waked ere yet the morn was nigh.
     No other could delight him;
     Ah! why did I e'er slight him,
    Coldly answering his fond tale?
      Which drove him far,
      Amid the rage of war,
    And left silly me thus to bewail.

But I no longer, though a maid forsaken,
  Thus will mourn like yonder dove;

For ere the lark to-morrow shall awaken,
 I will seek my absent love :
  The hostile country over,
  I'll fly to seek my lover,
 Scorning every threat'ning fear ;
  Nor distant shore,
  Nor cannon's roar,
 Shall longer keep me from my dear.

Nell. But, my dear girl, consider ; do you think you can cheerfully go through the toil and fatigue, and not repine after your own happy situation you left behind you ?

Nancy. O no ; I still must love, though I should regret the occasion of our difficulties.

Nell. Difficulty ! Why then, marry him at the drumhead, and that will end all your difficulties.

AIR.

What can our wisest heads provide,
For the child we dote on dearly,
 But a merry soul, and an honest heart
In a lad who loves her dearly ;
  Who with kisses and chat,
  And all, all that,
Will soothe him late and early :
  If the truth she tell,
  When she knows him well,
She'll swear she loves him dearly.

 Let the prude at the name or sight of man
Pretend to rail severely ;
 But, alack-a-day ! unseen she'll play
With the lad who loves her dearly.

> Say old men whate'er they will,
> 'Tis a lover still
> Makes day and night roll cheerly.
> What makes our May
> All holiday,
> But the lad we dote on dearly?

Nell. Well, my dear Nancy, you must endeavour to throw off that dress as soon as possible. I'll tell you what, here are some ladies in the camp, who condescend to notice me; I'll endeavour to introduce you to them, and they may be of great service to you. In the mean time, should you by chance meet with William, be sure you don't discover yourself. Hush! here is the sergeant.

Enter SERGEANT.

Serg. Why, Nelly, how's this? you have had a long conversation together. I began to think you had run away with my new recruit.

Nell. O there's no great danger, sergeant; he's no soldier for me. Pray, is he perfect in his exercise?

Serg. O, as handy a lad as ever was. Come, youngster, convince her.

[NANCY *goes through the exercise.*

Nell. Very well indeed; but, sergeant, I must beg of you to befriend him as much as you can, for my sake.

Serg. Any service in my power you may command; but a soldier's life is not the easiest in the world, so they ought to befriend each other.

TRIO.

> O the joy! when the trumpets sound,
> And the march beats around,
> When the steed tears the ground,
> And shouts to the skies resound!

On glittering arms the sunbeams playing,
  Heighten the soldier's charms;
The fife and the roll of the distant drum,
  Cry hark! the enemy come!
To arms! the attack's begun.

[Exeunt.

ACT II.—SCENE I.

A Grove near the Camp.

Enter NELL, *speaking without.*

William! come to speak to him another time; sure nothing could be more lucky! however, I must obey their ladyships' instructions, and keep him in ignorance, that they may be present at the discovery. Poor fellow! it's almost a pity too, when one has it in one's power to make him so happy.

Enter WILLIAM.

Will. I am sorry, Nell, to make you wait; but it was an old friend.

Nell. Ay, ay, some one from Suffolk, I suppose, who has brought you news of your dear Nancy.

Will. I wish it had: it's unaccountable that I don't hear from her.

Nell. Unaccountable! not at all: I suppose she has changed her mind.

Will. No, Nelly, that's impossible; and you would think so had you heard how she plighted her faith to me, and vowed, notwithstanding her parents were my enemies, nothing but death should prevent our union.

Nell. O, I beg your pardon.; if her father and mother indeed are against you, you need not doubt her constancy. But come, don't be melancholy. I tell you I want to have you stay somewhere near the inn, and perhaps I may bring you some intelligence of her.

Will. How! dear Nell?

Nell. Though indeed I think you are very foolish to plague yourself so; for even had Nancy loved you well enough to have carried your knapsack, you would have been very imprudent to have suffered her.

Will. Ay, but prudence, you know, is not a soldier's virtue. It's our business to hold life itself cheap, much more the comforts of it. Show me a young fellow in our regiment, who, if he gains the heart of a worthy girl, is afraid to marry her for want of a little wealth, and I would have him drummed out of the regiment for discretion.

Nell. Very fine! but must not the poor girl share in all your fatigues and mishaps?

Will. There, Nell, I own is the objection; but tenderness and affection may soften even these; yet if my Nancy ever makes the trial, though I may not be able to prevent her from undergoing hardships, I am sure my affection will make her wonder at their being called so. I wish I could once boast that the experiment was made.

AIR.

My Nancy quits the rural train
　A camp's distress to prove;
All other ills she can sustain
　But living from her love:

Yet, dearest, though your soldier's there,
   Would not your spirits fail,
To mark the hardships you must share,
   Dear Nancy of the dale ?

Or should you, love, each danger scorn,
   Ah ! how shall I secure
Your health, 'mid toils which you were born
   To soothe, but not endure ?
A thousand perils I must view,
   A thousand ills assail ;
Nor must I tremble e'en for you,
   Dear Nancy of the dale.

                       [Exeunt.

SCENE II.

An open View near the Camp.

Enter O'DAUB.

O'Daub. Well, to be sure, this same camp is a
pretty place, with their drum, and their fifes, and their
gigs, and their marches, and their ladies in regimentals. Upon my conscience, I believe they'd form
a troop of side-saddle cavalry if there were any hopes
of an invasion. But now I am alone by myself, 'tis
time I should be after taking my plan ; and here I see
are some of my directions for it. [*Pulls out a pocket-
book and pencil.*] I can't think what it is makes my
hand shake so, unless it is Mr. Blaud's wine that is
got into my head. So, so ! let me study my orders
a little, for I am not used to this business. O. P. and
P. S. Who the d—l is to understand that ? O ! here
is the explanation : P. S. the prompter's side, and

O. P. opposite the prompter. So I'm to mark down the view as it is to be taken on one side, and the other. Very well: P. S. and O. P. Let me see. Somewhere hereabout is certainly the best point to take it from. *[Retires.*

Enter SERGEANT *and the* TWO COUNTRYMEN.

1st Coun. There, you rogues, there he is!

2nd Coun. Ay, ay, that's him, sure enough. I have seen him skulking about these two days; if he ben't a spy I'll suffer hanging.

Serg. He certainly must be a spy, by his drawing figures.

2nd Coun. Do seize on him, or the whole camp may be blown up before we are aware.

O'Daub. Prompter's side.

Serg. Hush! we shall convict him out of his own mouth.

O'Daub. O yes, the star and garter must certainly be P. S.

Serg. P. S. What the d—l does he say?

2nd Coun. Treason, you may be sure, by your not understanding him.

O'Daub. And then O. P. will have the advantage.

Serg. O. P. That's the Old Pretender. A d—d Jacobite spy, my life on't.

1st Coun. And P. S. is Prince Charles, I suppose.

Serg. No, you fool; P. S. is the Pretender's Son.

2nd Coun. Ay, ay, like enough.

O'Daub. Memorandum—the officers' tents are in tho rear of the line.

2nd Coun. Mark that.

O'Daub. N.B. the general's tents are all houses.

1st Coun. Remember that.

O'Daub. Then the park of artillery; I shall never make anything of that. Oh! the d—l burn the park of artillery!

Serg. There's a villain! he'll burn the park of artillery, will he?

O'Daub. Well, faith this camp is easier taken than I thought it was.

Serg. Is it so, you rogue? but you shall find the difference on't. Oh, what a providential discovery!

O'Daub. To be sure the people will like it much, and in the course of the winter it may surprise his Majesty.

Serg. O, the villain! seize him directly. Fellow, you are a dead man if you stir! We seize you, sir, as a spy.

O'Daub. A spy—phoo, phoo. Get about your business.

Serg. Bind him, and blindfold him if he resists.

2nd Coun. Ay, blindfold him for certain, and search him too. I daresay his pockets are crowded with powder, matches, and tinder-boxes, at every corner.

O'Daub. Tunder and owns! What do you mean?

1st Coun. Hold him fast.

O'Daub. Why here's some ladies coming, who know me. Here's Lady Sarah Sash, and Lady Plume, who were at the *fête champêtre*, and will give me a good character.

Serg. Why, villain, your papers have proved you a spy, and sent by the Old Pretender.

O'Daub. O Lord! O Lord! I never saw the old gentleman in all my life.

Serg. Why, you dog, didn't you say the camp was easier taken than you thought it was?

2nd Coun. Ay, deny that.

Serg. And that you would burn the artillery, and

surprise his Majesty? So, come, you had better confess before you are hanged,

O'Daub. Hanged for a spy! O, to be sure, myself is got into a pretty scrape!

Serg. Bring him away, but blindfold him; the dog shall see no more.

O'Daub. I'll tell you what, Mr. Soldier, or Mr. Sergeant, or what the d—l's your name, upon my conscience and soul I'm nothing at all but an Irish painter, employed by Monsieur Lanternburg.

Serg. There, he has confessed himself a foreigner, and employed by Marshal Leatherbag.

2nd Coun. O, he'll be convicted by his tongue. You may swear he is a foreigner by his lingo.

1st Coun. Bring him away. I long to see him hanging.

O'Daub. Tunder and wounds! if I am hanged, what will become of the theatre, and the managers; and the d—l fly away with you all together, for a parcel of red blackguards! [*They hurry him off.*

SCENE III.

Part of the Camp.

Enter Lady GORGET, Lady SASH, *and* Lady PLUME.

L. Plume. O! my dear Lady Sash, indeed you are too severe; and I'm sure if Lady Gorget had been here she would have been of my opinion.

L. Sash. Not in the least.

L. Plume. You must know, she has been rallying my poor brother, Sir Harry Bouquet, for not being in the militia, and so ill-naturedly!

L. Sash. So he should indeed; but all I said was, he looked so French and so finical, that I thought he ran a risk of being mistaken for another female chevalier.

L. Plume. Yet, you must confess that our situation is open to a little raillery. A few elegances of accommodation are considerably wanting, though one's toilet, as Sir Harry says, is not absolutely spread on a drumhead.

L. Sash. He vows there is an eternal confusion between stores military and millinery; such a description he gives! On one shelf, cartridges and cosmetics, pouches and patches; here a stand of arms, there a file of black pins; in one drawer bullet-moulds and essence-bottles, pistols, and tweezer-cases, with battle-powder mixed with marechelle.

L. Gorget. O, the malicious creature!

L. Plume. But pray, Lady Sash, don't renew it; for see, here comes Sir Harry to join us.

Enter Sir HARRY BOUQUET.

Sir Harry. Now, Lady Sash, I beg a truce. Lady Gorget, I am rejoiced to see you at this delectable spot; where, Lady Plume, you may be amused, with such a dismal variety.

L. Gorget. You see, Lady Plume, he perseveres.

L. Sash. I assure you, Sir Harry, I should have been against you in your raillery.

Sir Harry. Now, as Gad's my judge, I admire the place; here's all the pride, pomp, and circumstance of glorious war! Mars in a *vis-à-vis*, and Bellona giving a *fête champêtre*.

L. Plume. But now, seriously, brother, what can

make you judge so indifferently of the camp from anybody else ?

Sir Harry. Why, seriously, then, I think it the
worst planned thing I ever beheld ; for instance now,
the tents are all ranged in a straight line : now, Lady
Gorget, can anything be worse than a straight line ?
and is not there a horrid uniformity in their infinite
vista of canvas ? no curve, no break, and the avenue
of marquees abominable.

L. Sash. O, to be sure, a circus or a crescent would
have been vastly better.

L. Gorget. What a pity Sir Harry was not con-
sulted !

Sir Harry. As Gad's my judge, I think so ; for there
is great capability in the ground.

L. Sash. A camp *cognoscente*, positively, Sir Harry ;
we will have you publish a treatise on military
virtue.

Sir Harry. Very well ; but how will you excuse
this ? The officers' tents are close to the common
soldiers : what an arrangement is that now ! If I
might have advised, there certainly should have been
one part for the *canaille*, and the west end of the
camp for the *noblesse* and persons of a certain
rank.

L. Gorget. Very right. I daresay you would have
thought of proper marquees for hazard and quinze.

L. Plume. To be sure, with festino tents, and opera
pavilions.

Sir Harry. Gad, the only plan that could make it
supportable for a week ; well, certainly the greatest
defect in a general is want of taste.

L. Sash. Undoubtedly ; and conduct, discipline, and
want of humanity, are no atonements for it.

Sir Harry. None in nature.

L. Plume. But, Sir Harry, it is rather unlucky that the military spirit is so universal, for you will hardly find one to side with you.

Sir Harry. Universal indeed; and the ridicule of it is to see how this madness has infected the whole road from Maidstone to London; the camp jargon is as current all the way as bad silver; the very postillions that drive you talk of their cavalry, and refuse to charge on a trot up the hill; the turnpikes seem converted into redoubts, and the dogs demanded the countersign of my servants, instead of the tickets; then when I got to Maidstone, I found the very waiters had got a smattering of tactics; for inquiring what I could have for dinner, a cursed drill waiter, after reviewing his bill of fare with the air of a field-marshal, proposed an advanced party of soup and bouilli, to be followed by the main body of ham and chickens, flanked by a fricassée, with salads in the intervals, and a *corps de reserve* of sweetmeats, and whipped syllabubs to form a hollow square in the centre.

L. Plume. Ha! ha! ha! Sir Harry, I am very sorry you have so strong a dislike to everything military; for unless you would contribute to the fortune of our little recruit——

Sir Harry. O madam, most willingly; and very *à propos*, here comes your ladyship's *protégée*, and has brought, I see, the little recruit, as you desired.

Enter NELL *and* NANCY.

Nell. Here, Nancy, make your curtsy, or your bow, to the ladies, who have so kindly promised you protection.

Nancy. Simple gratitude is the only return I can make; but I am sure the ladies, who have hearts to do so good-natured a deed, will excuse my not being able to answer them as I ought.

Nell. She means, an please your ladyships, that she will always acknowledge your ladyships' goodness to the last hour of her life, and, as in duty bound, will ever pray for your ladyships' happiness and prosperity. That's what you mean, you know.

[*Aside to* NANCY.

L. Plume. Very well; but, Nancy, are you satisfied that your soldier shall continue in his duty?

Nell. O yes, your ladyship; she's quite satisfied.

L. Plume. Well, child, we're all your friends; and be assured your William shall be no sufferer by his constancy.

Nell. There, Nancy; say something.

L. Sash. But are you sure you will be able to bear the hardships of your situation?

[*Retires up with* NANCY.

L. Plume. [*To* NELL.] You have seen him, then?

Nell. O yes, your ladyship.

L. Plume. Go, and bring him here. [*Exit* NELL.] Sir Harry, we have a little plot, which you must assist us in.

Nancy. [*Coming forward with* Lady SASH.] O, madam, most willingly.

SONG.

The fife and drum sound merrily;
A soldier, a soldier's the lad for me:
With my true love I soon shall be;
For who so kind, so true as he!
With him in every toil I'll share;
To please him shall be all my care:
Each peril I'll dare, all hardship I'll bear;
For a soldier, a soldier's the lad for me.

Then if kind Heaven preserve my love,
What rapturous joys shall Nancy prove!
Swift through the camp shall my footstep bound,
To meet my William, with conquest crown'd:
Close to my faithful bosom press'd,
Soon shall he hush his cares to rest;
Clasp'd in these arms, forget war's alarms;
For a soldier, a soldier's the lad for me.

L. Plume. Now, Nancy, you must be ruled by us.

Nancy. As I live, there's my dear William!

L. Plume. Turn from him; you must.

Nancy. O, I shall discover myself! I tremble so unlike a soldier.

Enter NELL *and* WILLIAM.

Nell. Why, I tell you, William, the ladies want to ask you some questions.

Sir Harry. Honest corporal, here's a little recruit, son to a tenant of mine; and, as I am told you are an intelligent young fellow, I mean to put him under your care.

Will. What, that boy, your honour? Lord bless you, sir, I shall never be able to make anything of him.

Nancy. [*Aside.*] I am sorry for that.

L. Sash. Nay, corporal, he's very young.

Will. He is under size, my lady; such a stripling is fitter for a drummer than a rank and file.

Sir Harry. But he's straight and well made.

Nancy. I wish I was ordered to right about.

Will. Well, I'll do all in my power to oblige your ladyship. Come, youngster, turn about. Ah, Nelly tell me, is't not she?

Sir Harry. Why don't you march him off?

Nell. Is he under size, corporal? Oh, you block-head!

Nancy. O ladies; pray excuse me! My dear William!
[Runs into his arms.

Nell. They'll never be able to come to an explanation before your ladyships. Go, go, and talk by your-selves. *[They retire up the stage.*

Enter SERGEANT, TWO COUNTRYMEN, *Fife, &c.*

Serg. Please your ladyships, we have taken a sort of a spy this morning, who has the assurance to deny it, though he confesses himself an Irish painter. I have undertaken, however, to bring this letter from him to Lady Sarah Sash.

Sir Harry. What appears against him?

Serg. A great many suspicious circumstances, please your honour: he has an O before his name, and we took him with a draught of the camp in his hand.

L. Sash. Ha, ha, ha! this is ridiculous enough: 'tis O'Daub, the Irish painter, who diverted us some time ago at the *fête champêtre.* Honest sergeant, we'll see your prisoner, and I fancy you may release him.

Sir Harry. Pray, sergeant, what's to be done this evening?

Serg. The line, your honour, turns out; and as there are pleasure tents pitched, perhaps the ladies will con-descend to hear a march and chorus, which some recruits are practising against his Majesty comes to the camp.

L. Sash. Come, Sir Harry, you'll grow fond of a camp life yet.

Sir Harry. Your ladyships will grow tired of it first, I'll answer for it.

L. Sash. No, no.

Sir Harry. Yes, on the first bad weather you'll give orders to strike your tents and toilets, and secure a retreat at Tunbridge.

A march, while the scene changes to a View of the Camp.

FINALE.

Serg. While the loud voice of war resounds from afar,
    Songs of duty and triumph we'll pay:
When our monarch appears, we'll give him three cheers,
    With huzza! huzza! huzza!

Nancy. Ye sons of the field, whose bright valour's your
        shield,
Love and beauty your toils shall repay:
Inspired by the charms of war's fierce alarms,
    Huzza! huzza! huzza!

Will. Inspired by my love, all dangers I'll prove;
    No perils shall William dismay;
In war's fierce alarms, inspired by those charms,
    Huzza! huzza! huzza!

Chorus. May true glory still wave her bright banners
        around;
Still with fame, pow'r, and freedom, old England be
    crown'd.

END OF VOL. II.

BALLANTYNE PRESS: LONDON AND EDINBURGH

www.ingramcontent.com/pod-product-compliance
Lightning Source LLC
Chambersburg PA
CBHW060533030726
47498CB00004B/1177